To Ros.
Enjoy! I
'The Dr
love   x

Sally Abbott is a former journalist and a PR director who lives in Central Victoria with her partner. She was the inaugural winner of The Richell Prize for Emerging Writers 2015. *Closing Down* is her first novel.

closing down

down

sally abbott

 hachette
AUSTRALIA

Winner of The Richell Prize for Emerging Writers

hachette
AUSTRALIA

Published in Australia and New Zealand in 2017
by Hachette Australia
(an imprint of Hachette Australia Pty Limited)
Level 17, 207 Kent Street, Sydney NSW 2000
www.hachette.com.au

10 9 8 7 6 5 4 3 2 1

National Library of Australia
Cataloguing-in-Publication data:

Abbott, Sally, author.
Closing down / Sally Abbott.

ISBN 978 0 7336 3594 6

Country life – Australia – Fiction.
Change – Australia – Fiction.
Australia – Social conditions – Fiction.

Cover design by Grace West
Cover photographs courtesy of Millennium Images
Author photo courtesy Marion Williams Photography
Text design by Bookhouse, Sydney
Typeset in 12/17.5 pt Adobe Garamond Pro
Printed and bound in Australia by McPherson's Printing Group

MIX
Paper from
responsible sources
FSC® C001695

The paper this book is printed on is certified against the
Forest Stewardship Council® Standards. McPherson's Printing
Group holds FSC® chain of custody certification SA-COC-005379.
FSC® promotes environmentally responsible, socially beneficial
and economically viable management of the world's forests.

For Mary Kidd

And in memory of Jill Gibson (1956–2017)

one

Through all his years away, when Robbie remembered his country he thought first of the white summer sun that seemed to light the land from within, sucking out all green and leaving only grey and brown and gold. He thought of his grandmother and her rose-petal perfume, and the sun striking the wooden kitchen floorboards in the House of Many Promises. And he thought of a horse screaming.

Apart from his grandmother, and Jonathon of course, Ella was the only person who knew the story of the horse.

'Tell me something that is only about you,' she said sometime in their first year together. 'Not a country, not a war, not a woman, not a politician, not a scandal. Something that is only you. A once-upon-a-time story.'

Robbie had left the bed and walked over to the window. The curtains were open to let in the light of the stars and the moon, which were only the ghostliest glow under the fog of the city's fumes. There was the smell of the sea and diesel and garlic frying somewhere and the scent from the giant ginger flowers Ella had bought two days earlier from a street stall. The big bedroom of the borrowed apartment,

1

with only the massive bed and their bags and computers on the floor, seemed to float above the world. Robbie looked at the play of the night lights and the soundless shifting of the South China Sea far below. He understood what Ella was asking.

'Okay,' he said. 'Once upon a time, when I was a little boy, perhaps eight, no, nine, I had a horse, a pony really, small, all black. I called him Timmy. I just loved that horse. I really did. You know, the way you love something when you're a child, like it's the whole world.'

He kept his back to her and she lay on her side on the bed, tangled sheet around her ankles, listening.

'One day my father held one of his long lunches. It seemed endless, like they always did. I can't remember who was there. My stepmother, the neighbours, maybe some of Dad's business mates from Sydney. Everyone got very drunk. I stayed in my room for most of the after-noon but I could hear their voices getting louder and louder, the music getting louder. I remember someone dropped a bottle of wine or beer. Anyway, my father was the drunkest of them all, as usual. He decided it would be hilarious to take Timmy out for a ride. I remember him shouting for me, telling me to saddle up the horse and bring him to the front of the house. What could I do? I knew it was crazy, but it was never worth arguing with my father when he was drunk.'

Robbie drew in a deep breath and then sighed. There was the slightest breeze, sticky and warm, through the window. He remembered his father standing in the doorway of the kitchen, blocking out the light, leaning against the frame to stay upright. He remembered walking through the dry grass to the back paddock to get Timmy, blinking through his tears, taking the small cracked saddle from the bench in the open shed that served as a stable of sorts, wood bleached grey by the sun. He could smell again Timmy's warm neck, damp and sweet in the heat. He could smell eucalyptus and dry grasses and the hot wind from the west that whipped the dust. He saw his own little boy hands, brown, nails bitten, shaking and slick with angry tears, pulling the girth strap as tight as he could, letting down the stirrups, all the time telling Timmy to be brave, be strong, get through it. Most of all he remembered Timmy's mute dark eyes.

Robbie turned around to look at Ella. From the sea far below a ship's horn sounded.

'My father climbed onto Timmy. It took him three goes. He couldn't even get his foot in the stirrup, he just kept kicking at Timmy's flank, and the first time he managed to get on he just slid over the other side. Timmy was stepping back and then forward, trying to edge away, ears way back. I was holding the chin strap, just whispering to him, telling him everything would be okay. I couldn't watch what my father was doing. I could hear him grunting and laughing and I could smell him, sour beer and wine. Finally he got on and stayed on. People cheered and clapped and there he was, this huge man sitting on little Timmy, swaying, laughing his head off. I could see Timmy roll his eyes back and try to settle the weight on his front legs. My father kicked him and Timmy tried to rear up but he couldn't, so he set off at a trot down the driveway, my father pulling too tight on the reins just to stay on. And then Timmy collapsed. One of his front legs snapped straight through. I saw it, saw Timmy buckle, then straighten, then the bone and the blood through the skin, and then he fell. Have you ever heard a horse scream, Ella? It's horrible, just horrible. My father was fine, the bastard. He lay on the ground laughing. And Timmy was on the ground too, shaking, foaming at the mouth. He'd try and pull himself up and then he'd scream again and sink back.'

Robbie remembered Timmy's eyes rolled back in fear and pain, soft black lips bared, the grey-white bone sticking through the flesh and blood, and his father like a whale beached on dust, belly shaking with laughter, face florid, dribble on his chin, the gasps of the other adults suddenly sobering up. He remembered he had taken off the bridle, gently easing the bit from the hay-smelling froth and foam around Timmy's lips.

'Get away. Get out of here,' Robbie had screamed over and over at his father, and finally someone had helped his father up and led him away, and someone else had said they would call the vet.

Robbie was left in the dust with Timmy, and he stayed by him, waving the flies from the blood, and cried as he had never cried before or since, whispering constantly through heaving sobs he'd felt even then were breaking his own body and heart in ways that would never quite mend, 'I'm so sorry, I'm so sorry, I'm so sorry'.

Ella sat silently on the bed, watching him. Robbie looked at his hands, as if perhaps they held the end of the story and then at Ella as she shifted her heavy hair from her shoulders. 'And then?' she had asked, gently.

Robbie sighed and shook his head. 'I waited with Timmy until the vet came and put him down. It must have been a couple of hours. I don't remember anything except the smell of him and holding his neck, stroking him, and saying sorry over and over, just trying to calm him while we waited. I wouldn't let anyone near. I told them all to fuck off. It was the vet who held me in the end, after he gave Timmy a needle. He was a young guy. He had some kind of weird birthmark on his cheek, and incredibly blue eyes. Jonathon was his name. He took me into the kitchen and sat me down and held me while I cried and cried. I could see the disgust on his face, the way he looked at everyone and all the empty bottles and the mess on the stove and the benches, the way he switched off the music.'

He smiled and shrugged. Enough, he had wanted to say. Enough.

'And then?' Ella asked again.

'I went to live with my grandmother after that. It was actually the vet who called her. He made me pack a bag and he took me home with him for the night. I don't think anyone even tried to stop him. We had to leave Timmy lying in the driveway and Jonathon promised me he'd come back and take care of him. I remember he reached over and took my hand when he said that and held it tight. Anyway, he called my grandmother and I guess they had a long talk. It was about an eight-hour drive to where she lived, still lives, and he took me halfway the next day. We stopped by a river and ate peanut butter sandwiches for lunch while we waited for her. His wife tried to be so kind that night I stayed with them. I remember she cooked me sausages and mashed potato for dinner, and she kept patting my shoulder. I tried to eat, but I felt so sick and I wanted Timmy back.'

Ella threw the sheet off and went to him. She took his hands and smiled and kissed his fingers. 'So,' she said softly, so softly he had to lean into her and the smell of her light peppery sweat. 'Well then. This is why I ask for stories, my love. They help me to understand.' She ran a finger over his lips.

Robbie looked down and then past her to his travel bag in the corner. He sighed. Ella would return home to Switzerland tomorrow and he would head to Cairo. Then where? The Africas again, probably. That was the panic of the month; the world tilting crazily from one food war to the next. More weeks and weeks of travel, of not seeing Ella.

There was the lonely bellow of a horn from another ship. The whole world is lonely, he suddenly thought, lonelier than it has ever been.

Ella leaned against him. 'Come to bed. There are still ten hours before we have to leave. Come and rest.'

When he finally fell asleep, head against her back, he dreamed of bones and light: bleached bones falling through white light; the grey broken bone pushing through Timmy's skin, wet with blood and veins and muscle; a horse's skull crying tears in moonlight; the crack of bone upon bone, body thrown upon body, in a grave that stretched to the centre of the world.

two

Clare McDonald, giant woman, walked the streets of a town called Myamba. It was what she did most nights. When she couldn't bear the sound of Phil chewing his food for another second, or when she lay on the sofa under her blankets, eyes wide open, cold but sweating, sleep impossible, listening to the creaks of the ratbag cottage in the night winds and Phil's snoring from the bedroom, she would heave herself up, put on her boots and jacket, and set off. Broad shoulders straight, hands in grubby pockets, one foot in front of the other, Clare just walked. Silently, steadily. Thinking, or not thinking. It was the moving that mattered.

She knew every back track into town, the shape of the footpaths, their lumps and holes, where the darkest shadows fell, where dogs barked and cats hissed and ghosts whispered, the good streets of solid bluestone and brick houses, and the mean streets where at two in the morning there might be a roar of rage, the smash of a bottle and the crack of a hand against skin.

If it was early in the evening, she would walk the streets south of what had once been the small river that neatly divided the town in two, and stop and look through the windows of houses as if at photographs of a world entirely unimaginable and incomprehensible. She saw the glow of computer screens, a small chandelier laughing with light, sometimes shelves with books, a gleaming wooden table set for dinner, beds with plumped pillows, a piano, boots and bicycles left messily by front doors. She smelled comfort and wood polish and food and money. She heard music and voices, even fragments of conversations. She enjoyed the looking and the wondering. Pieces of lives, she thought. That's what I see.

She wondered what it would be like to sit in a particular house, to be served food from the heavy red casserole dish sitting on a white dining table, to sip wine from a glass so delicate you could bite through it. She imagined knocking on a door. 'Please,' she might say. But then what? 'Could I just sit down for a little while? I won't bother you. I'm so tired.' And perhaps that might be enough, if she knocked on the right door. 'Yes, of course,' a smiling woman would say, shirt crisp and clean. 'Come in and make yourself comfortable. Sit down there. Would you like a cup of tea? Or some water? You've been walking all these years, of course you're tired.' And Clare would sit on a plush sofa and run her hand across the rich fabric, feeling the textures of a home.

On some nights she found herself drawn north, over the bridge that crossed the muddy river bed, away from the town centre, through the wrong-side-of-the-tracks suburbs and onto the highway. She walked past the auto centres and used-car dealerships, the garden-supply store, the hardware store with rusting metal gates fencing in lawnmowers and tractor parts no one wanted any more, everything half-price or less. She walked past a petrol station with its peeling plastic bunting hanging from every pump demanding permits and proof of identity, past a sandwich shop shuttered with a faded for-sale sign, past all the two-bit businesses – biscuit factory, cabinet maker, the Heaven Scent soap store, the picture framer with lurid blue and gold seascapes and sad portraits of forgotten grandmothers hanging in its dirty windows, water-recycling supplies, the concrete vault maker (*Protect Your Precious Possessions From Fire and Flood Forever*) – that hung on to the fringes of the long wide road that headed north, on and on across the wind-scarred plains and through the newly mapped inclusion zones and the slowly emptying closing-down towns; and all of it, the businesses, the sorry signs and the highway, were a tumbleweed wasteland in the dry, dusty night.

Clare would stop when she reached the rows of electronic billboards right on the edge of town where the road widened into a four-lane highway that had once been busy and noisy. The billboards were like a small army in the darkness, bristling silently under weak solar-powered floodlights that looked like giant stick insects, deformed and fragile.

Thank You for Visiting Myamba, Last Year's Fastest-
Growing Inclusion Zone Town
Your Government: Building Strong and Safe Communities.
Water–Safe. Fire–Safe. Food–Safe. Ready for the future
TODAY!
Are YOU Eligible? Assistance Available NOW for
Relocation. Call Your Land and Housing Relocation
Management Authority TODAY!
A NEW ERA: Energising Rural Australia
Travel Permit Essential for Highway Three. Heavy
Penalties Apply

Clare would read each sign, standing back so she could gather in the huge letters that glowed weakly in the dark. She would mouth each word slowly, to touch it and understand it. And then she would shrug and walk on, through the electronic tollway booths that hummed as if talking among themselves, and down the dark highway.

Forever, it seemed, Clare had always walked. She walked in the chill and the wind and wet of the flood years, and in the searing dry of the drought years. She walked through autumn leaves and over summer grasses that crunched like paper. She counted the trees that came crashing down across the town over the years, exhausted by too much rain or none at all. She counted the houses that were being built in the new designated estates and subdivisions, the businesses that opened, the businesses that closed. She counted the steps she took, the nights that would pass until the next full moon, the good things that had happened to her and the bad, and every futile dream she had ever had.

On the worst of the summer nights, when the searing north wind roared and the air sat hot in her throat, she let her heart turn to stone so it could not burn. She closed her eyes and ears to the chance there might be a shattering crack of flames and an explosion of trees. She barely breathed, in case her breath fanned a fire. Just walk. Just walk. One step and then another. Head down against the wind and dust.

And every night, when she was tired enough to return to the ratbag cottage, she would lie on the lumpy sofa scrounged from a footpath years ago and write in her journal of all the small and useless things from her day and her night: the half-moon hanging and the imagined rattles and footfalls of ghosts, if she had seen a kangaroo or a fox or a cat or a horse, what she had eaten for breakfast and what she had cooked for dinner, if someone had said hello to her, what the temperature was and if there was a fire warning, if she had lost weight or gained it.

How have I come to this, she would think. How has it all come to this? She would fold her hands between the familiar soft vastness of her breasts and the magpies would begin their dawn singing as she finally closed her eyes.

•

One night when Clare stood near the signs, leaning against a wind that was blowing in from the south, her eyes stinging from the cold autumn dust, she was startled by a voice beside her.

'Bullshit, isn't it?'

The man standing next to her was tall, as tall as she was, and she could see in the moonlight that appeared and disappeared between the rolling clouds that he had a short beard and was wearing a sturdy canvas jacket. He carried a backpack that seemed close to bursting.

'Those words,' he said, nodding at the signs, 'bullshit words. Bullshit signs.'

Clare looked at his heavy walking boots, and then at his face, which looked tired in the grey light.

'Yeah,' she said, after a minute or two. 'They scare me somehow.'

'It's like they're telling us how much things are changing and trying to make it normal,' the man said. 'They just sit like they've always been there. But they haven't.' His voice came and went on the wind so it was loud and then soft. 'I've been walking a long way. Hell of a lot of signs around. All bullshit.' He unbuckled his backpack and shrugged it to the ground.

'Walking where?' Clare asked. She watched two empty beer cans and a flurry of leaves roll across the highway.

'Been round different parts of the city for a while. Then up to here. Heading north. Going to walk till I come to somewhere. Still got to be a somewhere left.'

'But they're closing it down. The north. The west. Most of it.'

'That's what they're telling us. They been telling us that for a few years now. Not so easy, I guess.' He bent down and took a thermos from a pocket of the backpack. He undid the red plastic lid and poured something hot. She smelled tea on the wind. He took a sip then handed the cup to Clare. 'Have some. It's fresh. Made it this afternoon.'

The tea was strong and sweet and it warmed her throat.

He took back the cup. A beer can clinked up against the foot of a post supporting one of the billboards. A cockroach appeared in the opening of the can and Clare watched it struggle to pull itself through the space. She imagined she heard the rasp of its body against the tin.

'You know,' the man said, 'four years ago I had a wife and a house, kids, a job. Taught at uni. Natural science. The environment. Things like that.' He gave a bitter laugh. 'Anyway, job went. Should have seen it coming. The wife wasn't happy. Then the house went. They just came in and bought the whole block, bought six blocks. Eighty houses. Paid nowhere near what anything was worth. A thousand apartments going up now on the land. Couldn't have fought them even if we had the money to. They've changed all the laws. Anyway . . .'

He sipped the tea and watched the cockroach. After a minute it gave up and retreated. A thick dark antenna waved weakly from the opening.

'How the hell did it get in there if it can't get out?' Then he shook his head. 'Anyway,' he said again, 'we found somewhere new to live, but the rent was a fortune. Kids had to change schools. Nothing seemed to work any more. It was too much for the wife. She buggered off with the kids, back to her mum's. Left twenty thousand dollars for me in the account. That doesn't buy anything any more. I could have fought her, but they told me the waiting list to get the case heard was three years. Didn't want to spend three years waiting or hoping. So, I'm walking.' Some of his words were lost in the wind but his voice was strong. 'Plenty worse off than me left in the city. It's crazy what's happening.'

'But how can you go north?' Clare asked. 'They're moving people out.'

'Like I said, that's what they're telling us.' The man sighed deeply, and shifted on his feet, as if to ease muscles that were aching. 'I don't believe they can close down half the country. Don't want to believe it. Everything that's happening – it makes me feel strange. As if I've lost my footing. Figure I'll find an empty house somewhere and lie low, wait for things to change. I know how to get by in the bush. Always have.' He laughed. 'I did get a new job, you know. Landfill quality monitoring officer, out at one of those new dumps past the airport. That was bullshit too. Thought they might want me to actually test for what's in the stink that's over that whole place, but no. Foraging for scrap metal and wood was about all they wanted me to do. Anyway.' He looked at her. 'Why are you out here?'

Clare looked at the signs, at the dark road ahead. 'I walk a lot,' she said. 'Something to do.'

He didn't respond.

Clare wondered about his wife, about how some women seemed able to throw away one life and find a new one. It was something that had always been beyond her.

'And I like to look at things. Watch things.' She shrugged. 'Then I can think about them. I walk most nights.'

'Do you get afraid?'

'Of what?'

'The dark, maybe? Of the other people who are walking?'

'I never meet anyone. I've never seen anyone. You're the first person I've talked to.'

'You need to be careful,' he said. 'There's lots of people walking. Walking away from the cities. For every hundred people they bring in, a dozen walk away. And they're not all like me.'

The man bent and pushed the thermos into a pocket on the side of his backpack, adjusting a strap. He was getting ready to leave. His movements were steady and certain. A plastic bag tumbled past them. Clare pulled her jacket down hard across her shoulders.

'Animals,' the man said. The wind fell suddenly so his voice was almost a shout.

'Animals?'

'They're on the move. Too many left behind all over the place. They're acting weird. Everything's weird. Be careful is all I'm saying.' He looked directly at her and smiled. 'You married?'

What was the honest answer to that, Clare thought. That there was a shadow of a man in her house? 'Sort of.'

'Seems you are or you aren't.'

Clare shrugged. 'I don't think there's much any more that's either one thing or the other,' she said slowly. She surprised herself by asking, 'What about you? Do you get scared?'

'Not any more. When my wife left me, I was scared. Not now.' He was pulling his backpack onto his shoulders, swaying to adjust it. 'Anyway, I have a knife. Big old hunting knife. Used to belong to my granddad.'

'Would you use it?'

'If I had to. I've thought about it. I don't know. You can break a life with just words. Why is using a knife so bad? In these times, anyway.'

He seemed ready to leave, rocking on his heels. The wind swirled around them again and the moon briefly appeared, throwing a bright light on them both before clouds rolled across. There was a brief roar of aircraft far overhead. Military most likely, Clare guessed, from the droning weight of the sound.

The man started speaking again. 'You know, one of the guys I worked with for a bit at the landfill, he was on security, used to come on as I was leaving, but we started talking. He said he couldn't believe how many people came out in the night to see what they could scrounge. He said it was really sad.' He looked at his feet. 'Anyway, he told me that one night he heard this huge crashing sound, like a massive hail storm or something. Out of nowhere. He comes out of the security hut and he can't believe what he sees.'

'What? What did he see?'

'Bones.' He looked at Clare as if expecting her to laugh, but she was listening carefully. 'That's what he said. This crazy heap of bones just tumbling down from the sky, crashing onto his office, onto all the rubbish and the piles of tin and wood and cans. Five, ten minutes this went on. He nearly shit himself, he said. Like it was some sort of ghost scene. He sat in a corner of the hut on the floor all night. In the morning there was nothing. No bones. But he swore that's what he saw. And his car had three huge dents, on the bonnet and the roof. Nothing could have caused them, he said, except things falling onto it. Crazy, huh?'

Clare thought for a minute. 'I guess.'

'Even crazier, I believed him. Don't know why. But I did. I still do.' He stepped forward so that he was in front of her. 'I'm going to keep moving. Patrols could start soon and I want to get off the highway. So, good to talk to you.'

He held out his hand. Clare looked at it, then reached out to shake it. His skin was warm.

'Be careful,' she said.

'You too. Strange woman in the dark.' His smile was gentle.

He started walking down the black highway and Clare watched him until he disappeared. She turned to walk home. A small black cat was sitting in front of her, staring gravely at her knees. Now it looked up to her face and its eyes were a vivid green. Clare stared back, and then the cat stood up and suddenly darted off down the highway, following the man.

Clare walked slowly back into town, thinking about the man and what he'd said about bones and about carrying a knife, and she remembered the warmth of his skin when he had shaken her hand. She wished she had asked his name. That was a conversation, she thought. A real conversation. It would be something to write about when she got home – what he'd said, what she thought about the things he'd said, what might be in his backpack.

Clare felt and then heard a convoy of large trucks coming into town from the north and she stepped off the road. Their headlights cut briefly through the night, and as they passed her, over the whine and shake of the engines, she heard animals screaming, a wail of pain and distress, and she saw the heads and tails and ears and wild eyes of pigs and sheep and cows and, in the last and largest truck, horses, all of them straining against the bars of the double-decked containers, broken legs hanging out like sticks, snouts and muzzles bloodied and mangled. Some animals seemed to be upside down, Clare saw, or sideways, or hanging across the backs of other animals sagging and crumpled beneath them.

When the unbearable noise and stench had passed, Clare realised she was crying. Too much, she thought. Much too much. She started walking again.

A few blocks from home, a patrol car pulled over and then drew away as the officers recognised her. They used to ask for her identification, watching quizzically while she held her phone to the scanner, but now they could rarely be bothered. Clare imagined them laughing. She's weird, that one, they'd say.

·

Over the next few weeks and months, as autumn became a too brief winter and spring edged in, it became clear to Clare that the walking man had been right about the people and the animals. Or perhaps she was paying more attention. She went regularly to the blinking, silent billboards and began counting the silhouettes trekking silently north, skirting the road and following instead the darker lines of fences and scrub. Only one or two people on some nights; some nights none at all; but more on others, and twice at least she thought she saw a child.

One night she heard the faint pull of rubber on the road behind her. Turning, she watched a woman pushing a heavy pram steadily up the middle of the road. She stopped when she saw Clare and there was a sudden shrill wail from the pram, but it subsided as soon as the woman, with a toss of her head, began walking again. It seemed she would walk past Clare and the signs, just keep walking down the lonely highway, but she stopped when she was level with Clare. There was another brief cry and the woman rocked the pram gently with one hand and swept back her hair with the other.

'Are you a walker?' she called across to Clare.

The night was still and so the words were loud and sharp, like a glass breaking. It seemed to Clare the soundless shadows and shapes that darted through the low scrublands by the sides of the highway stopped and stiffened.

She shook her head and then realised the woman probably couldn't see the gesture. 'No,' she called back. 'Where are you going?'

The woman was silent for a minute. 'There's places. That's what they're saying in the city. Places. You know.'

The baby in the pram cried again. The woman bent over and touched it and the crying stopped.

'We'll be right,' she said. 'They're selling stuff, you know, in the city. For people who are walking. It's like a black market. Special maps. A thing that blocks the drones spotting you. Tablets that clean water. Lots of stuff. I pawned my jewellery and sold the car and bought everything I could. The city stinks anyway. It's crazy. Too many people coming in. We'll be right.'

Clare didn't know what to say. 'Sure,' she said with a shrug.

The woman nodded and set off again, crooning softly to the baby.

Clare followed her. 'You have to get off this highway,' she said with an urgency prompted by a feeling that she wanted, somehow, to be kind. 'Take the left three kilometres along, and then the first right. It'll keep taking you north but it's safer. They don't bother patrolling so much.'

The woman raised her hand to acknowledge she had heard and kept walking. The lights from the billboards behind her spilled across the pram and for a few seconds Clare could see the baby, one tiny arm raised stiffly. She saw that it wasn't a baby but a plastic doll, red mouth and empty eyes open, black plastic curls on an oversized head that jerked from side to side. Clare shuddered as the woman disappeared into the darkness.

The next night a pack of dogs walked past the signs, single file. They were thin, collars hanging loose, and they ignored Clare, simply walking patiently towards the town as if they knew where they were going.

On another night a few weeks later, she stood outside the high mesh and barbed-wire fence surrounding the vast old canning factory. When she had first moved into Myamba she had liked to come here and watch the lights and trucks and the people smoking on their breaks by the factory doors under the signs that read *No Smoking* and breathe in the sweet smell that on certain days had scented the air across Myamba with a syrupy fruit salad perfume. Phil had even scored a month's work their first December here, and for those few weeks had seemed happy and busy, using some of the money to build her a couple of garden beds. But the factory had closed just a year later, a few years before all the rumours began about the closing-down towns and inclusion zones and cities and the buy-outs of farms and forests and water by one day China, another day the US or the Arabs, whoever, who knew? For years now the factory had sat empty in the shadows of weak floodlights and the red blinking of an alarm system.

On this night, Clare was startled by a sudden hissing and growling that seemed to be coming from the empty car park. She walked the long length of the fence, through empty plastic bottles and bags and fast-food wrappings and dry leaves, and stopped at the corner. She sucked in her breath. Dogs were circling a mob of kangaroos. The kangaroos stood tall, ready for flight. A large lean dog, growling

deep in its throat, leaped forward and slammed against one of the
kangaroos, burying its teeth into the animal's side. As the kangaroo
reared up and forward the dog sprang back, ripping flesh and blood
with it. The kangaroo screamed and a frenzy of growls and hisses and
screams was unleashed, animal against animal. A dog stood in shock,
its entrails at its feet, ripped open in one brutal swipe, and then it fell.
Another kangaroo screamed as it collapsed under the force of muscle
and jaws of dogs gone crazy. Clare smelled blood and wildness and
she shrank back against the fence as finally the remaining kangaroos
took off, thudding past her.

At the same moment a truck roared into the car park, headlights
on high beam. Dogs fell back into shadows, but some remained at the
body of the kangaroo, too intent on meat and blood. Clare watched
as two men in council uniforms got out of the truck, immediately
raising rifles to their shoulders. There were six quick quiet shots, each
a punch into the night. Then there was silence, except for the hum of
the truck engine. One of the men lit a cigarette while the other made
a phone call. They stood for a few minutes before putting their rifles
on the back of the truck. They climbed in and the truck moved away,
down across the field.

Clare looked at the bodies of the animals and shook her head.
Later, when she lay on her sofa, a mess of blankets around her, she
thought of the dead animals lying lonely on the cold, hard cement
and the screaming, bleeding animals in the trucks she had seen on
the night she met the walking man and her heart ached in a way she
couldn't have explained.

When she fell asleep towards dawn she dreamed of cockatoos flying
backwards down empty midnight streets, a cat and a possum curled
together on a car bonnet, kookaburras laughing at the moon, a hen
killing a fox, pecking out its eyes and nose. A small boy cradled a
dying horse, crying. The images rotated repeatedly, one after another,

every detail clear. *Pay attention, Clare*, a voice kept saying. A gentle voice. Clear and careful with the pronunciation of each word, as if this was not a first language. *Listen now, Clare.*

She thought about the images throughout the day that followed and the kind singsong voice and wished she could talk to the walking man.

three

On many nights I walk with Clare. Or, perhaps, she walks with me. Her legs are long and thick and strong. Tree trunks. Her stride is almost a metre. With four thousand steps she walks nearly four kilometres. Most nights she walks for eight thousand steps, but sometimes it is more. Twelve thousand steps and she has covered ten kilometres. It is nothing. Not for Clare and, of course, not for me. When I began in this country, toppling off the great boat that heaved and crashed against a teeming dock, I walked eight hundred and sixty-one thousand steps from the endless coast north to here. Here, where I fell in love with the stars, and the colours in the stones and rocks, and the promise of gold.

Yes, I am a ghost. Really. A visitor from the past. My own once-upon-a-time past. Or yours.

Clare sometimes talks as she walks. 'Love this one,' she might say, stopping in front of a little weatherboard cottage painted blue with a pink trim, chimney crooked.

And I talk back. 'Mary Johnson died there in 1863, Clare. Whooping cough. Her father was so grief-stricken he boarded up the front door and those little windows for two years to block out the sunshine.'

Or she might stop on a winter's night, startled perhaps by the hollow ringing howl of a dog in the distance. Or empty beer bottles clinking in a brittle breeze that rips along a broken gutter. Or a gunshot. She will pull her old coat more firmly around her. She is thinking, perhaps, of her mother standing more than forty years ago in her tidy white kitchen, shivering suddenly as she pulled a tray of roasting fish fillets, golden and buttery, from the oven. 'A ghost walked over my grave,' she exclaimed to a startled Clare. 'I swear it did. Sweet Jesus.' And they found out two hours later that at that precise moment, at the very second on an ordinary Friday evening when Clare's mother was pulling Friday night's fish fillets out of the oven, Clare's father had died in a freezer room at Al's Supremo Smallgoods, where he was assistant manager. The roof fell in and buried him under ice and frozen pork legs and ribs and belly and pipes and plaster. It was, her mother always said, a ridiculous way to die.

Clare often stops and listens intently for her past, looking at and considering the dark trees, the moon, the cracks in the pavement, as if they might offer clues. Clues for getting by. For coping. For not giving up. For finding something to believe in. For answers.

That is all a ghost is, Clare. An attention to the past. Listen for the stories and they will come. Listen now, Clare.

Oh, Clare. You walk upon bones that lie upon bones that lie upon bones. We all do.

This way, come this way. On that hill there, past the sports oval. A thousand of us once upon a time, digging and scraping and washing for flecks of gold. Just on that one small hill. Can you imagine? Can you see? Not a tree anywhere. Every scrap of wood needed – for building shafts, for fires for cooking. I was only a boy. Quick hands, quick fingers, quick eyes to see the gold. It was crazy then. Yes, it's crazy now. Crazier. I see that.

See the half-moon hanging? Just four hundred and seventy-eight million steps from here to there, Clare. Give or take.

four

Years after telling Ella the story about Timmy, Robbie asked her to marry him. It wasn't the first time. In fact, he had lost track of the number of times he had asked and the number of times she had said no, firmly and definitively. 'It will change nothing,' she always said.

This time they spent a day walking in the Kander Valley, a few hours drive north on empty roads from Ella's apartment in Geneva, wandering slowly in brilliant sunshine, talking about their work, about the population dislocations and closed-down states across North America, and the refugee processing in what was once Cuba and was now International Refugee Station Five, where Ella had spent the last three months.

'As bad as I've ever seen but worse,' was all she would say, and he could see she was tired and unsettled.

They talked about the impending buy-out by China of the South African States, the drought in India, the blackout across California, now in its fifth week, the latest oil price.

Robbie told her there had been, briefly, photographs on the internet of bones falling from the sky in Australia. The photographs had been removed but he had called his grandmother and she swore it was true.

23

'She also said the ghosts were walking.' He shrugged. Then he laughed. 'Well, she would say that, wouldn't she?'

Ella smiled and then frowned and said she had heard something about falling bones in Alaska. 'I can't remember where I heard it. But your grandmother, she is well?'

'Yes, I think so. But I think . . .' He paused. 'I don't know. She's worried. About the world. The town. Everything.' He laughed again. 'I asked how she was and she said, "I am being vigilant, my dear boy. Very vigilant. More people should do the same." I have no idea what she meant but I sort of do.'

'Time for a visit,' Ella said.

'It's so far. There's enough travel.'

'You miss her.'

'Sometimes. Yes, of course.'

'She is remarkable. I would like to see her again.'

Robbie had an image of his grandmother sitting on the wide wicker chair on the front verandah of the House of Many Promises, night shadows gathering, a candle burning on the side table, her cat sitting on the verandah railing, watching her. He remembered her capacity for stillness, and the brightness of her brown eyes, and how the last time he had visited, her love for him had broken his heart when it was time to leave.

'Geese,' said Ella. 'That was the other thing. A friend in Toronto says the geese haven't arrived this spring. He waits for them every year by Lake Ontario and even last year there were still a few. But not now. There are no geese. He is weeping for the gone geese, he says.'

They sat on rocks by the river and ate cheeses and tomatoes and bread, and peaches that Robbie had been surprised to find. So surprised he had bought the whole box despite the exorbitant price and struggled to carry it up the narrow street back to Ella's apartment, where it took up the length and width of the small kitchen bench.

'What will I do with so many peaches?' she had asked.

'I don't know,' Robbie said. 'Just smell them. They smell beautiful, like real peaches.'

And over the past two days the peaches had slowly scented the apartment with a smell as elusive and wistful as early spring sunshine.

The night before, Ella had poached half a dozen with some sugar and schnapps and a bay leaf she had taken from her ground floor neighbour's flower box, and they had sat, not talking, on her window seat and fed each other spoonfuls of a perfect summer's day.

'It is still possible,' Robbie had said. 'A beautiful day. It's still possible.'

And she had pressed a peach-flavoured finger gently to his lips.

The peaches were a bright rose-orange and now they each ate one slowly, and waved away with sticky peach hands the curious goats that had come high-stepping down the mountainside. While they were sitting, an elderly couple walked past, the first people they had seen all day. The woman was wearing a pink cardigan, with her walking permit prominently pinned to it, and hiking boots; the man held a sturdy walking stick and binoculars hung around his neck.

'Good afternoon,' he said in German. 'Beautiful day.'

'Very warm,' Ella replied.

'Too warm, I think.' The man touched his binoculars. 'We have been hoping to see a chamois or an ibex, but there have been none so far.'

Ella smiled. 'Like the geese in Canada,' she said.

'Pardon?'

Ella shrugged. 'Animals are going missing everywhere it seems.'

The couple looked at her. 'Yes, I have heard of this,' the woman said. 'And no snow again. It is gone so soon. Still, we have the goats. There is still just enough for them, I think. I am glad the goats are happy.'

For a few seconds they all looked up at the peaks of the mountains, grey and purple and black, the spring dusting of snow already melted.

Then the man and woman nodded and resumed walking. Robbie watched as the man reached out and took the woman's hand.

Ella and Robbie began their walk back to the valley entrance. Robbie walked ahead, lost in his thoughts. It had taken forever and cost a small fortune to arrange this day – the permits for the car, and the driving and access to the valley. That didn't matter. What did matter was that ten hours had felt like fifteen minutes. For the umpteen millionth time, he wondered how this happened whenever he was with Ella. Even last night it had felt as if time had stood still, but then he realised that it had simply gone. Vanished. He hadn't managed to hold even a minute in his hand. And he thought, yet again, that he did not want to catch a plane tomorrow. He did not want to leave her. He did not want to go to . . . where was he going? Shanghai. That's right. A three-day conference on global water pricing and transport. He shuddered at the thought. Three days that would feel like a year. And he would file stories on the empty talk and decisions that would barely be read, that would disappear within a second in the continual cascade of news and reports from other conferences and committees and parliaments and wars and famines.

One single day gone by in minutes, he thought. I want to stay in this valley and walk forever.

He heard Ella calling him. 'Robbie, please.' Her voice sounded thin under the soft, slow trickle of the small river and the music of goat bells.

He turned and was surprised he was so much further along the track. Ella stood with her hands on her hips, rucksack thrown to the side. She looked as if she had been superimposed onto a postcard: behind her was the sweep of the valley, pure greens and greys under the bluest sky, ringed by the Alps. He moved back up towards her.

'My feet are killing me. Truly.' She was genuinely upset. She ran a hand through her thick hair.

Robbie looked at her quizzically.

'I can't walk another step. I mean it. I should never have worn these shoes. We should never have walked so far. Damn it.'

The goats had followed them from their picnic spot and now they began to nudge her, forcing her to take several steps to the side. She swore loudly, in German.

'Move the goats, Robbie. Get them away. And then tell me how I'm going to walk back to the car in these shoes.'

Robbie looked at the shoes she was wearing: light yellow loafers. He had stepped over her hiking boots in the hallway that morning and should have thought to throw them in the car. He looked up at her and burst out laughing. She was impossibly beautiful.

'Marry me,' he said.

'Robbie. Please.'

'Marry me.'

A goat butted her from behind and Ella lost her footing and sat down heavily.

'Please just tell these goats to piss off.'

He clapped his hands loudly and stamped towards the goats. They scattered. He picked up her rucksack. 'There. Goats gone. Yes or no?'

Ella eased off her shoes. He could see huge blisters emerging on both heels.

'Give me one hundred reasons,' she said.

'A hundred reasons why you should marry me? That seems unreasonable.'

'A hundred reasons why you love me, so that I know you're asking the right woman to marry you.'

Robbie sat on a large rock at the side of the path and put their rucksacks between his legs. 'A hundred reasons is a lot.'

'Marriage is a lot. I do not even know why we are having this conversation but I want to sit down for a while. You have five minutes starting now. Oh, goat, go away! Go.'

A goat had come back and was nibbling at her hair. Robbie leaned forward and clapped again and it backed away.

'Marriage is about compromise,' he said. 'Thirty reasons.'

'Why thirty? Fifty would be a compromise. Thirty means you win.'

'I met you when I was thirty. One reason for every year I waited to meet you. Thirty is still a lot of reasons.'

Ella stretched out her legs. 'Damn you, Roberto Adams. Okay. Thirty reasons. Two minutes. Go.'

Robbie drew a deep breath. 'Because you are beautiful.'

'No, that doesn't count.'

'What do you mean it doesn't count?'

'I know you think I'm beautiful. But that's hardly a reason to love someone, let alone get married. You'd have ten thousand wives by now, for God's sake. Perhaps you do.'

Robbie shook his head. The afternoon sun was warm on his shoulders. He took another deep breath. 'I love you and I want to marry you because . . .' He looked at her sitting on the path, leaning back on her hands, legs and sore feet stretched in front of her. 'Because . . . of the straightness of your back and the slope of your shoulders, because of the work you do despite the pain you see, because you wear yellow shoes and red shoes and you keep and wear every scarf I have ever bought for you and that touches my heart, because you speak four languages, because of the way your breasts fall when you sit on me, because you let me be who I am, because you still read real books, and because you found for me the last English-language copy of Bolaño's *Antwerp* that was left in the world and I carry it with me everywhere although the back has fallen off, because you always wear the same perfume and whenever I smell it I feel I can breathe again and sometimes when I'm at an airport and missing you the most I find the perfume in a shop and I stand there smelling it like a fool, because there is a tiny freckle on your clitoris—'

'Really?' Ella interrupted.

'I've told you before.'

"Okay. Yes, you did. One minute.'

'Because there is also a freckle on your left earlobe and three freckles on your right shoulder, because the world is so damn crazy now that love may be the only lifeline that's left, because you are never scared of how crazy the world has become, because you are magnificent when you are angry and because you can sulk like a schoolgirl—'

'Not true.'

'Very true, and two minutes isn't long enough.'

'One more then.'

'Reason or minute?'

'Minute.'

Robbie sighed. Two goats nuzzled at the rucksacks between his legs. He let them be.

'Because you listen to Beethoven concertos and *Madame Butterfly* and you taught me to listen too, because that speech you made against the refugee processing stations at that last press conference before the United Nations shut down was one of the best I've ever heard, because you know the story of Timmy, because you never panic, because you've met my grandmother, because we've made love in nineteen countries although some of them don't exist any more which is not our fault, because you can be so very still, because every summer you grow red geraniums on your windowsill, because nothing has changed in your apartment since I met you except your computers, because you can rarely be bothered cooking and because when you do it's wonderful, because there is nothing you have needed from me, because you make me laugh, because I can always find you in this world no matter where we are . . .'

He paused for breath. One of the goats looked up at him, as if surprised by his sudden silence. It had a grey beard and eyes. It butted his knee gently.

'One more,' Ella said. 'That's only twenty-nine.'

'Goddamn it, woman. Okay. One more. Because your heart is the only home I know.'

'Aaah.' Ella drew her knees up to her chin and wriggled her toes. 'That one.'

'What one?'

'The last thing you said. Okay then.'

'Okay what?'

'Okay, Robbie, I give up. Truly. I give up. I'll marry you.' She rested her forehead on her knees for a few seconds and when she looked up her face seemed, briefly, bright and young. 'Because, yes, your heart is also the only home I know any more. Because I don't know what else there is that matters. Or what else there is that I can understand.'

Robbie leaped up from the rock and the goats scattered, bells tinkling. He laughed and went over to her, helping her to her feet. As she was slowly and painfully putting on her shoes, a goat butted her from behind again and she fell over and started crying. 'Stupid, stupid goats,' she said.

Robbie helped her up again, and, carrying their rucksacks, led her gently the mile down the valley to the wooden chalet at the entrance gate where they still served wine and beer to the few hikers permitted into the valley each day. He sat her at a table on the patio and went inside, where he threw a fifty-franc note on the bar and asked in his terrible German for some soap and a bowl of hot water and a carafe of white wine.

He sat at Ella's feet and washed them gently, while she sipped the wine.

'Stupid, stupid goats,' was all she said, but she was smiling.

five

Once a week Clare went into Myamba town centre. It was something she looked forward to. She would wake early, put away last night's dishes, and shiver through a shower that was painfully cold because the hot water system had broken long ago and the owners simply ignored requests to fix it and she couldn't afford to. Then, while she had a cup of tea on the rotting front verandah, she would begin to prepare her list for the day. She paid careful attention to this, writing every word slowly and neatly, as a child might. I will do these things and the day will pass, she thought. I will breathe and move and remember to smile.

Petrol, she wrote today. Then, in a separate box, under the heading of *Shopping*: *lamb chops, oranges, cabbage, onions, bread, milk, soap, notebook*. She knew the list of items was largely superfluous. She would collect her Food Essentials Pack and buy whatever was on sale, although lamb chops would be a real treat if she could manage it. But she would buy herself a new notebook. It was one of the most expensive purchases she made these days because of the cost of paper, but only

thirteen blank pages remained in her current notebook. She needed
to know she had more pages. More space.

Phil was still sleeping when she drove into town. Useless bastard,
she thought.

Myamba had outgrown its sole supermarket long ago. Efforts to
build another were thwarted over the decades by every conceivable
interest group, from the environmentalists, who opposed every proposed
site because it would undoubtedly damage what remained of the town's
heritage aesthetics and add to traffic woes and only serve the interests
of multinational businesses, to the developers, who opposed every
proposed site if it wasn't their own or couldn't become their own,
to many of the old-time locals, who expected things to remain the
way they always had been thank you very much despite every shred
of evidence making it clear this was impossible. When Myamba was
declared an inclusion zone town two years earlier, far higher and
more moneyed powers than any local interests had intervened swiftly.
Three old houses and gardens adjoining the supermarket were demol-
ished, and an extra fifty square metres of shopping area and ten more
checkout lanes were added, along with another hundred car parking
spaces, and a Food Essentials Distribution Depot opened, for those
who qualified.

Despite its upgrades the Myamba Maxi Store, through no real
fault of its own, had become about as dysfunctional as it was possible
for a supermarket to be. Six thousand people had been moved into
Myamba during the past two years. How did any town cope with
that, the locals asked. The queues for a parking space grew longer and
moved more slowly month by month, and caused traffic jams on the
main road as drivers waited to turn into the parking lot. Draconian
fines were introduced for people overstaying the thirty-minute parking
limit, which of course everyone did because it was impossible to get
in and out of the supermarket in that time.

The matter caused intense discussion, in the streets, over fences, in the long queues at the supermarket's checkouts. What were the odds of finding a parking space at seven in the morning? Excellent except for Tuesdays and Thursdays, the 'specials days', when pensioners and the poor in general would be queuing by six thirty for the doors to open to save five dollars on a tin of cat food and buy two-day-old bread at half-price and collect their Food Essentials Pack. What about seven at night? Hopeless usually because somewhere about that time, give or take, the leftover cooked chickens that had been sitting in a vast bain-marie since the morning were reduced to twenty dollars each, and again, you know, the pensioners and the poor. Lunchtime? Impossible. Even if a parking space was available, it meant waiting behind dozens and dozens of teenagers on their school lunch-break, each purchasing a soft drink or a chocolate bar and swearing they'd topped up the funds on their phone just yesterday and so it was, like, just unbelievable that they couldn't pay.

It was, people agreed, far worse in summer, when people went to the supermarket simply because it was the only place in town that ran air conditioning eighteen hours a day, thanks to the solar panels and batteries the owners had installed on the roof and the back-up generators they had purchased. If it was forty-five, forty-six degrees outside, hundreds of people crammed the aisles, studying cereal boxes or gazing intently at lemons or sausages, or they simply stood in the cool, arms folded, eyes closed, no pretence at all.

People still talked of the long autumn and winter two years earlier when members of a group calling itself Educators for Food Democracy staged an apparently endless sit-in up and down the supermarket aisles, chaining a fair-trade-cotton-clothed ankle or wrist to a barrel of oranges or bin of nuts or box of no-brand tuna, which was the only tuna for sale anywhere any more, assuming it was tuna, and handing out leaflets containing impassioned pleas for shoppers to preserve the integrity of Australia's food chain and wheat farmers and the Indian and Pacific oceans and garlic growers, and almost unintelligible lists of preservatives and food modifiers and chemicals that were in everything from salt to sultanas, and graphic descriptions of hundreds of ten-year-old girls burning to death when a fire ripped through a two-hectare food-packaging factory on the outskirts of a town with an unpronounceable name somewhere in the Greater China, the girls having worked weeks, months of fifteen-hour shifts sealing up boxes of cereals and dry biscuits for the careless glazed-eyed shoppers in towns like Myamba or cities like New York. And a woman like Clare would gather every leaflet handed to her and later spread them over her rickety kitchen table, a finger moving slowly across the words and blurred photographs, trying to understand what she should eat, or could afford to eat, if making a tuna casserole took the world a step further to shutdown. Then she would stuff the leaflets into a drawer and sweep up the dust that had blown into the kitchen again and peel some carrots and potatoes and grate some cheese to make a vegetable bake because it was what she had and could afford.

The Educators for Food Democracy seemed to attract more people than ever to the supermarket: the curious, the lonely just wanting a conversation even if they couldn't understand it, sympathisers happy to talk for hours about the smells and textures of foods they were increasingly suspicious of. The increased traffic pleased the owners because everyone inevitably bought something and so they let the protesters be, provided they stopped boiling pots of pungent herbal tea on portable gas burners in the aisles, a matter that was resolved amicably. The protesters looked thin and hungry but they were also clean and peaceful and earnest, and the conversations they tried to strike up with the local shoppers were so harmlessly convoluted that more and more people found the weeks of the sit-in vastly entertaining. Despite the inconvenience of stepping over bodies to reach for something on the shelves, and the delays in getting a trolley down an aisle, and the fact that people went home wondering if the fifty-five pesticides, fungicides and herbicides in the knob of garlic they'd bought meant the bolognese sauce they planned to cook up that evening would be toxic, the supermarket was briefly more interesting than it had ever been.

For many people it had been easier for years to simply drive south or east to a bigger town with a bigger supermarket, or even a choice of supermarkets, but the inclusion zones were becoming more congested and not everyone could afford a travel permit every week, and anyway food everywhere seemed to be more and more the same, with less choice, often only the basics, whatever items whoever was in charge of these things decided on as the basics; and then there was the price of petrol, more fearsome than the thought of squeezing the car inch by inch, breath drawn, into one of the allotted parking spaces at the Myamba Maxi Store once one eventually became available.

Clare always thought of a trip to the Maxi Store as an Outing with a capital O. It was a phrase her mother had often used, grimly, to establish that a forthcoming event, such as a visit to the cinema, would be exhausting and even the contemplation of it was arduous. But to Clare it was the opposite. There would be things to see and hear and touch and count and to take away and think about.

Today she collected her Food Essentials Pack and waited patiently for her phone to be scanned, staring resolutely ahead while the grubby little girl, or maybe it was a boy, straddling the bony hip of the woman in front of her asked loudly, pointing at Clare's face, 'Are you too fat?' She was disappointed to see the FEP was more or less the same as usual: long-life milk, orange juice – Clare hated orange juice, but if it was free she'd drink it – a loaf of bread, a kilo of white sugar, a tin of peas, two tins of fish paste, a tin of some sort of ham, two tins of peaches, a packet of ten teabags, six small apples, and a packet of biscuits in

plain brown wrapping labelled Snacks for Health. She would read all
the labels carefully when she got home, although they would be the
same as the ones on last week's food. But still.

Then it took her an hour to fill her trolley, every item slowly scru-
tinised, for cost mostly, out of curiosity partly, but also for usefulness,
for how she could prepare it, reinvent it, stretch it as far as it would
go. The lamb chops were too expensive after all, but she could get
four meals from a pack of stewing steak on special, another two from
chicken thighs use-by date tomorrow. She got the new notebook, one
hundred and twenty pages, for her lists and notes and little drawings
(there were one hundred and seventy-six already filled notebooks in
eleven boxes in Clare's shed, rimmed by rat bait and gathering dust),
a cabbage, four onions, toilet paper on special, a bottle of cooking oil,
Weight Watcher's double chocolate chip cookies ten dollars off, and
a huge bag of carrots on sale that could be good for soup. She looked
longingly at the bananas, but they were far too expensive.

At the checkout she watched the woman in front of her. It was
Granna Adams, wearing black cashmere and pearls and the faintest
perfume that smelled to Clare of red roses in sunshine. Everyone knew
Granna Adams, who lived alone in the House of Many Promises on the
hill. 'Bloody town matriarch,' Clare had overheard someone describe
her, but she understood it was meant as a compliment.

'I was astonished, just so surprised,' Granna was saying to the young
checkout girl, who seemed to be recording and packing the contents
of Granna's shopping trolley in slow motion.

Clare couldn't believe the amount of food being unloaded: lamb
roasts and chickens and mincemeat, potatoes, slabs of cheese – real
cheese, Clare could see – and dozens of tins of tomatoes. Six bunches
of bananas.

'How old is he now, then?' asked the checkout girl.

'Oh, too old, he says. Roberto and Ella – well, I just never thought . . .' She threw back her head and laughed. It was the sound of water playing on stone.

'I saw him just a few weeks ago,' the girl said. 'One of the cable channels. We were at the pub and the news was on. He was in China, I think. Something about water.'

'Well, I've never heard him so happy.'

Clare listened to the conversation with her head tilted to one side. She would collect it and file it away along with the countless other stories and pieces of information about the town and its people that drifted her way. Gossamer thin threads that held lives together.

The girl handed Granna the last of her shopping bags. 'That will be one thousand and thirty-five dollars, Mrs Adams. And I'm so happy for you.'

The amount of money caused Clare to shift slightly. What on earth did an old woman who lived alone need with so much food?

Granna turned to her. 'I'm so sorry, dear. I've been chatting away and taking up everyone's time.' As she spoke, she took her phone from a soft brown leather bag and touched it to the screen to pay the bill. Clare imagined the bag smelled of money. 'And I do like your scarf,' Granna went on. Clare's eyes narrowed. 'You made it yourself, of course. I think I've seen you selling them at the market sometimes.'

It wasn't a question, but Clare nodded clumsily and rubbed her hand back and forth along the front bar of her shopping trolley. Granna flashed Clare a smile of such warmth that she was moved to smile back. She was suddenly ashamed that for a moment she had wanted to lean over and take the old woman's bag from her and put it into her own trolley. She had imagined Granna might understand this, might say, 'Of course you can have it, dear. Take it and enjoy the money. I don't need it.' Now it seemed to her that Granna had known exactly what she was thinking.

She looked at Granna's hand, now putting her phone away. It was elegant, with a simple gold wedding ring on the third finger, but there were liver spots too and a network of veins under soft faded skin. Clare suddenly remembered the thin dogs, the animals dead on the cold ground, and felt the same jolt of pointless, hollow sadness. Then she smelled the perfume again, or almost smelled it, because it was lighter than air, like rose petals falling.

'Tell that young man of yours to be careful at cricket training. The oval's hard as a rock,' she said to the checkout girl. She smiled again at Clare and left.

It was Clare's turn. She watched each item being checked, anxious that perhaps she had miscalculated, that perhaps the bill would be twenty or even fifty dollars more than the amount of money she held tightly in her hand, for which she had waited patiently for an hour to take from the town's sole remaining bank machine because she refused to fully trust that her government-issued phone could reliably pay out the right sums of money to the right people at the right time, and the small receipt stating her balance reassured her and the smell of the notes was comforting.

The assistant paid her no attention at all. Fine. Why would she? The total bill was only ten dollars higher than Clare had expected. That was fine too.

After shopping, Clare liked to go to Maisie's Bakery Café for two egg and bacon sandwiches and a coffee. The sandwich and coffee were a daily morning special that cost forty dollars, and the second sandwich was only twenty-five dollars. It was the type of café where no one looked at her as if to say a big woman shouldn't be eating two egg and bacon sandwiches. Clare could listen to the chatter of the women behind the counter and the talk of other customers.

She was comfortable sitting at one of the chipped and cheerful wooden tables, although she worried a chair would one day give way

under her weight, and she always put her list carefully on the table
to give the impression that she was a woman with things to do. She
drew a line through *bank* and *supermarket*, and took a mouthful of
sandwich. The egg was soft and warm. A drop of yolk fell on her scarf.
She wiped it away with her hand then licked her finger. She chewed
slowly. I am a big woman but I am not greedy.

Two men sat at the table closest to Clare, drinking cups of tea.
They wore scuffed boots, shabby work pants, flannel shirts; in town
from one of the few outlying hobby farms that remained. They were
talking about a neighbour who had committed suicide a week or two
ago and Clare listened intently while she ate. The man had hanged
himself in his work shed and his wife had found the body when she
went to call him to dinner. The man telling the story spoke slowly,
as if there was nothing particularly unusual about it, just a thing
that happened.

At another table in front of Clare, a woman in a dark blue cardigan
was complaining loudly to a friend about the cost of complying with
the latest mandatory regulations for a garage she and her husband were
building. The cost of cement. The cost of iron sheeting. The cost of
bloody insulation. All the bloody new climate-safe rules.

Clare let herself drift between the conversations, which ebbed and
flowed like the cold spring wind that gusted and receded whenever the
door opened or closed. She started her second sandwich and doodled
on her shopping list. She drew Granna's frail hand with its wedding
ring. It looked like a claw. She drew a dollar sign. Glancing out the
dusty window she thought she saw a small black cat trotting down
the footpath, tail high, its tip swishing.

The older man was saying the whole place was fucked, everything
was fucked, and this seemed to make the women uneasy. They drew
closer together and lowered their voices. Clare heard the woman in

the blue cardigan say something about sixty-five thousand dollars and
where on earth to get it from.

'Eighteen suicides here so far this year,' the younger man said.
Then, as if he had thought about it, he added slowly, 'That would be
about two a month.'

'They're the ones we know about, mate,' the older man said. 'Only
the ones we know about.' He stretched out his long thin legs and
scratched his knee. Clare saw he was wearing frayed red socks. He
raised his voice. 'Maisie, love, two more pots of tea.'

Clare drew a foot next to the hand. It also looked like a claw.

The woman's friend was saying she didn't understand all the new
rules and the travel permits. Life seemed more complicated than it
ever had, she said. Still, worse for people in the closing-down towns.

Maisie edged to the men's table with two teapots on a plastic tray.

'How you holding up, love?' the older man asked.

She put down the tea and folded her arms across impressive breasts.
'Not good. The operation's delayed again. Can you believe it?'

'That's too bad.'

'Tell me about it. Twenty-four hours' notice they gave me. I been
waiting four years and every damn day it gets harder to move.'

She turned to Clare. 'Finished love?'

It was the second time that morning that someone had smiled so
warmly at Clare. She smiled back, and nodded and stood up slowly.
She folded her list, covered now with doodles and phrases and odd
lines, and put it in her bag and moved carefully around the small
tables and out into the cold. She would tape the list into her new
journal that night.

Before she got into her car, she checked her phone. There were two
identical text messages from the offices of the Housing Relocation
Management Authority and the Long-Term Under-Employment

Assistance Bureau: Clare was to report for work in the closing-down towns the following Monday.

She put her head to one side and read the messages carefully. Well, that will be something to do, she thought. She felt oddly pleased. Perhaps it would be interesting. But then immediately she was scared: new people, people who might think she was fat or slow. Be positive, she told herself in her mother's voice. Be positive.

On the way home, she stopped at the small bottle shop on the way out of town as she did every week, the cheap bottle shop where people went to buy alcohol they didn't want other people to know they were buying. She picked up three flagons of rotgut sherry for Phil and, as she paid for them, she felt, as she always did, a tug of hopeless pity and anger that his world had shrunk to the size of the next mouthful of drink.

six

Clare spent the last two months of spring working in the closing-down towns. Whether she wanted to or not, she had no choice: anyone unemployed for more than two years was assigned to a local New Horizons Workgroup, which trawled the towns to record, suck out and put to rest what life remained. Where houses and shops had been knocked down, timber and bricks and pipes and chunks of cement and wire were separated and stacked for future collection. Where buildings still stood, rat bait was laid, stray animals were counted, doors and windows were secured, and the lonely scraps of gone-away lives were collected – a towel hanging on a clothes line, a garden rake, a child's tricycle.

The New Horizons Workgroups were under the supervision of the Housing Relocation Management Authority, which was under the administration of the Climate Assets Relocation Program, which was under the jurisdiction of the National Water and Food Security Taskforce, Emergency Bureau One, which in turn reported to the Bureau for Climate Impact Minimisation and Management, which reported, finally, to faceless and nameless shadows in the office of the President of the Republic of Australia, who were known only to themselves and absolutely no one else, under threat of maximum-security imprisonment in accordance with the Water, Food, Land and Agribusiness Security Protection Legislation, article 74, subclause 126c, as the ERA Committee, which stood, people were told, for the Energising of Rural Australia. Clare watched the announcements about the new taskforce and bureau and workgroups and she never understood a word that was said.

Clare hated working in the closing-down towns, but not because it was work. In fact, getting up each morning with somewhere to go and something to do for a whole day, and then the next day and the next, was so surprising that it was almost invigorating. A little of her energy fell onto Phil. Several times he surprised her by being almost sober and having a dinner of sorts on the table when she got home. One chilly night a fire was blazing; each week a load of laundry was done. Sometimes she would tell him where she had been and the things she saw and she could see he was trying to understand the details of what she was saying.

When she told him one week that her team was working in Crescent, he looked at her, startled. 'That was a pretty town,' he said.

They had lived there for seven months, renting a caravan in the town caravan park while Phil worked shifts at a small nearby gold mine and Clare cleaned houses. Then the mine had closed and they had moved again.

'Well, it's closing down,' Clare told him. 'That whole area isn't in an inclusion zone. All around there most of the towns have gone already.'

'That's not fair. Shit.' His face brightened for a moment. 'Remember there was that great pie shop? And that pub with the verandah all around and the garden? We went there Friday nights.'

'The pub's still there but it's boarded up. The pie shop's gone. All the shops are gone.'

'Shit,' he said again, shocked. 'That's crazy.'

'Yep,' Clare said.

He looked as if he might say something more, but after a minute he simply shrugged and shook his head and reached for the flagon of sherry.

And it was crazy. That was part of what Clare hated: the sense that a mighty unseen hand was redesigning the country at its own whim, sweeping away a town here, another town there, moving roads and tracks as if they were bits of string.

But it was more than that. It was the unutterable sadness of it all. Clare tried to find the words on her night walks. She felt she was a gravedigger, silently helping to prepare for the inevitable and heart-breaking and final end of endings.

•

One clear spring morning, Clare stood outside the Myamba Town Hall waiting with her New Horizons Workgroup team members to be collected by the bus that had *New Horizons: Energising Rural Australia (The New ERA!)* emblazoned across all sides and would be driven who knew where today. While she waited she read the news headlines on the jumbo electronic screen that had been installed by the government on the side of the town hall. The screens were being installed in every inclusion zone town, on the sides of all public buildings, on the walls of apartment blocks, inside shopping malls, to deliver the World News Stream that also played constantly across all television screens. The delivery stream was tailored to each location so as well as portentous-sounding world news there were local edicts and announcements and items approved to be of community interest. *Hellish Heat Closes US States*; *Canada Outbids China For Brazil*; *Myamba Mandolin Quartet Plays Tonight In Town Hall And Bring Your Own Chair*; *Power Crashes In UK*; *Global Commodity Prices Up Four Per Cent Overnight*;

International Refugee Station Seven Nears Completion: Will Shelter Twelve Million; Have You Seen Ditzy, Missing Since Saturday Morning?; Two Hundred Thousand Dead In Northern Africa Drought; Remember Your Vitamin D Every Day Twice A Day.

There was always some desultory chatter on the bus above the whine and thump of music leaking through earphones. The youngest person was nineteen, the oldest close to seventy, and they talked lazily and slowly of small things: if someone had something to sell, if someone had sold something and had extra cash and what that might be spent on, the cost of bread and meat and fruit and petrol and the struggle to make ends meet, the keenly felt and obvious inefficiencies of the bureaucracies that had them trapped like flies in a web, drugs and slam-kill music, and whatever someone might have noticed on news stream screens.

There was a younger man Clare always watched. At least, she assumed he was young. All his exposed flesh – his hands and fore-arms, his ankles and calves beneath his baggy cargo shorts, his face and neck – was covered by lurid scrolling tattoos, black and red and purple and green. She could see eagles and bones and crosses and a blue heart, but there seemed to be no meaning to the design except an agonising application of a second skin of colour. It was his ears that made her think he was young: they were small and pink and soft, like a baby's ears. He was usually silent, staring straight ahead at the top of the seat in front of him, lost in whatever he listened to. But today he was pissed off.

'Only one hundred koalas left. Do you fucking believe it? One hundred. In the whole country. Hey, dudes, how much does that fucking suck? How did that happen, hey? Who let that happen? Who wasn't paying attention? Man, that's so fucked.'

'So what?' someone called out.

'Yeah, so what?' said a young woman with short green hair waxed into sticky sharp spikes. 'Only four hundred polar bears left in the whole world. Only one thousand humpback whales, they reckon. There's no bees. Everything's extincting except people.'

'I don't care about whales. I don't care about polar bears,' the tattoo man said. 'I care about the koalas. It's wrong. It sucks big time. Hey, driver, turn off the crap.'

The screens on the bus were showing a press conference. Men in grey suits looking important and serious. 'Proud to introduce a new chairman to steer us through these exciting challenges . . . investment in three thousand social housing units and eight thousand private market apartments in Melbourne, and a further nine hundred and fifty townhouses for multi-family accommodation in the strategically critical outer inclusion zone city of . . . In Sydney, a further twelve thousand seven hundred apartments . . . allowing us to complete stage two of the transition to a safer, more secure Australia, and move to stage three of inclusion zone design and construction . . . The harnessing of our resources to serve centralised population destinations will deliver new food distribution efficiencies, improved services coordination and help ensure no family need fear the extremes of heat, of drought, of rainfall . . . detailed briefing regarding stage three planning in six months and a full budget accounting . . . And now I'll hand over to Jonathon Watson . . .'

The driver switched off the screens.

'They should be talking about the koalas,' the tattoo guy said. 'They should talk about something that matters.'

'Aw, shit, here comes the phone jam,' the green-haired girl said.

Clare checked her own phone. All signals were down. The exclusion zones were dead – no internet, no reception, no way at all to message anyone about anything. How did they do this? She thought of the walking man.

The bus deposited them at Lilac Town, somewhere to the north-east of Myamba. *Lilac Town: Population 1,668* read a faded sign standing on the roundabout at the southern end of the only main street. *Tidy Town Award Winner 2005*, said another.

The spring morning had been overtaken by the sun and the air shimmered slightly with warmth. Another bus from somewhere had joined them and now eighty men and women were gathered in the main street waiting for instructions. A black cat sat on the doorstep of what must have been a small general store and its tail snaked and twitched. The old post office building had red and white tape around it and a piece of laminated yellow paper nailed to its double wooden doors: *Historic Building Number 376. For Preservation Under the Order of the Housing Relocation Management Authority Heritage Division. Do Not Enter.* The Dutch elm tree in front of the building was dying.

Today Clare's task was to search the houses on three blocks on the north-west side of the town. She would check that all furnishings had been removed, that there were no squatters, no water leaks, count any animals, goats, sheep, chickens, whatever, and make sure all doors and windows were fastened.

She collected two bottles of water, a packet of sandwiches – processed chicken and lettuce again – and a canvas bag with a clipboard and pen, hammer, nails, a piece of red chalk and a few dozen thin strips of plywood, and set off down the wide street.

•

Clare put a big red chalk tick on the front door of the fifth house she had checked: a tidy grey weatherboard, empty except for a stuffed pink elephant that had been left sitting on a neatly folded white blanket in the front room. It had been placed there very deliberately, very gently. She had stared at it, then shrugged and left the house.

A lemon tree in the back garden was bowed under the weight of its fruit, and dozens and dozens of lemons, some rotting, lay on the dead lawn. Clare put three in her bag, then decided to sit in the shade of the tree to eat her sandwich. The air was warm and still. She was thinking about the stuffed toy when she saw the black cat she had noticed earlier on the main street. It was sitting on the path that ran down the side of the house past the lemon tree and small patch of dead garden. She saw now that it had one white front paw and a small streak of white on its tail.

The cat stood and stretched, arching its back. It turned and walked four steps towards the gate that opened to the street, then stopped and turned back to face Clare. The cat looked at her with eyes that glowed white-gold and then stretched out the leg with the white paw. It held it in the air, just above the ground, and curled and uncurled the paw. The gesture was unmistakable. Follow me.

Clare got to her feet and, leaving her bag and half-eaten sandwich under the tree, moved towards the cat, which now ran happily up the path. It waited for her at the gate, which Clare opened and closed, then led her at a brisk trot to the last house on the block. It turned into the overgrown driveway and trotted through a garage, empty apart from faded green picnic chairs leaning against a wall, and across a back garden that was part weeds and part dirt. Without breaking its stride, the cat checked that Clare was following. It passed through a small open gate in a sagging wooden fence, across another garden grown over with blackberry bushes, and onto a street. Come, come, its golden eyes said.

It crossed the empty street and took a right turn down a laneway sheltered from the sun by loquat trees. Here the cat stopped and sat by a wrought-iron gate painted a dark green. There was a mailbox, also painted green, and an old-fashioned pillar lamp. Clare and the cat looked at each other. It seemed to Clare it was smiling at her. The cat inclined its head to indicate Clare should go through the gate. She unlatched it and again the cat jumped ahead of her, brushing her ankles, leading the way along a stone garden path towards a crooked little wooden cottage painted in shades of green, some light, some dark.

The cottage had a rusted red tin roof, and all around was the flutter of birds and butterflies in a green, green garden, and the smell of water. There was a wicker rocking chair on the narrow front porch and a hanging basket of pink geraniums. By now the cat was at the front door, an old-fashioned flywire with green trim, clearly unlatched, and again it inclined its head. Go in. Go in.

Clare felt oddly cool and refreshed and a little dazed, as if she had walked through a small waterfall. She stepped into the narrow hallway. It was quiet and dim and every inch of wall space was covered in photographs and small paintings. The ceiling almost touched Clare's head. She eased past a hallstand holding a vase of fresh violet roses and the floor of the hallway dipped and groaned under her weight.

'Come in, dear, come in,' said a bright voice. 'I can't wait all day, you know.'

Clare stepped into a kitchen unlike any she had ever seen. And yet it was somehow instantly recognisable, like a coming home. A sprawling wooden table with mismatched chairs, some painted white, some plain wood, one green and one red, was set for ten people with bread-and-butter plates and dinner plates, and silver knives and forks and spoons, and old-fashioned teacups and water glasses, and neatly folded linen napkins. The floor was faded yellow linoleum, and there was a big timber window with bright yellow and white curtains that shifted in the breeze, although Clare knew there was no breeze today in Lilac Town. But here it was, dancing and playing. Hanging from a hook in the ceiling near the window was a very large birdcage painted a dark red. Inside was an intricate arrangement of perches and swings and a miniature tree made of the same red wood. Several-dozen small brightly coloured birds hopped and fluttered from perch to perch and swing to swing with a constant low chirping and chittering.

Watching the birds from the windowsill, and watching her, Clare saw, was a large duck, its dark eyes impassive. It took a step to the left and then to the right.

On the other side of the window from the birdcage, a piece of purple glass hung, by a string or wire that was invisible, from the ceiling. The glass turned and spun, throwing purple moonbeam spotlights across the yellow and the white and the sunshine breeze. The colour from the glass, and the colours of the birds and their chittering, and the dark eyes of the watching duck combined in a dancing circle to make Clare feel slightly dizzy. There was a smell from the birds, like old soil and rotting leaves, and a fainter smell of grease, as if someone had recently fried onions and sausages in the kitchen.

Standing against the stove, arms folded, was a short woman in an old-fashioned blue dress gathered at the waist, her dark hair swept back in a tight bun. The woman's face had a thousand lines and wrinkles crossing over each other every which way, an ancient creek bed baked dry, and her eyes glowed like beaten gold.

Clare took a step back. She is like the cat, she thought. And then she looked around. Where had the cat gone? Ah, there it was, sitting on one of the chairs, gazing gravely at the plate in front of it.

'Hmmm. You have absolutely no idea who I am, do you?' the woman said, head to one side. 'Well, of course you don't, and why should you, after all. Joon,' she turned to the cat, 'you were a clever, clever girl to find her. Lunch for you, I think.'

The woman dragged a chair back from the table. Climbing onto it, she reached for the door of the birdcage, unlocked it and put her hand in. The birds jumped and hopped and knocked into each other and the chattering and chittering became a frenzy. The woman's hand moved quickly and then she withdrew it, shutting the small door so firmly that the cage swung on its hook. She was holding a small blue bird with delicate black markings on its face. A budgerigar, Clare thought.

Climbing down from the chair the woman swiftly and sharply tapped the bird's head against the edge of the table. There was a small cracking sound. The duck gave a short, deep quack that sounded like a groan. The woman threw the bird onto the plate in front of Joon. The cat reached out a curled paw and buffeted the bird, gently pushing it away and pulling it back. It seemed to be smiling again. Then it lazily climbed onto the table and circled the plate. It crouched, hunching its shoulders, tail swishing, and Clare heard a low grumble from its throat and then a crunch as it bit into the bird's head.

'The cat is called June?' Clare asked. It was all she could think of to say. She took a step to the table and put a hand on it to steady herself. The table felt real. Smooth and cool.

'Spelled J-o-o-n. Not the month. Persian name, of course,' the woman said. 'Well, it would be, obviously. It means "dear", "dear one". Joon has been called Joon for the longest time and, quite frankly, we'd be lost without her.'

There was another growl and a crunch of bone. Joon shook her head and small pale blue and black feathers drifted upwards.

'Anyway, you are here simply so I can pass something on,' the woman continued. 'We do have a few mutual acquaintances, you and I, odd as that must seem.'

She was looking at Clare and her golden eyes were both warm and unrelenting. She had a blue feather on her head. Clare frowned.

The woman went to a cupboard and opened it and took out a long slim package clumsily wrapped in a piece of brown paper. She handed it to Clare.

'It's from the walking man. He said to tell you it's a gift. And he said to tell you it is safe where he is and that he has seen the bones.'

Clare opened the package. She couldn't remember when she had last unwrapped a present, and then thought it was absurd to think this, in this strange house with this strange woman and the dancing colours. Putting the paper and string on the table, she looked at what was clearly a piece of bone, long and thin, and crudely scraped and carved to resemble a knife. The side meant to be the blade was blunt, and on the handle she could see the walking man had tried to carve her name, but the letters were rough and he had given up after 'a'. The bone was light in her hands, but felt dense as well, as if it was something that couldn't be broken, and she wondered if it was from an animal or a human. And then she remembered – I never told him my name.

Joon had finished eating the bird. She sat up and began to rub the right side of her face with her right paw. Her tail still twitched slightly.

'You saw the walking man?' Clare asked.

The woman had been watching her. 'Of course,' she said. She went to the refrigerator. 'I should feed you something. That's what I usually do. Let me see . . . hmm, no, there's no food here today. Not much anyway.'

Clare could see that the fridge was, in fact, full of food. Three loaves of bread, a plate of sausages and chops piled high, a leg of lamb, a tray of vegetables neatly cut and waiting to be roasted. Butter. Milk. Bottles of beer.

Finally the woman pulled out the remains of what looked like a fruit cake. There was a film of green mould along the top and at the edges. She cut this off with a knife, and then cut a small square, which she wrapped in a piece of tinfoil.

She handed it to Clare. 'Here you are, dear.' Then, abruptly, 'It's time for you to go.'

Clare thought she saw a shadow pass by the window, and the birds in the cage rose and fell again and fluttered.

'Joon will take you back. You'll never find your own way.'

The cat jumped down from the table and went to the door. She looked at Clare.

Well then, Clare thought. She put the cake in her pocket. 'Thank you,' she said to the woman.

The duck squawked loudly.

'Oh, you are most, most welcome,' the woman said. 'And by the way . . . you do know, I am sure, that this is very real. This place, this moment. Very, very real, and not just because I say it is, although of course if someone says that something is real then indeed it is. For them at least. It's always been a shame, I think, that most people don't necessarily understand that. You might be tempted to think, when you climb back onto your bus or when you go for your walk tonight, that this has perhaps been a dream. You would be wrong.' The woman cocked her head to one side. A blue feather fell to the floor. Her eyes glittered. 'Of course,' she continued 'if it's not a dream you presumably should tell your nitwit group leader about me. But that would be wrong too, my dear. Very wrong. We think you like secrets. You do, don't you?'

And Clare nodded, because, yes, she did like secrets, and she kept secrets, because she had no one to talk to and because secrets were free and they might be useful one day. She kept secrets the way she kept her old journals and empty jam jars and clothes that didn't fit any more. You just never knew.

The woman considered her, and then she also nodded. She tapped her foot impatiently. 'Good. Go now.'

Clare followed Joon out of the house, along the lane, and through the sunlight to the lemon tree. She sat down again and Joon nudged her hand before bounding off down the path. Her bag was where she had left it and she gently put the bone inside. Ants crawled over her half-eaten sandwich and she picked them off one by one.

I don't understand anything, she thought.

•

Clare finished her houses, leaving big red chalk ticks on lonely doors. There was another stuffed pink elephant in one house, a large bright yellow giraffe in another, and an old-fashioned teddy bear, one button eye missing, in a third. They all sat on neatly folded blankets.

It's some sort of sign, Clare thought. Or a message maybe that I don't understand.

She looked for Joon when she went to board the bus, but the cat was nowhere to be seen. When she sat down, she remembered the cake the woman had given her and she took it out of her pocket and unwrapped it. She turned it around carefully, looking for mould, then smelled it. It was dark and rich with sugar and dried fruits and Clare took a small bite. It was the most delicious cake she had ever tasted.

At the end of the main street and turning left onto a feeder road that would take them back to Highway Three to head south, one of the guys gave a loud shout.

'Man, look at that swarm. What the hell?'

Heads turned. A white-grey cloud was falling from the skies onto Lilac Town.

'Locusts maybe?'

'No way. Wrong shape. Wrong colour.'

'Cockies, that's what. Huge fucking flock of cockies. Coming in to eat up what's left.'

'No way, man. Cockies'd be wheeling offa each other. Not comin' straight down like that.'

Just as the bus turned onto the highway, for the briefest second Clare saw and knew. It wasn't cockatoos. Bones were falling from the sky. Grey-white, brittle-dense bones: jaws and skulls and tiny finger bones and hip bones and femurs and kneecaps. She shivered.

'Probably fucking koala bones, I bet,' said the tattoo man. 'Fucking giant skull fuck going on up there.'

•

Three days later there was an item on the local television news. Clare stopped peeling the potatoes and listened.

A government spokesman, a burly red-faced pork-pie man bristling with indignation, denied 'absolutely and categorically' reports that bones had been seen falling from the sky in the north.

'These are malicious, absurd, dangerous and indeed we would go so far as to use the word subversive rumours aimed at undermining the integrity of the Republic's critical agricultural resources management program that is restoring opportunity and new beginnings to tens of thousand of people. Resorting to fantasy to undermine this effort and this government is not only un-Australian in intent and principle, it is an insult to the many, many hard-working families who understand they will ultimately benefit from these important changes, and an activity that, at the end of the day, is punishable by the full weight of the law.'

Bullshit, Clare thought.

seven

Robbie called at exactly the time Jonathon had asked him to. He pictured Jonathon, thin and grey, slightly stooped now, eyes a shocked and shocking blue, sitting on a chair on the expansive terrace of his Sydney apartment, the harbour and bridge hidden in the darkness.

'Robbie.'

'Hello, Jonathon.'

'How are you? How's Ella?'

'We're good. Well, Ella's travelling so much. Seems there are more refugees than the rest of us these days. So she's in a losing battle to try to make something, anything, better for someone, somewhere. She's tired. Very tired. How's Sarah?'

Robbie imagined Sarah in the vast kitchen, cleaning up after a roast beef dinner, the television switched on low, tuned to that awful reality refugee race show Jonathon had told him she liked to watch.

'Sarah is Sarah. Some things don't change,' Jonathon said.

He had tried to explain to Robbie the last time they had shared a meal and several bottles of wine that he could never decide if Sarah had changed more than he would have thought it possible for anyone to change over the years, or if she hadn't changed at all.

Robbie knew Jonathon thought he had married a woman who would be content to be the wife of a country vet. But Sarah had planted the idea of him moving into politics, something she openly and proudly admitted; and Robbie had imagined her, the quiet woman with the worried eyes who had fed him sausages and mashed potato for dinner after Timmy died, encouraging and pushing and goading Jonathon to do more and be more in the needy and needling way quiet and worried people could. What he had never fully understood was why Jonathon had agreed, or when he had become intrigued and immersed and enjoyed more and more the fact that he was good at it, good at the talking and listening and number-crunching and the ideas and the waiting.

It was clear enough that Sarah enjoyed the money and privileges, and that Jonathon enjoyed the thinking and the planning. But Robbie had known for a long time that the world had sold its soul, and therefore it followed that the men who ran the world, or parts of it – because it was, astoundingly, still mainly men who decided who ran a country, or who would be bombed, or who could turn on a tap and drink the water that ran from it, or who could buy a house or their favourite coffee twice a day – were also soulless. They had to be or they could not bear to do what they did each day. Robbie had thought for several years now that Jonathon was not, in his heart, truly one of these men. He was too kind. And he felt for his friend, for the man who was more of a father to him than anyone had been, and he worried that the strain of being what he fundamentally was not would break him.

'Thought you were determined to stay retired?' Robbie said.

'I got bored.'

'But this?'

'This what? Talking to you?'

Robbie waited. Jonathon cleared his throat. 'I just thought . . . Well, I thought if it was me, me doing this, I could try, somehow, to minimise the damage. Make some things better.'

'I watched the press conference,' Robbie said. 'But I think the new chairman of Energising Rural Australia is going to have to do more than damage control. Aren't you?'

Jonathon cleared his throat again. 'It's as bad as anything I could have imagined. Worse maybe. I know it's what people have always said – I never knew, I never even guessed. But now I know that sometimes it's true.' He paused. 'You know, in the beginning it made some sense. I mean, this country is just so damn big and we couldn't afford to go on paying for all the infrastructure – every school, every highway and back road, every hospital, every bridge and footpath. So sure, consolidate, and do it before we went completely broke. It's not like we were the only country with these problems. Close down some towns, expand others. I think most people were even behind it, and the ones that weren't didn't much matter.'

Robbie heard him sip a drink. It would be brandy, he knew.

'You were here, weren't you,' Jonathon continued, 'when they rolled out the plans and the slogans and the timeline for it all? Energising Rural Australia – a new ERA?'

'A few years back,' Robbie said. 'I was visiting Granna. I went to a couple of the launches. Usual bells and whistles and bullshit. I filed on it.'

'I found out a few weeks ago ERA never stood for Energising Rural Australia.'

'Oh?'

'The E is for euthanasia. The Euthanasia of Rural Australia. That's the new ERA. That's what it all means.'

'Jesus,' Robbie said. 'The Euthanasia of Rural Australia. Okay, I'm listening.'

Jonathon took another swallow of brandy and then, for the next half an hour, he talked. The one thousand six hundred towns that were being gutted – five hundred gone already, the ones that were known, but so many more to come – the four hundred million or so hectares of agricultural land that had been sold, the several million people being rounded up and sent to cities that couldn't cope, the annexation of part of the Northern Territory for the Greater Southern Pacific Refugee Station, the arrangements for shipping out the water and food, the bureaucrats and troops arriving from China and the Arab States, the Greater Americas interests that were involved somehow but were not in any way clear, the money – who was paying who for what, the money given over for the Australian Government to secure its inclusion zones and build enough housing and schools, and the new entry points and exit points to the country that the new owners wanted. He described all the justifications he had heard, from the President down, the excuses, and the faint and absurd hopes that all this could be made to work; the confidential reports and analyses on the scheme from half-a-dozen independent bodies, all buried because not one could offer a ringing endorsement of the plans. The bones that were falling, the people that were walking, walking away from the overcrowded and dirty cities and the tiny apartments with no sunlight or fresh air, the suicide rate, strictly secret, hundreds of people every day.

At times Jonathon's voice broke and he had to stop and take a deep breath; at times it trembled with anger and frustration. Robbie listened and took notes. He wouldn't risk recording anything.

'It's real people, Robbie. Real people being torn away from what they love, what they know, where they've always lived, no matter how tough it's become,' Jonathon said at the end. 'It's as if the last few years have just been an elaborate hoax to have us thinking and looking one way while they redesigned the whole country.'

'But it's the same the whole world over,' Robbie said. 'It's like a Monopoly game gone mad. Everyone's buying and selling, but now they're buying and selling countries and cities and water and people. It's shocking, I know. It's awful. It's beyond awful. Remember you asked me a while back why I was giving up, why I was just doing boring stories about currencies and energy and stuff? Remember?'

'You said you were tired of being constantly abused for being a greenie, communist, leftie, do-gooder, cock-sucking tree-hugger. I think those were your words. And the death threats. All that stuff.'

'It was all of that,' Robbie said. 'But more too. I finally got that no one cares. I mean, some people care. They say endlessly how much they care. But it doesn't mean they actually do anything. Or want to. There was nothing I could write, no story I could find, that would make any difference where it really matters – which is in the minds and hearts of the sorts of assholes who have written the plan for the euthanasia of rural Australia, the assholes who are doing this stuff the world over.'

Jonathon was silent.

'So,' Robbie said, 'they want you to do what specifically?'

'Try and make it sound okay. Smile a lot on all the news channels. Pat dogs, because people can still apply for permits to own dogs. Sorry. One dog. If they're lucky. Open new housing blocks and schools and food distribution depots. Everything normal and happy, happy.'

'You could get out of it. Health problems. Whatever. Just retire again.'

But Robbie knew that wouldn't happen. If Jonathon thought he could make even one person feel comfortable with the concept of the death of rural Australia he would stay in the job.

'No. I'll do it. I said I would. I can't bear sitting around here anyway. And sure, maybe it's not such a big deal any more with the way the world's going.' His voice broke. He began to sob. Softly.

Robbie put his head in his hand and listened. He heard the shake and gasp and rasp of each breath Jonathon took, he imagined the tears curving and falling through the dunes and folds of the older man's cheeks and chin. He imagined he was there, and could hold Jonathon's thin hand in his. And then he felt, again, his own grief rise, the grief that every life was finite; the grief in Timmy's black eyes; the grief in Granna setting and squaring her shoulders to face another lonely night. The impossibility of the sadness would obliterate him one day, crush him. I am going mad, he thought briefly. I cannot bear this.

He held up his free arm. It was enough. The movement, the gesture, shifted the moment.

'I'm sorry, mate,' he said. 'I'm so sorry.'

Jonathon took a deep breath. Then another. And another. Robbie heard him take another sip, then a swallow. 'You know, I loved it out there, on the farms, in the bush. The choices we make, Robbie. The choices we make.'

'I know. I know.' Robbie let another minute pass. 'Now listen—'

Jonathon cut him off. 'There's just one thing. One last thing. That I've been thinking about.'

'Sure.'

'Well, I shouldn't be surprised about anything really, but I want to say this to you. It's what I've been thinking about. It seems to me there's a line, a direct line, from a drunken man breaking a horse and a boy's heart, to a whole country breaking. It's just a monstrous carelessness. Isn't it? Or an unforgivably careless cruelty. Both. And there's never a way back.'

Robbie swallowed and bit back tears. 'That makes sense to me,' he said. 'Yes. That's about what it is.'

He heard a clink of glass and a woman's voice. He heard Jonathon say, 'Two more minutes.'

'Okay, my favourite old man, you have to go. So, tomorrow you need to drop the phone you're talking to me on in the ocean somewhere. The harbour's fine. You wouldn't believe how many phones are in there. Then activate one of the other phones I gave you. We'll talk again soon.'

'Seriously, where are these phones from?'

'Seriously? A basement apartment in a place called Scarborough in Canada. Near Toronto. Nice guy lives there. He's clever too.'

'Will you write this?' Jonathon asked.

'Yes. Absolutely. I'll give it a couple of weeks, but yes.'

'Will you remember the place you're writing about? In some ways it's hardly your country any more but there has to be context, you know.'

Robbie felt a flash of irritation mixed with a wry nostalgia. 'I remember.'

And he did. The lazy buzzing of a blowfly's wings as it hovered over blood-slicked bone. The smell of bone-dry dust carried on a hot wind. His grandmother cutting red and yellow and pink roses, their petals like small silk flags that fell gently across tables and sideboards throughout the house. He remembered the kelpie that slept on a faded brown mat at the side of the narrow bed in Jonathon and Sarah's small house, the house where he'd cried himself to sleep the night Timmy had died, and the dog's soft eyes and tawny eyebrows and old-dog smell that had been some small comfort. He thought of that house and the tens of thousands of houses like it, nondescript, humble, quiet, where mainly humble and quiet lives were lived, and understood that for those homes still standing in the new exclusion zones their days were numbered. Going, going and gone.

I remember, he thought. And I try very hard not to. It is too sad.

'Where are you now?' Jonathon said. 'I never asked.'

'London. Going to be in Germany and Africa over the next few weeks. You go to bed, Jonathon. It's late for you. We'll speak again soon, but on the new phone. You'll be okay.'

They hung up, and Robbie looked out the wide bay window of the huge room he rented and called home in Chelsea. There was a small bathroom and kitchenette at one end and a king-sized bed at the other, with oversized sofas and tables in-between. The afternoon traffic was at a standstill and late autumn gloom was closing in. He loved this room and he enjoyed London, its busy and eccentric shabbiness, its odd loneliness. It reminded him of an eccentric aunt who had perhaps made a series of flamboyant but serious mistakes throughout her life and now lived off the memories, with neither regret nor celebration, in splendid and stubborn and cobwebby isolation.

He thought about his conversation with Jonathon. He knew the information was shocking. He knew he would write about it. He knew no one would care. Similar things had already happened, after all. In parts of the United States and Canada most especially. And Europe. And the former Central America. Countries closing down. Razor-wire fences and walls closing in.

It was only lunchtime but he poured himself a scotch and raised a glass to the empty room. 'Jonathon,' he said.

He sat on a sofa in front of a computer and decided to write the story now, this moment, because otherwise he might not write it at all. He looked at his notes and wrote about the inclusion and exclusion zones, and the money and the takeovers and powerful men in dark suits blustering and lying, and the people being moved and empty towns where tumbleweed rolled down empty streets, and water rations and fires and tent cities, and men and women and children and dogs and cats walking. Walking.

It was evening by the time he finished. He poured another drink and thought of the stories Jonathon used to tell from his few years as a country vet. The stark beauty of the back roads he used to drive along; the hard men mute above their love for cows and sheep and the smell of the earth after it rained. He thought of a gum tree towering alone in a white-brown field, skeletal sheep motionless in its blistering shade. And he remembered Jonathon's strong big hand holding his small sweaty one.

He thought of Jonathon's comment and knew he was right. If a man could break a horse, break a boy, then a man could break many things. A woman. A town. A country. Everything. And it *was* just a monstrous carelessness. That's all it was.

Robbie wished, suddenly and strongly, that he could see Jonathon, and shake his hand, and put an arm across his thin shoulders.

•

He had visited Jonathon's apartment only once, the night he had met Ella. There had been some sort of fundraising dinner and concert for refugees at the Sydney Opera House, and he had been seated at a table at the front of the room that included two other Sydney-based journalists and Ella and several of her colleagues who, he learned later, were touring and assessing refugee detention stations in Australia and Indonesia and Thailand. It was before the United Nations was disbanded, and just as the real upheavals began.

Robbie was bored and wishing he was anywhere else – somewhere in Africa, for example – and was sharing reasonably crass jokes with the man he was sitting next to and drinking too much too quickly, so it wasn't until desserts were placed in front of them all that he realised he was sitting across from one of the most beautiful women he had seen, and that she had stopped talking with her colleagues and was regarding him as if he were a scruffy stray dog that had wandered in off the street.

He straightened in his chair and drank a glass of water. 'We were introduced earlier,' he began.

'We were indeed, Roberto Adams. How do you do. Again.'

Her English was pronounced and impeccable with a strong accent; German, he thought.

'I don't quite remember . . .'

There was a slight pause and a raised eyebrow. 'Ella Yoder.'

'Yes, of course. And you're . . . ?'

'One of the speakers this evening.'

'Yes, of course,' Robbie said again. He felt himself flush. He hadn't bothered to look at the program. He was here for a good meal, and afterwards he would walk a few blocks up to the city and have a nightcap with Jonathon. 'Well,' he said, 'I've blown it, haven't I? Completely. Most unimpressive. I admit it.' He held up his hands and shrugged.

To his surprise she laughed. 'At least you are honest that you can be stupid.' She tapped a finger on the table. 'I know who you are, Mr Roberto Adams. I liked your piece on the detention and processing centres on the eastern Mediterranean islands. It was good. Thoughtful. So I know you can, in fact, be thoughtful. Which is lucky for you.' She tapped the table again and leaned forward. 'I am at the Hyatt. Not the nice one by the harbour. The other one. Call me. Tomorrow. Before nine.'

And with that she turned back to her colleagues, and then was taken to meet people at an adjoining table, after which she gave a gracious and, Robbie thought, interesting speech on the emergence of the major regional refugee processing centres, and then she seemed to be gone.

By the time he reached Jonathon's apartment building he had forgotten the speech and what he had eaten for dinner and was annoyed that there were still nine hours until he could, reasonably, call her hotel. Surely seven o'clock wouldn't be too early?

When Jonathon opened his front door Robbie burst out laughing. 'I've fallen in love,' he said. 'I'd like a drink.'

And Jonathon laughed too and found at the back of his bar fridge a bottle of French champagne, which he opened on the terrace. 'To the feeling of falling in love,' he toasted.

Robbie remembered it had been before all public lighting was shut off at night, and so the lights of the Sydney Harbour Bridge and the Opera House and the office towers looked perfect and beautiful.

He smiled as intermittent rain hit his London windows, then thought again of his conversation with Jonathon. He imagined people standing in their homes as he was standing now in his, but looking out through old wood-framed windows and flywire doors onto gardens or lawns or rolling fields or granite hills or red, red dirt or the neighbour's picket fence or an old dog waiting for a ball to be thrown or a wire pen with chickens scratching or a child's swing set, yellow plastic, or a clothes line with sheets and pillowcases and work overalls swinging in the wind or a storm rolling in or wisteria or pink roses climbing a verandah post. Each single and simple thing precious to someone, and each single and simple thing to be taken away.

He closed his eyes. Impossible, he thought. Except it clearly wasn't. And, of course, it was the story of the ages, wasn't it? What there is can be taken away, can be made to be gone. Always. Over and over.

He and Ella had spoken of visiting Granna after the wedding and their honeymoon. He would speak to Ella tonight. They should do it. It was important. For the first time in a long time he wanted to go back, back to Australia and to Granna's home and his home, and it surprised him.

eight

W ho is to say what is home? Nearly two hundred years ago I fell in love with these low brown hills and the blazing white summer sun and the stars that hung so low and heavy in the clear night sky I felt I could pick each one and put it in my pocket. I built the House of Many Promises stone by stone and brick by brick. I dug through the granite to build the channels and shafts that would feed the vast underground vat beneath the foundations of the house where the water, better than gold now, still whispers ceaselessly. Who could have known then the wealth that water would be?

I planted the lemon and orange groves, the pomegranate and fig trees. I carved furniture, and I sold my fruits and vegetables, and used an abacus to keep the books for the butcher, the seamstress, the blacksmith and the publican. I read books to teach myself about things I didn't know and to imagine worlds I would never see, and if there were frowns or taunts in the town about the slitty-eyed Chinaman who spoke better English than most I ignored them.

I married an Irish girl who gave me good children, and I taught her to cook rice and use the spices that I liked, and twice a year I took the tins of gold nuggets and flecks and shavings from the hole I had built in the stable floor, hidden by straw and manure, and touched and weighed it and added to it, and slept like a king for another five months and twenty-nine days.

But now I am only cold and restless bones. For years and years and years I have been wandering and I have wondered if loving the way stars hang in a night sky or the colours in a line of rocky hills – the purple, the orange, the grey, the brown – are the wrong reasons to say a place is a home. Perhaps I should have gone back to the noisy village and the wet heat and the rice fields and the rumblings of war and been content with nothing and then I might have slept peacefully forever. Who is to say?

I talk to Clare, and she talks to me as we walk together. Ghosts and how things once were. We walk on bones that lie upon bones that lie upon bones. We all do. We always have. When I was a boy trotting along the bullock tracks and through dry dusty grasses to reach the promise of gold, I was treading on bones. The bones of men and women and children, monstrous bones from lumbering creatures long gone, infinitesimal bones from vanished seabeds, invisible fish bones on a limestone wave. Turn the world upside down and shake it hard enough and the bones will tumble and fly.

Sometimes I go much further. I visit the closing-down towns, the empty houses and buildings. I visit where towns once were, and where now there are only empty homes and mud or dust and weeds growing through the roads and the wooden verandahs. I see the ends of the stories of lives, and I tip what I see into the dreams of those I know. Clare, and Robbie, poor Robbie. But never Antonia Adams. She has always seen everything. She has always known.

•

On the outskirts of a tiny town many, many miles north from here, a woman is sitting in an armchair looking through the window at the brown-grey plains that stretch forever. She is a stick, this woman. A twig. She draws her breaths heavily, in slow and low gasps, through an oxygen tank, and it can take her ten minutes to move from her armchair in the living room to the kitchen.

For thirty-three years she and her husband have bred toy poodles, and for thirty-three years people have driven from all over to her immaculate weatherboard home with its rows of immaculate kennels and pens to select one of her puppies. They wince at her thinness and her efforts to breathe, but after half an hour of listening to her husband talk on her behalf from written notes in plastic sheets about the dogs and their breeding lines and their personalities and how they should be fed and trained, and after they look at the immaculate paperwork, they only see her energy and love.

She has turned people away over the years: a child who was too greedy and grabbing, a man whose lips were too thin and cruel. All her life she has loved her husband, the view of flat grey-brown plains through the living room window, and the dogs that unravel and roll at her feet every morning from the joy of being alive. Now she has been told that she and her husband will lose their home and the view and the dogs, and will be compensated with a one-bedroom townhouse in an inclusion zone town two hundred and thirty kilometres away. The apartment will be on the second floor and there is no elevator. She will never be able to walk up the stairs. It will be impossible.

After weeks of arguing and pleading with hollow voices far away, who apparently cannot see the details of her myriad medical conditions on the screens in front of them, the man and woman make their own decisions. The vet does as she is asked without question, because what else is there to do. The stick woman cradles each dog, whispers to it, says goodbye, and barely feels or smells the dampness as the bowels and kidneys of each small dog loosen when the injection takes effect. Tears roll down the woman's face, a tidal wave of tears.

Her husband gathers the small bodies, gently, gently, and burns them in the furthest corner of the yard that afternoon. He has closed all the windows of the house so his wife will smell nothing. He cleans out the kennels for a final time. Then he cooks the woman's favourite meal, meatloaf wrapped in bacon with gravy and mashed potatoes and peas, and slowly does the dishes afterwards. They open a bottle of sparkling wine that has been sitting in the fridge for years and sip it and hold hands for a long time. He traces the bones of her wrist gently with his fingers. Finally he nods.

With a surge of strength, the woman picks the rifle up from the kitchen table, the old rifle they used to shoot foxes and which last week the man patiently cleaned and oiled and loaded. With one shot she kills her husband, taking away half his head. Without looking or thinking, she opens and closes the breech to eject the casing and loads a new one. She jams the butt of the rifle against the edge of the table, balances the gun in a line across her body and takes the barrel in her mouth. Steadying herself against the recoil, she finds the trigger guard and then the trigger, which she presses hard and firm. Her last feeling is relief.

When they come to the house they will find it immaculate except for two rotting bodies in the kitchen and a tumble of small bones sitting on ash and dust in the yard. The bones collect themselves and clatter and skip away as they approach.

•

In a town that is barely on any map anywhere, and if it is, soon won't be, two men sit on the front porch of an empty brick building. Inside, the walls are painted in rich reds and greens, and the ornate cornices are cream, and there is a huge country kitchen where people gathered around a table big enough to seat sixteen. The building has been their home and business for more than twenty years. The men are holding hands and watching a savage storm play across the northern foothills of the valley. They have managed to sell most of the antiques and books to collectors in the inclusion zones, and tomorrow they leave for their new home in a city they had never planned to return to. They are shocked and sad but determinedly optimistic. They still have each other, after all, and this is what they have been saying over and over these past few months.

But they will miss the neighbours, who became their friends, and the morning music of magpies singing, and the beauty of the building they have lived in, and the sound of children playing in the street. They will miss cooking sausages and hamburgers at the monthly school fundraisers, and taking hot dinners twice a week to old Margaret Ambrose three doors down who broke her hip two years ago and was never quite the same since and who was taken literally kicking and screaming to the brand new nine-hundred-bed aged care home in the nearest inclusion city one hundred kilometres away. They will miss babysitting the Mitchell children from time to time, and the gossip and wine at the historical society committee meetings.

'Remember when we first—'

'No, don't.'

'Don't what?'

'Let's not start remembering. Please. I don't want to. It hurts. Maybe later. Not now.'

'Okay.'

•

From where Clare and I are standing, under the branches of the massive peppercorn tree that fall like a curtain over the high iron gates at the House of Many Promises, it is one hundred and thirty-five thousand steps to where a farmer is hanging his head in rage and shame.

Tomorrow the trucks will roll in, and the cows will be taken to one of the new agribusiness central stations, and the house he was born in will be dismantled and taken south. Planks from the beautiful old hardwood floor he played on as a boy will reappear as design features in sharp-edged coffee bars. The tractor will go, the milking sheds will go, the irrigation pumps and water tanks will go, the generators will go, the fertilisers and feed bales. Before she left for the city with the kids and the one dog they are allowed to keep, his wife, crying silently, pruned for a final time the roses that his great-grandmother had planted. The Borderer, the Marjory Palmer, the Diana Allen, the masses of hybrid tea roses, the Sunny South. They will go too.

The farmer puts his bag in the car. He says goodbye to Micer, the big old ginger cat who has slept for years in the sheds and helped keep mice out of the feed. She'll be alright, he thinks. There are birds and rats and mice.

Then he kneels down in front of Girlie, the golden-eyed kelpie he has loved for eleven years. Last night he sat on the front steps of the wide verandah and fashioned a collar and lead from scraps of rope and leather he found in the sheds. Now he pushes the collar over her head and checks that it isn't too tight. He pulls Girlie's head to his own, rubs his hands over the soft ears and the mouth that seems to smile, and lets her lick his ears and lips. He feels the puzzlement in her.

'You and me, okay?' he says to her. 'You and me.'

He leads Girlie to the car and settles her on the floor on the passenger side. He throws some old rugs and water bottles and a bag around her. She will have to be hidden when he goes through the checkpoints, but for now she can sit up and he can put his left hand on her head while he drives.

When he leaves the old house for the last time and turns onto the road he feels the sting of tears. He pulls over before he reaches the highway and puts his head in his big rough hands and sobs, and Girlie stands up and nudges him with her black gummy lips.

By the time the man reaches the city he has been stopped four times at checkpoints and asked to show his travel permit and had his phone scanned for identification. Girlie has stayed curled under the mess on the floor. He is confused and shocked by the amount of traffic on the roads, the bypass around the huge sinkhole, the army trucks, the bicycles, the food vans, the security and the police, the razor wire blocking turn-offs to towns and back roads, the instructions and information streaming from the radio. As he tries to find his way to the townhouse in a new suburb where his wife and children wait, he is thinking that none of this can be happening. It must be a dream. Surely.

'It's not our fucking country any more, is it, Girlie? That's for sure,' he says. 'Fuck them all.'

•

One night a few years ago, I stepped through the stars to examine the wider world, only to find it wasn't worth examining. It is better and easier to see only the small things, the very small things, in fact.

I saw Robbie sitting in a desert in north Africa. There were a few dozen dead bodies near him, wrapped in stained blankets and bandages. International Red Cross vans and some army jeeps were parked close together, and some soldiers with Kalashnikovs over their shoulders were laughing and smoking cigarettes. They should have been travelling at night, but there were landmines and it was not safe. The soldiers were laughing because they were afraid.

The night was very cold and Robbie was writing a letter on a small scrap of thin card he had perhaps torn from the cover of a book. His writing was small and spiky, as if ants had been swatted on the page. He was a man not used to holding a pen. I looked over his shoulder.

. . . so if something happens to me, darling Ella, which it won't but sometimes I am frightened, I would have wanted to say this to you: your beautiful heart is the only home I know any more . . .

When he was finished, he folded up the letter, wrote Ella's name and street address and email address on it, and wrapped it in a small piece of plastic and put it inside his phone cover, so that if he was blown apart someone would find it and she would eventually know what he had needed to say.

nine

Robbie's flight was the last to land at Charles de Gaulle ahead of the storm front. All the departures and arrivals boards flashed *cancelled, cancelled, delayed, cancelled* and it was obvious he wouldn't be getting to Berlin tonight. He was almost relieved. The flight in had been a lurching, tossing hell that had him gritting his teeth hard for nearly eight hours.

He thought of going into Paris and finding a room, but looking at the weather and the queues and the chaos he realised it would be pointless. The airport was a steaming stew of exhaustion, frustration, fury and resignation, an incessant shrill spit of announcements and voices shouting down telephones and computer hum and the babble from the televisions and news streams. And there was a grey stink, the smells of stale perfume and cheap soap and sweat and coffee and liquor and disinfectant.

Robbie made his way slowly to terminal one from where his flight to Berlin would eventually depart. Or not. He passed a man pissing into a flowerpot, and a small girl vomiting copiously onto the blue carpet while she held her mother's hand. At an internet kiosk three men, bald and tattooed, wearing black vests, fought loudly over a computer terminal. An old woman in a bright green tracksuit sat in a wheelchair wringing her hands while a younger man, her son perhaps, yelled in Italian into his phone. A contingent of Chinese troops sat stoically, looking only at each other. People had propped themselves against hallway walls, suitcases and bags around them, sipping coffee and water and staring blankly at the floor. Others had made pillows and blankets from whatever they had and lay down against walls and doorways, under seats.

Waiting to edge onto an escalator, Robbie was pressed into the back of a huge man who had an arm wrapped tightly around a young woman with pink stripes in her hair. The man, American, was speaking loudly into his phone. 'Sure, babe. I'll keep you posted. Nothing I can do about it . . . Yeah, a crazy mess . . . Give my love to the kids, huh?' He nuzzled the young woman's head with his heavy chin.

The Western Europe Internal Flights lounge was full, but Robbie was a premium member. The two women at the front desk, immaculate and charmingly determined to ignore the chaos, let him through with a shrug that he took as an apology for what he would find.

Walking past the guards and the overflowing baggage racks, he saw the lounge was the same as outside, but there were more people in suits, the lights were dimmed and the noise volume was one notch lower. Every seat was taken by men and women slouched over their computers or phones or watching the news streams with glazed eyes. The air smelled flat and stale.

There was some floor space near the windows and Robbie left one of his bags and jacket there. Carrying his computers and chargers, he went to the dining bar. There wasn't much left. He filled a glass with scotch, and took another glass and a bottle of water. He put these on the floor by his bag and went back for food.

A small fat man with a moustache stood at the empty soup tureen. He brought out the ladle with a last smear of soup and licked it, then dropped it angrily on the table. 'I'm fucking hungry,' he said loudly to no one. Seeing Robbie approaching the sandwich bar, he pushed in front and grabbed a plate. He piled it with the last of the tatty sandwiches and dried brioches. 'I'm fucking hungry and this is fucking shit.' He glared at Robbie as he left.

Robbie put some packets of cheese and stale biscuits on a plate. It would do. He made himself comfortable on the floor, back against the window. The glass shuddered slightly in the driving wind and rain, and lightning streaks lit the room and then faded. He looked at the radar on his phone – band after band of storms were moving across France, Switzerland, into Germany.

He messaged his news desk to say he'd miss the opening of the conference in Berlin, but presumably so would most people, and for a few minutes he watched the news stream that covered the wall to his right: *Major Storms Cause Transport Chaos Across Western Europe; Power Down In London; Yuan Edges Higher; World's Largest Refugee Holding Pen To Open In North Africa; Ceasefire Holds As Negotiations Continue Over Kazakhstan Oil, Wheat Reserves; Eight Hundred Dead In Rio Food Riots; China Building World's First Ever Proteins Processing Plant With Aim To Help Feed The World; Australia Announces Successful Resettlement Of Twelve Thousand Farmers And Farm Workers In Queensland; Global Discussions Reopen On Recommencing Olympic Games Within A Decade; City Of Boston Completes Sea Wall.*

It was almost nine o'clock and he decided to call Ella.

She picked up after one ring. 'Hello, my darling. Where the hell are you?'

'Charles de Gaulle. Sitting on the floor of one of the lounges.'

There were bursts of static and he missed most of her response.

'. . . the power's . . . across western France . . . probably next.'

'I'm still hoping to get to Berlin tomorrow. Then back to London before Nairobi.'

'Can't . . . you. Guess what? The approval . . . yesterday . . . three months . . . work out a date . . .'

'I can't hear you, sweetheart. You're breaking up.'

'Robbie? . . . you . . . when . . . I see you?'

Robbie hung up and sighed.

A man eased himself onto the ground next to him. He was wearing a business jacket with a shirt and tie, faded red cargo trousers and leather sandals. His blond hair was greasy and Robbie felt him flex his muscles and shoulders against the glass of the window, defining the space around him.

The man smelled dank and stale and was shaking his head up and down while he untangled his earphones. Finally he plugged the headset into his phone and, before he switched it on, flashed Robbie a smile of such unexpected simplicity and joy that Robbie shivered. It was as if, for less than a second, the smile blew away the storm and birds sang and Robbie was somewhere easy and Ella's head was on his shoulder. Then the smile disappeared just as suddenly and the man switched on whatever he was going to listen to and there was another lightning flash and shudder through the thick glass.

Robbie mixed some scotch and water and ate the cheese. There was suddenly a roaring drawl from the man's phone, the sound of a shock jock or preacher on steroids. Robbie could hear every word, as if the device had been turned up to over maximum volume, or as if the words were magnifying themselves in their transmission to the strange man's brain the better to be heard on arrival there.

'The psychiatric fear of radiation. The psychiatric fear of radiation,' the disembodied voice howled. 'Do you feel it? Can you feel it? Listen to this fear closely. This most fearsome of fears. This fear that is distorting you and the whole world. Never let them give it another name. Never. It is the psychiatric fear of radiation and it is in everything you see and touch, it is in you and through you. It is, and you know this if you think about the non-messages within it, the shadow that walks with us and through us. It is in you now. It is in you now. And you, my friend, you . . .'

The man's eyes were closed and he was smiling. Christ, thought Robbie. He nudged the man, who didn't move or open his eyes. Robbie nudged him again. 'Hey,' he said sharply.

The man whipped out his earphones but the raucous droning continued. He looked at Robbie.

'Just turn it down a little, man,' Robbie said.

'I can't.' His voice had no accent. It sounded empty.

'Sure you can. Just a little.' Robbie didn't like the light in the man's eyes, a faint crazy bad light. He wished he hadn't started this.

'No, I fucking can't,' the man said loudly and slowly. 'That's the point. And now I have to start again at the beginning. The very beginning. That's the fucking rule. And now it will be even louder because that's the fucking rule too.'

He put his earphones back in, hit a button and, sure enough, a few seconds later the ranting began again, louder than before.

Robbie gave up and took another mouthful of scotch. Looking around the lounge he thought how impossible it was to know any more what was pouring into people's heads. Maybe that woman over there, in the smart trousers and jacket and brown-rimmed glasses, was listening to the sounds of people fucking. Maybe the man with the neat grey hair and the walking stick propped against his chair was listening to a woman reading poems. Or the shrieks of a child being tortured. The young guy in the expensive business suit, red tie loosened, was probably listening to instructions on detonating a bomb. The two nuns with the soft smiles, knitting away, could be following a Bible reading or listening to the latest slam-kill music.

Who the hell knew? The world was a tsunami of sound that broke against thoughts and words and ideas and crushed them, and sent the debris tossing and spinning to the end of the world and sucked it back again, all in a second, in a blink of an eye, over and over.

Robbie watched the nuns. He was surprised to see them. He realised he had forgotten they might still exist, presumably because he had forgotten God might still have meaning for some people.

'Disembowel the leaders,' came the scream from the phone of the man next to him. 'Gather the mutants and disembowel the liars and the cheats and the liar . . .'

Robbie got out his own earphones and switched on the sound of waves breaking on a beach. It was what he always listened to now when he was waiting somewhere, and half his life was spent waiting. There was another flash of lightning.

He wrote to Ella: *Still sitting on floor of CdG and will be for a while. There is a strange man sitting next to me. Do you know what the psychiatric fear of radiation is? Have booked Nairobi. Only two weeks until I see you again. Good luck with coordinating refugee transfers. You know I'm thinking of you.*

Then he took a thin book from his bag and eased off the elastic band that held it together. Half of the front dust jacket was missing and he had lost the last two pages somewhere. He heard the slow crash and hiss of a wave and opened the book gently to a random page. As he read, a large hand came down on the page. It belonged to the strange man. Robbie stared at it. The big fingers, with thick tufts of reddish hair on the knuckles, slowly and softly stroked the page for several minutes, as if stroking a kitten or a newborn child.

'A book,' the man gently said.

The hand withdrew and Robbie kept reading and thinking and sipping scotch and listening to water until he fell into a restless sleep in which he walked on a black sand beach and watched a little boy with brown hair build a complicated castle from shells and rocks and bones and sticks and sand that was like clay. As soon as the castle was nearly finished a bright, white wave would roll in to wash it away, and the boy would start again. At the other end of the beach was a large woman, big and broad and strong. She was no one Robbie knew but in his dream he watched her watching him for the longest time.

When he woke it was almost dawn. His back was stiff and he was hungry. He took out his earphones. 'The psychiatric fear of radiation' was the first thing he heard. The crazy man in the red trousers was still listening, still nodding his head, eyes closed.

Robbie quietly gathered his bags and stood up. He could see the storms had passed, leaving a steady rain. He could get lucky with an early flight. As he was about to move away, the crazy man opened his eyes and flashed him that shocking smile again.

Robbie went down a hallway to a vast white bathroom and stopped in the doorway. The small fat man with the moustache who had been so angry about the food the night before was dead on the floor. Two knitting needles had been jammed through his neck, just under his right ear. The points protruded under his left ear, grey with streaks of blood. There was blood on the tiles. From a cubicle at the far end of the room came loud gasps and groans of people having sex.

Robbie looked over his shoulder. There was no one behind him. He quietly backed into the hallway. I do not want to know about this, he thought. No. No.

He walked briskly to the reception area, looking straight ahead. Before he left the lounge he glanced quickly at the mess of people. The nuns were asleep and there was no sign of their knitting. The elderly man with the grey hair and walking stick had a large ball of thick red wool in his lap. Robbie shook his head.

He left the lounge, then turned back to the front desk where the receptionists were asleep, heads on their arms, the slightly older woman snoring loudly. Robbie leaned over the counter and shook the snoring woman's shoulder. He tried to remember the little French he knew. '*Cadavre*,' he said loudly to her startled, pale face. '*Salle de bain. Cadavre. Pardon.* I'm sorry. I'm very sorry.' Then he walked away.

He got himself a seat on a flight at ten. While he waited, he found a small table, covered with crumbs and coffee rings, at a patisserie and ordered coffee and a baguette. The baguette was stale and there was no butter. He read a message from Ella.

It stormed for hours here, and I sat on the windowsill and watched. The psychiatric fear of radiation is what they're calling the trauma of the fear of possible exposure to radiation. No one has radiation poisoning of course, only the fear of it. A fertile field these days as exposure to depleted uranium increases, which we're not supposed to know about. Remember I was telling you about the mutant butterflies and lizards? Why do you ask?

Ten thousand refugees leave for African Federation station Monday. Tibetans, Koreans, Sri Lankans mostly. I feel I'm herding cattle onto a truck for the slaughterhouse. I don't believe a word they say about it, but you know all this.

Marriage approval papers have come through and we have three months to make it official. We can talk dates in Nairobi, where I want to sit in sunshine on our balcony and drink cold beer for a whole long afternoon. Can we? Read your piece on the currency issues and liked it, but think a move to two currencies will be the final line in the sand, as it were. Imbalance will be too great. Loving you and wish you were here to hold my hand for just a little while.

Robbie smiled and wondered what to write back. *There was a body in the bathroom this morning, sweetheart*, he could say. He told her he would call when he got into Berlin, and then he checked his emails.

He saw the Republic of Australia was still chasing him for payment of a fifty-thousand-dollar fine for *the utilisation of comments and false interpretation and imposed nuances of undisclosed singular or multiple anonymous alleged government sources in the construct of a purported media story designed to discredit or cast aspersions upon the motives of the government under Revised Media Reportage Law, section . . .*

Robbie forwarded it to his lawyer. *Fuck this*, he wrote. *Can't afford these forever. Have to find another job.*

Then, on a whim, he sent a message to his grandmother: *I am missing you.* And then it was time to leave.

ten

Clare was wheeling an empty shopping trolley back to the Myamba Maxi Store car park. She was disappointed with the Food Essentials Pack. Six tins of apricot quarters, two tins of mandarin segments, a packet of vitamin D tablets and a half-kilo bag of potatoes. 'Like, really?' she said to no one in particular.

A beep from her phone told her she had a message. She stopped and looked and tried to understand what she was reading. *Clare, sorry but rental contract on Treedown Lane will now expire in sixty days. Final inspection three days prior. Nicole.* There was the garish blue and green logo of the Myamba Property Agency underneath the message.

Clare jammed the trolley into another at the supermarket, pushed in the chain and retrieved her ten-dollar coin. Her hands were shaking. She read the message again. She walked through the sliding glass doors and stood in the sun. For a few minutes she couldn't see anything but the sunlight. There were no horns blasting in the car park, no children laughing, no people pushing past and around her. She felt the edges of her small world begin to unravel – unravel again, fuck it – and the knot of anger and anxiety she carried uncurl. What to do?

She turned abruptly and walked the three blocks to Myamba Property Agency, past mostly empty shops, or shops and stores being converted into boarding houses. There were a few people outside the real estate agency scanning the sale and rental notices on the computerised wall. Most had sold or leased banners flashing across them. Inside it was hot and crowded, people queuing at desks waiting to speak to agents. A woman and three children were sitting on the floor in the middle of the room. The woman was talking urgently on her phone and the children were eating ice-creams that dripped onto their clothes and chubby legs and the blue carpet. The oldest child knelt by a red plastic cage and Clare could see a small white dog inside. For no reason she suddenly thought of Joon. The dog put its paw through the bars and the girl slapped it.

Nicole's desk was in the far left corner. There were four or five people in front of it. Clare planted herself firmly with them and folded her arms. She'd wait all day if she had to, although she knew it was hopeless.

A tall man in a smart grey jacket was talking at Nicole. 'I've got the money, okay. We don't care what we pay. Two thousand a week. Three thousand. Or we'll buy something. Look, look,' he was thrusting his phone at her, scrolling through the screens, 'see what's in the bank. Look, job contract, travel permit for the job, references, how many references do you want, security check, provisional loan clearance—'

'Mr Johnston,' Nicole swept her hands back through her hair, 'you've got all the necessary qualifications. I'm simply trying to say that right now there is nothing available. Nothing. What I suggest is you register on our waiting list.' She gestured to a row of computer terminals that lined the opposite wall. 'Fill in the forms, transfer your data, and I hope we can be in touch very soon.'

'And how long are we talking about?'

'I honestly don't know. The Flatland Estate was supposed to start coming on the market in six weeks but they're running behind. There should be a few listings coming up from people on blocks they can't afford to make climate-safe—'

'Not a problem for me,' the man interrupted. 'Tell them you've got someone ready to make an offer. A bloody good offer. Cash down—'

Nicole sighed. 'I'll do that. Regardless, you need to lodge your data with us, okay?' She pointed again to the computer terminals, then pulled a card out from a drawer. 'You could also go down to the caravan park. I know there's a couple of cabins left. Say I sent you. If you're happy to spend the kind of money you're talking about, you might get lucky.'

He took the card. 'Beats staying with the frigging in-laws,' he said, and pulled his wife away with him to wait at the computers.

Then it was the turn of an Indian man and his very pregnant wife and young child. They stepped up to Nicole's desk and the man held out his phone.

Nicole took it and pressed it to the scanner. 'Ah, yes, Mr . . . ah, Mr Mukho . . .'

'Mr Mukhopadhyay,' the man said politely in a thick Australian accent. 'People call me Mucko.'

Nicole looked relieved. She held out a hand for the folder the man was holding and flicked through the papers. 'So, um, Mucko, your townhouse is all ready: 84A, Designation C. There are no problems that I can see. I'll need the final payment and you'll need to sign the final contract.' She scribbled an address on a piece of paper. 'Unfortunately no one can take you to the property until this evening. You can see we're swamped here. So look this up,' she handed him the piece of paper, 'make sure you understand everything, and maybe set your funds transfer for around five.' She flashed him a dazzlingly tired smile. 'Then we'll take you to your new home.'

'Is it really our new home, Daddy?' the little girl asked. She was shifting things around on the edge of Nicole's desk, keys and phones and a framed photograph of a large smiling brown dog.

'Really, truly,' the man said.

Have you seen it, Clare wondered. She had often walked through the designated estates and marvelled at the horribleness of them. Dark small boxes sitting against dark small boxes, red-tiled roofs. No verandahs or porches, no trees, no gardens, no shade or shadows, no softness or surprises. But then the man in front of her had a home, which was apparently more than she did. And a home was a home and it was all she wanted. It was all she had ever wanted.

Eventually, Clare stood in front of Nicole. Two phones on the desk both began ringing and Nicole stared at them. When the ringing stopped, she looked Clare.

'I am really sorry,' she said.

'There isn't a mistake?' Clare asked.

'No, no mistake. Look, the owners really don't have a choice. They have six months to comply with the latest residential climate-proof regulations or they will have to sell it to someone who will fix the place up. But bottom-line, no one lives there any more until the climate-proof renovations are done.'

Clare had met the owners once. They had visited at the end of her first year in the ratbag cottage, an inspection they were entitled to make: two short stocky women with severe haircuts, black jeans, belts, T-shirts. One had rings in her nose and upper lip. They had praised Clare's work in the garden, apologised for the slope of the bedroom floor and the state of the shower, and looked around at the bush and trees and dust as if they were an alien landscape. She thought they had both looked at her breasts.

'Make any changes you like,' they had said. 'Feel free to paint the walls, whatever. Really. This is just a little retirement dream for us. Maybe. One day. We won't be bothering you.'

Clare didn't explain she had no money to fix or change anything, and she somehow suspected they didn't either. She was grateful for the reasonable rent they charged and simply smiled and nodded.

'Fucking dykes,' Phil had said when they left.

Clare had watched them walk up the driveway to the road and saw the slightly taller woman press her hand gently against the small of the other's back. She felt a stab of jealousy. For what, she had wondered.

'But what am I supposed to do?' she asked Nicole.

'I don't know,' Nicole said. She looked away. 'Honestly? I don't know.' She cleared her throat. 'They're opening up a new campsite soon—'

'I don't want to live in a fucking tent,' Clare said loudly.

A thin woman talking to the property agent at the desk next to Nicole's looked up sharply. Clare saw that under her straw hat she was bald and her skin was a translucent star-white, like thin paper. She seemed to have been crying. Clare felt herself flushing.

'It's okay,' she said to Nicole. 'Sorry. It's okay. We'll be gone in sixty days.'

On her way out she saw the girl hit the small dog's paw again.

•

Phil was at the kitchen table when Clare shoved open the front door and dumped the bags of groceries. He was wearing black trackpants and a grey T-shirt that was once white and he was eating baked beans from the tin. He didn't look up. There was an empty tin of sardines on the table with dirty tissues stuffed in it. The room smelled fishy and salty and dark.

Clare pulled out the second chair and sat down. The table was nothing more than an old-fashioned card table, thin legs and scratched red laminated surface. A blob of tomato sauce from the baked beans sat like a dirty puddle. It isn't much of a table, Clare thought. And it isn't much of a kitchen. But it's been mine. I've done the best I can. And, as always, it hasn't been enough.

She looked at Phil. He was all grey. Grey skin. Grey hair. His feet were a mottled grey and blue. Where Clare had grown over the years, her grief and confusion swelling her, he had shrunk, collapsing inwards. Phil had barely left the house for six months.

'Phil,' she said. Then louder. 'Phil.'

He finally looked up. There was a piece of mashed bean on his chin.

'We have to move.'

'Huh?'

'We have to get out. We have to leave.'

'What?' He was finally looking at her. He licked the spoon and put it on the table.

Clare took her phone from her pocket and, slowly through clenched teeth, read him the message from Myamba Property Agency. Her hand shook slightly and she thought suddenly of Granna's hand in the supermarket.

'So,' she said, 'sixty days. Two weeks before Christmas, we've gotta be out of here.'

Phil's eyes twitched. 'Can they do that? They can't do that, can they?'

'Of course they bloody can. They have to anyway. Legally this place is unlivable. All these new fucking rules.'

'But . . .' There was silence. Phil twitched in his chair. He looked at the spoon and the empty tin and the television on the bench next to the sink.

Even now he wants to turn the bloody thing on, Clare thought.

'But . . . where will we go? They can't just throw us out.'

'They can throw us out. They have to throw us out. And I don't fucking know where we're going. I don't have a fucking clue.'

More silence. The warm dark air sharpened the smell of the empty food tins. The kitchen window rattled in a sudden short breeze. Help me, you useless bastard, Clare wanted to say. She put her head in her hands.

'We can't afford to move,' Phil said. 'I don't want to move. I'm not moving. I can't move. I like it here.' He was whining now. 'You have to think of something. You can fix it.'

Clare couldn't bear to look at him for another second. She got up and began to put meat and groceries away. That was the thing. No matter what happened, things had to be done. Meat for a stew had to be put in the refrigerator. Toilet paper had to go in the bathroom. A sticky glob of baked bean sauce had to be wiped from the table, whether the table was an expanse of polished mahogany for twelve or a collapsing card table just big enough for two. If you just kept doing the things that had to be done, one at a time, one thing and then the next thing, a moment could pass. A day could pass. A disaster. A lifetime even.

Phil went to switch on the TV.

'Don't,' said Clare. 'Don't you dare.'

He looked at her blankly. 'Well, what am I supposed to do? Huh? It's not my fault. You can fix it.'

Clare dumped a bag of frozen peas on the table. 'How do I fix it?' she shouted. 'How do I fucking fix it? You tell me. You tell me, for once.'

She watched him shrink a little more. He was terrified of her anger, she knew. She was mostly too tired to be angry any more, but now she felt the black wave rising and rising. She sat down heavily at the table.

'Do you know how much money we've got in the fucking bank? We've got all of six thousand eight hundred and seventy-six dollars. That's it. That's all we've got. You know one of those crappy little cabins at the caravan park? Maybe close to two thousand a week. I went into the agency to see if there's any way to fix this and that's what Nicole was telling someone. You don't know what's happening out there. You don't know how much is changing. All these people coming in from the north and west, from all the other towns, like the closing-down towns I was working in. You don't know. You watch that garbage refugee reality show, that other rubbish. You don't know anything.' She took a deep breath. 'We've been fucking lucky for a few years and now the luck's run out. Again. As usual. As fucking always. I've been fixing things for us for nearly thirty years, Phil. But you know what? I can't fix this. It's about money. We don't have any. We don't have a house. We've got fucking nothing. Nothing. We've always had fucking nothing.'

It was more than she had said to him for years. She made herself breathe. Just breathe, breathe.

'There has to be something,' Phil said. His fingers picked at each other. 'We could maybe put a sign up in town. You know, couple wanting room or something. We can pay for a room.'

She looked at him in disgust. Who would want him in their home? She could perhaps pull herself together and pass on her own, but not Phil.

'Look at you,' she said. 'Just look at yourself, for God's sake.'

Phil stared at the floor. There were breadcrumbs on the brown linoleum, which was scratched and greasy although Clare washed it down with her old mop once a week.

He lost the plot so long ago, Clare thought, lost his grip on the threads that tied a life together. Somehow he had tumbled to a depth she hadn't reached, would not let herself reach, or had perhaps climbed back up from. All he did, each day, was eat tinned food and whatever she cooked for dinner and watch the World News Stream and the refugees scream and fight and cry and die on his favourite television show and drink his rotgut sherry. She watched his throat work anxiously, the twitch in his right eye. And then she looked past him, through the old window that she had never been able to get clean no matter how she tried and where two blowflies were buzzing and crashing against the scratched glass.

Clare thought slowly about what to say next and how to say it. She sat up straighter and looked at him again. 'I want you to listen to me very carefully. Really listen,' she said.

He nodded, and clasped his hands.

'We've lived here for seven years,' she said, breathing deeply to keep her voice steady. She felt she was talking to herself, pulling words from every lonely step she had taken on her night walks, and she understood that she had been thinking the words for a long time. 'It hasn't been much but it's been a home. It's been the only real home I've had for so long. And I like this town. People say hello to me. They nod. It's safe. I like walking here. After what happened to us, to me,' she heard her voice harden and she held up a hand to him to remind him to keep listening, 'after everything that happened, we said we were better off pooling our money and keeping an eye out for each other, that we'd somehow build a little life somewhere. Somehow. And that's what we've tried to do. What I've tried to do anyway.

'So, I haven't figured out what happens next. I'm going to have to think about it. But here's one thing I do know. I've worked hard to get myself together, okay? I'm not going back to the streets. I'm not living in a fucking car again. I'm not going to grovel and plead my way back to some social housing dump. I'm not living in a campsite where kids laugh at the size of my bras hanging on a public line and my tits and where the showers smell of piss. Not ever. I won't ever, ever do those things again. Do you hear me? And living here with you and trying to take care of you, it's been okay. I haven't minded. But you've let yourself go so much that I really don't think I can carry you any more. Even if I wanted to. So, I'm going to figure out what happens next for me, and if that won't work with you around, then I'm sorry, I'm going it alone. Somehow I'll get myself somewhere decent to live. But

I don't know if I care what happens to you. So, what I'm saying is, you need to think too. Okay? Start thinking about what you're going to do. Not us, not me. You. Okay?'

Phil stared at her. There was only the buzzing of the blowflies.

'But—' he started.

Clare held up a hand again. 'No,' she said. 'Don't even try to talk to me. You've had years to do that.' She pulled herself up.

He looked around the room as if he didn't recognise it. Then he cleared his throat. 'Um. The sherry?'

Clare took a deep breath. Again. 'In the bags by the door. You'll have to actually move to get it.'

And then she walked out, slamming the door behind her as hard as she could. Fuck, she thought. What to do? What to do? Through the thin walls she heard the TV come on.

•

For a long time, Clare sat on a rock at the end of the dirt path that wound down past the cottage through the scrubby garden, all acacias and old buddleias and grasses already drying out in the early summer sunshine, to the chook pen she had built herself and where she had kept chooks until a fox killed them all and she didn't have the money to replace them and the old wooden shed that leaned precariously to the left and sheltered the belongings that wouldn't fit anywhere in the cottage: the debris and souvenirs she had collected from her years of walks, the items she couldn't fix and sell on, or the pieces that struck her as worth holding on to. One day, if I have a proper house again, she would think. One day.

On her knees was a battered tin, grey-yellow with a dark scorch mark on one side and *Arnott's Family Biscuits* in swirling old-fashioned writing across the top. One bright and breezy afternoon a long, long time ago Phil's mother had brought the tin of biscuits and two bottles of lemonade over to the house Clare and Phil had been putting the finishing touches to. All shiny brick, three bedrooms, a big rumpus room where Phil had built a wall-long bar of wood and glass and cupboards for his sound system and bottles of fancy liquor and beer. They had been oiling the new back deck that afternoon and had stopped to enjoy the biscuits and lemonade and admire the view of the grey-green low hills rising to the rear of their property. That was one week before the fire.

Inside the tin now was the money Phil and the unemployment office and the bank didn't know about, more than five thousand dollars in cash and coins saved arduously and patiently through her years in Myamba by selling the scarves she knitted, and cleaned-up pieces of junk and food items from the Essentials Pack she didn't want, and giving fifty dollar cash-only haircuts at the market at the end of every school holidays. There was also the credit card she had held on to through thick and thin for twenty years, two hundred dollars in credit with a ten thousand dollar limit and kept that way no matter what happened. Buffer money, she had always thought. If the car collapses, if my teeth fall out, if I get cancer, maybe I'll be able to do something about it. See a proper dentist or doctor, at least. She had also vaguely thought that if she could ever find or keep a job again, the money might pay for a bond on a house that was just a little brighter and cleaner and bigger. Just a little. But somehow that had never happened and today she realised it never would and that she would only ever have nothing, because that's the way it was for some people, whether they deserved it or not.

Clare kept her money tin in a plastic bag inside another plastic bag pushed into one of the boxes that held some of her journals and notebooks and scraps of paper, underneath a grimy Tupperware container full of rusty nails. She hugged the tin close to her chest and watched the afternoon close in around her. She should put the meat on to braise, with some onions and potatoes and carrots and a tin of chicken stock. She should tidy the kitchen. She should. She should.

But instead she kept sitting and thinking, what now, what now, what now? Shit.

•

When she walked that night, she heard the voice of the walking man. She saw the shadows of dogs and men and women and children slip past her and melt into the highway as she watched the signs. She remembered the two women who owned the ratbag cottage, she remembered Joon and the pale veins under the thin faded skin of Granna Adam's hand and the small birds hopping and chittering in the red cage. She tried to remember the very first time Phil had smiled at her and the first time he had held her hand and the first time he had stretched his long, strong body against hers, but she couldn't.

She stood under a dim streetlight in a cloud of orange and black butterflies that fluttered and rose and fell, trapped in the patch of warm light. It was the first time she had seen butterflies at night. One settled on her left breast, rising and falling with each breath she took, and then it slowly spun away.

I have some things, she thought. Things that I have seen, and things that are only mine, things to remember. And there are surely people doing it sadder and rougher than me in these strange, strange times. I know there are.

She watched the butterflies for the longest time, watched their ceaselessly beating tiny wings carry them up and up to the light.

eleven

Clare and Phil said next to nothing to each other for the next few days. Clare slowly wrote lists of all the things that needed to be done in order to vacate the cottage in fifty-nine days, then fifty-eight days, then fifty-seven. A list of what she wanted to keep – the television, the table, the refrigerator and freezer, her sofa and blankets, her journals, her saucepans and her clothes – and a list of what could or should be thrown away, which was far longer. She cursed herself for all the items she had scavenged from sidewalks over the years – the bookcase with no shelves, the rocking chair with an arm missing, garden pots, a wheelbarrow with a twisted front tyre, all the junk stacked in her shed in the belief that one day things could be fixed and find a home.

She wrote a list of what and who should be notified and by when, which was very short. She wrote a list of meals she could make using up the meat and fruit in the freezer. She wrote where to go, what to do, several dozen times in small letters across two columns and added question marks. She ate far too much and felt her stomach bulge and stretch, squashing down her panic and anger. Phil watched her cautiously and made an effort to keep the kitchen clean and the television volume low.

She telephoned the storage business in the north of town and was told there was a three-month waiting list but anyway, from the sound of it, she had too few possessions to begin to fill even the company's smallest container and would be wasting her money. She had known this but had simply wanted to hear a voice that belonged to a person who was functioning efficiently in the world. For the same reason she called the electricity company, but there was only a recording telling callers all accounts were to be activated, cancelled or monitored via the website.

She called the unemployment office and after she'd pressed every available option and waited for three hours, a voice did come on the line.

'Doesn't make any difference to us where you live,' the voice said, after Clare explained she was ringing to tell whoever needed to know that she would no longer be living at 17 Treedown Lane, Myamba, fifty-three days from now.

'I've always had to tell you guys everything. Otherwise I can't get my benefit.'

'Used to. Not any more. Now we know everything. All the time. No telling necessary.'

The voice was curious. Male, Clare thought, but unusually high-pitched and with a soft lisping hiss, so that 'necessary' became a long and slithering 'nethesssssary'.

'How do you know?'

'Your phone, of course.'

'But I've always had my phone.'

'Well, that was your phone then, honey, and this is your phone now. No one does paper any more. Not here. I can't remember when I last touched the stuff. Now, I'm looking at everything I need to know about you. Let me see . . . so, you were once a hairdresser. And you did cleaning work. Lovely. Ah, you're in D segment.'

'What's D segment?'

'Doomed, dear. Doomed.' The voice broke into a high-pitched giggle. 'Disaster. Dead. Doomed.'

Clare said nothing. This seemed entirely plausible.

'Just our little joke, of course.' When Clare stayed silent the voice became anxious. 'Really, sweetie, just a joke. After all, we're all doomed, aren't we? Well, the humans anyway. Don't take it personally.'

'Personally' slithered through the phone as 'perthssssssssssonally'. The ethssses and the sunlight and the late morning crescendo of the cicadas created a white shimmering of sound.

Clare was sitting on the uneven back steps watching a blue-tongue lizard start its slow scrambling walk from the broken front fence down the long path towards the shed. Most summer days the lizard patrolled the perimeter of the property, usually twice and always in a clockwise direction, hauling itself through dead grasses and between rocks. Clare often watched it for hours.

'Anyway,' the voice was saying, 'back to business. No, there is no need any more to fill in silly paperwork or tell us where you are going or not going. Where you go your phone goes and that tells us everything we need to know. Where you are. Where you've been. Your phone is the naughty lover who tells us all your secrets.'

'I don't really believe you.'

'Well, you should. For example, I can tell you exactly where you were one year ago today. I just press this, and this. Yes, you were at the fire station hall exactly one and a half kilometres north west of your house.'

Clare thought and then remembered. Yes. It had been a meeting of the local fire authority, the last as it turned out. She had gone to every meeting since moving to Treedown Lane. In the early years she had occasionally volunteered to bring a platter of sandwiches or her homemade sausage rolls, carefully planning her budget to ensure she could manage her small contribution. But then the new personal health and hygiene directive outlawed the serving of any food at any public or community gathering unless it was prepared in professional kitchens. The directive saved everyone some money but it also shut down some of the spirit and energy of the volunteers, breaking already under the increasingly bizarre and complex regulatory codes covering fire, water, land clearing and the new mandatory volunteer profile clearance checks. Clare still went to meetings and every spring she helped to clean down the old trucks, although she made it very clear that in the event of a fire she'd be unable to help. She was terrified of fire, to her very core.

Then last year a special meeting was called and two young men in cheap suits from the newly formed Centralised Catastrophe Coordination Unit, which was part of the Inclusion Zone Emergency Services Management Authority, arrived to announce that all volunteer firefighting services were being disbanded, and, as an aside, so were all bush and environment regeneration organisations.

'I'm sure we all appreciate the days of amateur efforts are well behind us,' one of the men had read tiredly from his computer, and at that point Clare's neighbour Cutter had leapt to his feet and, pointing at the men, denounced them as useless pompous idiots with no respect for the traditions of rural communities or for the men and women who for years, decades, had done more to keep small towns safe than all governments combined.

The men had tried to explain how the drone fire surveillance system – 'accepted with great gratitude from our ally in rural restoration, China' – would work, but they were shouted down again and again by Cutter and then others who became bolder and angrier as the minutes went on. Weeks later Cutter had told Clare he'd been fined a thousand dollars for inciting disrespect.

'Let's see,' the soft, lisping voice resumed. 'What else? Dear, oh dear. Haven't held a paid job for eight years. Just the closing-down towns. But I'm sure there's been a bit of fudging around that. Always is. Should I put an alert out? Get the teams to find out everything, and I mean everything, you've done these last few years? Hmmm? Husband last worked at the canning factory. How you survive on our handouts is truly beyond me. Truly it is. There's a few photographs of you here on file. Let's have a look. Well, I'm going to be brutally honest, honey. You could lose a bit of weight. Quite a bit, if I may say so. You'd feel better for it.'

'Where are you?' Clare asked.

'A long, long, long way away.' There was a sigh.

'But where?'

'You're not really supposed to know,' the voice said. There was a brief pause. 'But I can't see what difference it makes to you. I'm in China. Well, under China somewhere really.'

'China?'

'Oh yes.' Another pause. 'They tell me it's raining here. It's been raining for weeks and weeks and weeks and weeks and it's not even the wet season.'

The lizard was now a fair way down the path. It had stopped and was swinging its head slowly from left to right. It's like me, Clare thought. Slow. One foot in front of the other. It would make a list each day if it could. *Stop at the red rock. Hide behind the herb bed.*

'People really have no idea,' the voice was saying. 'There's drones, there's CCTV, there's vehicle and travel permits, there's fingerprints on file, there's phones with their cameras and location tracking and financial identification and verification sensor. Of course we know most things about most people, and especially where they are. It is so very expensive to hide. It really is.'

'What if someone's outside the inclusion zones?' Clare asked. 'Can you watch them?'

Every day she wondered about the people who were walking and the walking man.

'Only if they've been silly enough to take their phones with them,' the voice said. 'Of course they won't actually work, but even if they are just carrying a phone we can know where they are, if we want to. But I don't think many walking people take their phone. Why would they?'

Clare got up and walked to the front verandah, where she sat on the old wrought-iron chair. The sun was too hot now. Her arms and feet were pink.

'I think it's kind of weird, what you do,' she said.

'Oh, honey, I couldn't agree more. It's very weird indeed. And boring. And lonely too. That's why I'm so enjoying talking to you. I truly am. I think you're the only person I've spoken to for days. Because the point is, with phones the way they are now no one needs to ring anyone any more. All anyone does any more is press buttons to get or say what they want. And all government does is watch people pressing buttons. Boring, boring, boring.'

'You don't have other people working with you?'

'Oh goodness, there are thousands and thousands of us, working in thousands of rooms. People often get lost here. They walk for hours looking for their room and their desk and their computer. We watch them looking. It's very funny. Well, we are only human after all. Sort of.'

'Do you have a name?' she asked.

'Everyone has a name. Even me. But I mustn't tell you. I must not. I'm just a lady-boy voice.'

'What do you look like?'

'Beautiful. Quite beautiful.' There was a pause. 'Has anyone ever told you that you're beautiful?'

Clare thought the voice suddenly had an edge to it, something cold and hard.

'Tell me, Clare. You can tell me. Has anyone ever, ever said, even once, that you're beautiful? Have they?'

Clare closed her eyes. She felt the hot sting of tears and blinked rapidly. I don't like this any more, she thought.

The voice went on and on, a merciless soft chant. 'Has someone ever said that, Clare? Has someone ever said that?'

'Yes,' she roared. 'Yes, they fucking have. Fuck you, fuck you.'

The tears and the sobs came now, and as she switched off the phone she heard a chorus of giggles and laughter. She let herself cry. She felt fat and alone and defeated.

After a while she went inside and made a cup of tea. I have to figure something out, she thought. I just have to.

•

The day after the conversation with the voice, Clare got up early and went down to the shed. She took out the boxes of journals and notebooks, spreading them around wherever there was space. She dragged out the broken rocking chair and the greasy wicker coffee table with only three legs. Then she felt on top of the bookcase with no shelves and pulled down a thick black satchel. Wiping off the cobwebs, she tipped it upside down. A heavy white ceramic doorknob fell out, along with some black and green tiles in various shapes and sizes, a half-used tube of putty, a pair of size fourteen red lace underpants with the price tag still on them, a bright pink pen and a small heavy glass bottle.

Clare picked the bottle up from the dust and wiped it with her T-shirt. Sitting on her rock, she turned it over gently in her hands. When she took off the carved glass lid there was still a faint elusive scent. She thought she could smell pine needles and laughter and a mild summer sky.

Phil had given her the perfume on their second Christmas together. He had made a six-hundred-kilometre round trip to the city and back to buy it, along with a silver bracelet with a large heart as a clasp. She remembered arriving on Christmas morning at the small flat he lived in over his parents' garage and seeing the two gifts, professionally wrapped, on the kitchen bench. He made her open the bracelet first and she'd loved it, the sparkle of the silver, the weight on her wrist.

Then he'd picked up the second present, and cleared his throat. 'I went into Sydney to get this. You know when I told you we was having a boys' night at the river? Wasn't true. I wanted to get you something special, something different that none of the girls here would have, so I went into Sydney, one of those big fancy stores.'

He had handed the package to her and she undid it slowly. She gasped when she took the small bottle out of the box. She knew from the thickness and sharpness of the glass and the French words on the box that it was expensive.

Phil cleared his throat again. 'It's just, well, it's not a big thing and it was hard to decide what to pick. But I wanted to find something that said, well . . .' He'd stuck his hands in the back pockets of his jeans and looked at the ceiling and then back at her and spoken in a rush. 'You're beautiful to me, you know. I don't think I've ever told you. Not properly. So I wanted to find something beautiful to give you. And I thought of perfume, not cheap stuff but real perfume, because, I don't know, it's sweet and strong, like you. And every time you put it on you can remember I think you're beautiful.'

Clare had pictured Phil in his jeans and flannel shirt towering over shiny counters of glass and brass, his big bricklayer's hands sweaty, scratching his head. She had imagined the women behind the counters with their make-up and red lips and nails and streaked perfect hair not knowing whether to laugh at him or flirt with him, and Phil probably flirting just a little in his rough boyish way. She imagined him getting

back to his car and sighing with relief that the ordeal was over. Her
eyes had filled with tears.

'Anyway, I liked the smell of this the best,' he had said. 'And the
bottle. You only need a little bit, the woman told me.'

Clare held the small empty bottle. So there, lady-boy voice, she said
to the sky that was a motionless sheet of heavy cloud. Yes, someone
once told me I was beautiful. Someone wanted me and touched me.
I was beautiful to someone. So bloody there.

After a while she focused again on the mess around her, the scrappy
boxes and broken furniture. She got up, pushing the bottle into the
pocket of her trousers, and went to a box that had *One* written in large
red letters on all sides. She took a notebook from it and again used
her T-shirt to wipe away the dust and mouse shit. Sitting back on her
rock, she opened the thin, tired pages. A receipt fell out. She picked it
up and looked at the faded print. Three meat pies, two sausage rolls,
four lamingtons, a bottle of lemonade, twenty-nine dollars. Only
twenty-nine dollars? But why would she have kept such a thing? She
screwed up the scrap of paper and threw it aside.

I'm so angry with him, Clare read. *Bastard. Bastard. It was his fault
the insurance didn't come through. He said it would be okay to move in
before the occupancy papers, that everyone did it. But it meant we only
had our building insurance after the fire, not the proper insurance. We
still owe money to the bank. I hate the bank. And fucking Phil. And
me. I was so stupid. If he was too busy I could have done our insurance
properly. I let him do everything. That's how he liked it. Me just the little
wife. Smiling, smiling.* She saw she had written *angry, angry, angry,
angry* over and over on the rest of the page in an ugly scrawl, huge
exclamation marks everywhere.

The next page was the same. And the page after that. On the next,
she had drawn what she must have imagined was the face of a mad
angry person, with wild eyes and hair and a mouth that was screaming.

On another page she had drawn a kitchen with captions and little arrows pointing to different things: *This was my beautiful oven. Phil made all these cupboards. Separate fridge and freezer!*

She flipped through to the middle of the book. *My mother is a very sick woman*, she read. *Saw her today just to ask one last time for help. Even a loan. We'd pay it back. 'I have fulfilled my earthly obligations to you,' is what she said. 'I gave you and Phillip money for the deposit. You managed to lose it. Now you must trust the universe to provide.' What crap. She was mixing up one of her stupid herbal teas at the stove. Her stupid bottles of potions and lotions were everywhere. Fucking astral charts all over the walls. She gave me a cup of the tea. 'This'll help unblock your negativity,' she said. Cunt. Maybe I wouldn't be so fucking negative, Mum, if you'd give us some fucking money. The universe doesn't provide. Never has. Never will. I hate you. I hate you.* The writing was uneven, some words in capitals, some barely legible.

She turned to the end of the book. *Too hot today. Good fire day. I can smell the burning. I hate the hot days. And it's getting hotter. One day everything will burn.* She had drawn a picture of a cat and flames. Under it she had written: *Phil didn't let me get the kitten from the laundry. He said there wasn't time. The fire was coming that quick. Poor fucking Muffin. I hate the animals burning in fires.*

Clare threw the notebook on the ground. There was a hiss and she saw the lizard was watching her. Then it looked at the boxes, as if contemplating a way through an unexpected obstacle course.

She picked up another notebook. Inside the front cover she had pasted a rental agreement. She remembered the house – a small timber box in a vast suburb of identical timber boxes on the edge of a dusty desert.

Phil starts the new job tomorrow. He says he's not scared going down the mine. I'm going to like it up here. I think I can get some cleaning work. Phil says we can pay the bank back by the end of the year if we're careful. I'll make bloody sure we're careful. He's stopped drinking, well, drinking much anyway. I'm going to make curtains for the windows. Maybe things will be okay. I weigh a hundred and ten kilos. That's good.

They were okay, Clare remembered. For a few years. Until the mine was sold and a new workforce brought in. They had paid back the bank and they still had nothing.

Towards the end of the notebook: *One hundred and eighteen kilos. Oh well, it's been Xmas. I made barbecue chicken and coleslaw and Phil bought a fruit cake and a huge tub of caramel ice-cream. We had a happy time. Need to stop eating so much bread. Thinking grains not good for me.*

She stood up and looked at the dark sky. There was no smell of rain. She couldn't remember when it had last rained. She picked another journal from another box and went back to her rock. The lizard had gone.

This journal had a blue vinyl cover. Fancy, she thought. In the front was a card with a picture of two hands, fingertips touching, and inside were a dozen or so messages. Clare touched the card lightly, then opened it. She remembered the women giving it to her the morning she left the refuge. *Beautiful Clare. Go well,* one message read. *You're big and strong and brave and beautiful. I'll miss you,* read another. That's a second beautiful, she thought. I'd forgotten.

She put the card carefully on her knee under the journal, which she opened at the middle to a sprawl of furious and barely legible writing. There were circles and boxes and in some places the pen had been pressed so hard against the paper that it had torn. Clare snapped the journal shut. For the second time in as many days she put her head in her hands and cried.

There wasn't, she thought, a single page in all the boxes that was worth keeping. For twenty-seven years she had written the same things over and over.

It was a grief counsellor who had recommended Clare start keeping a journal, after the fire and the miscarriage that she never told Phil about because he was, in his own way, as shattered as she was. It was a way of beginning to articulate her feelings, the woman had explained, and Clare remembered her sad, earnest face and the huge weight she gave to the word 'feelings', as if they were something Clare could take out of herself and put on a table and carefully untangle and separate and tidy up. And perhaps, for a little while, it had helped. It had given a small focus to each long day. But what had she been thinking, to paste shopping lists and meaningless receipts onto the cheap pages, to write over and over and over that she was sad or angry or okay? I only wrote what I felt, she thought. I never wrote what I saw. I never wrote what I did. I never wrote that I've made it this far.

She stood up and looked at the boxes and the mess around her. 'I'm getting rid of all this shit,' she said aloud. 'Wherever I'm going next this crap is not coming with me.'

She took out her phone. 'Inclusion Zone Three landfill,' she said, and was connected to a recording that detailed opening hours, costs and an endlessly long list of what items would be accepted and what items had to be separated from what. No wonder the country's becoming a scrap heap, Clare thought when she hung up. Used to be you could burn your own rubbish but, of course, for most of the year now no one was allowed to light a fire or a barbecue, not that she would want to. But still, an arm and a leg just to get rid of rubbish and broken things. Clare got her tin and counted out six hundred and forty dollars. Enough for petrol and four carloads of crap to be dumped.

Over the next two days she made the trips to and from the landfill, more than six hours of driving and twelve checkpoints. Phil offered to help load the car but she said no.

The landfill itself set her teeth on edge. Armed guards checked her through the electronic gates, and others were posted at various points across the low hills that surrounded a heaving muck of garbage and waste and debris that an assortment of trucks and diggers and loaders were sorting and shifting. There was a stink she couldn't name; a rotting blood-metal smell that was profoundly primal and made her want to gag. Black crows swooped and circled viciously. On her third visit, she heard shouts and saw a pack of dogs running down the far eastern side of the hills, raising dust, and into what looked like a black molasses swamp, a fenced-off pool of something thick and steaming. She saw the guards raise their guns and then lower them as the dogs began to sink. She watched them scramble and bark and heave their bodies up out of the muck and then sink again. She shuddered.

As she was leaving after dumping her last load, she stopped the car by the guard who was waving her through the checkpoint.

'Have you ever seen bones falling?' she asked.

'Get outta here,' he said, jerking the butt of his gun.

•

On her final trip back from the landfill site Clare braved Myamba's Maxi Store and bought a new journal and a pen and a bag of apples on sale for only thirty dollars. She was disappointed to find half the apples were bruised, mushy and dark, but she cut up what she could and stewed the pieces with some sugar and butter and some rosemary she picked from the small herb garden she had planted years earlier. She panicked when she looked at her plants, but bit it down. I will grow herbs again. Somewhere I will grow herbs again.

She boiled some eggs and toasted bread and made curried egg sandwiches for dinner, two rounds for herself and one for Phil. They ate in silence in the small hot kitchen and watched the news feed on the television. Another earthquake in California. A dust storm in central Australia. Something on the global population management program. Travellers arriving at major airports in China could now collect an oxygen tank as they left the arrivals hall. The warmest winter days on record across Scandinavia.

When Clare had finished washing the few dishes, Phil switched the channel to *Race For Home*. Clare glimpsed a small green tub of a boat lurching over a mountainous wave, terrified people screaming, someone vomiting. She shook her head in disgust and went outside with a bowl of stewed apples and her new journal.

She ate the apples slowly, watching the summer white of the day turn to shadow. She put the bowl down and picked up her new journal and put it on her knees. She listened to the squealing of cockatoos and the cicada hum and the hiss and scream of cats fighting somewhere

What is the next piece of the plan, she wondered. What do I do next? What do I do? She sat for hours and didn't write anything in the new journal.

twelve

Ella and Robbie had their three days together in Nairobi, and they did spend one sweltering afternoon sitting in sagging wicker chairs on the balcony of their room drinking beers. Robbie would remember Ella pressing a cold bottle against his thigh, the condensation on the glass mixing with his sweat and the momentary, minuscule chill, and then her finger tracing the coolness.

'One smile, please, my darling,' Ella had whispered, sweat beading across her upper lip. 'One smile.'

And so he had smiled, finally, and, taking her hand, wrapped it around the cold bottle of beer he held and then pressed it again against his thigh. He would remember that one moment, the cold of the bottle on his leg under Ella's fingers, the sweat gathering on her lip and under her eyes and jaw, and ache to have it back.

Ella had spent a week at the new refugee station that sprawled across the recently created United Central African Federation. She arrived in Nairobi wind-burnt and grimy and hungry.

Robbie waited for her in the hotel lobby. He had always loved this particular hotel and was always surprised it continued to exist, surprised

110

it hadn't been ripped down and replaced with an eight-hundred-room megabrand monolith. The absurd ancient mock-Tudor décor, the shadowy wings spreading out from a central garden, the dark panelling and eclectic furnishings, the dusty plastic palms, the ridiculously haphazard service: it was a last eccentric oasis in a city that was now nothing more than a purpose-built platform, all glass and steel and concrete, for the round-the-clock negotiations and bullying and money-counting and denials that tried to keep the continent functioning.

While he waited he watched the guards and their guns, and the grim-faced businessmen and women who came and went, or greeted each other and headed off to a private room to talk or deal or whatever they did, or stood by the vast double doors at the entrance waiting for an armoured limousine to pull in and whisk them down the potholed roads that snaked around the city, through the smells of fruit and flesh and spice and easy money, to another room somewhere.

He watched a beggar in torn shorts and a T-shirt that might once have been yellow approach the wide steps leading to the entrance, thin arms outstretched, holding a tin with a wrapping showing bright red tomatoes; and behind the beggar, a child, perhaps six or seven years old, wearing only a disposable nappy that bunched under his swollen taut stomach. One of the guards walked down the steps slowly and raised the butt of his rifle and brought it down against the side of the beggar's neck. Robbie imagined he heard the snap of bone and a scream of pain and the crack of the tin on stone as the beggar fell and folded. But he could hear nothing through the thick doors, not the snap of the guard's fingers as he summoned staff to take the beggar away, not the click of the polished boots worn by a businessman walking briskly up the stairs and stepping over the body with a scowl of disdain, not the crying of the child who squatted now by the beggar, dirty little hands scratching through his hair in anguish, and not the thud as the same guard kicked the child, and then kicked him, or her perhaps, again and then again, not the bray of the guard's laughter.

I am seeing this from far away, Robbie thought. I am looking at pictures on a screen. That's all. And he continued to watch because he wanted, urgently, for the body of the beggar and the child to be removed before Ella arrived. That seemed to him, in this minute, to be the most important thing there was.

The businessman in polished boots walked past him. He was wearing oversized reflective sunglasses and he smelled of melting hair wax and sweat and something dark. Robbie instinctively stepped aside. He watched three guards throw the beggar and then the child into the back of a small van, which had the hotel's name written in purple and gold lettering down the side. The van took off and Robbie sighed with relief.

Ella didn't notice him when she arrived. She walked straight to the empty reception desk and, after waiting for a few minutes, leaned over it as if someone might be hiding behind the panels. 'Hello?' she called. 'Hello?'

Robbie put his arms around her waist. 'Hello,' he said.

She spun around and laughed. 'Hello, darling.' She cradled his head between her hands. 'You shouldn't do that, you know. I could think you were just anybody and knock you out cold.'

'You wouldn't.'

'I would and you know it.' She kissed him lightly. 'So, I am here. And I want a shower, clean clothes and food. In that order. And then, whatever.'

She turned back to the reception desk, where an attendant had materialised and was glaring at her. When Ella smiled and pressed her fingertips to the identity scanner, the attendant stood a little taller and brushed his collar, as if there might be dust on it.

•

Robbie watched Ella while she showered. The nearness of her and the ordinariness of watching her rinse shampoo from her hair and the smell of the shampoo, something crisp and clean like cut grass, made him feel, for a moment, sharply lonely, as if her sudden and lovely presence was a challenge to all his imaginings of her.

He stepped back into the room and put the shirt and shawl he'd bought for her in Berlin on the bed, and waited on the balcony, watching a tiny iridescent bird sunning itself on the leathery leaves of an old frangipani tree.

'Oh, Robbie,' he heard and turned back to the room. Ella had put on the shirt and was doing up the buttons. It was a fine white cotton shirt with small hand-painted red roses scattered across it. 'It's just beautiful,' she said.

'No. You are.'

They held each other then, a long hello-again hug. After a few minutes, he pointed to the bottle of champagne in the ice bucket.

'Can we save it for later?' Ella asked. 'I don't think I've eaten since last night.'

'Then let's go eat.'

They took a table in the corner of the terrace restaurant and watched the dusk begin to fall across the gardens. Behind the gardens and the far wing of the hotel the lights of the city's new towers and buildings hovered and shimmered, and there was a steady low wail of sirens and the thrumming of helicopters and trucks and tanks. Despite a slight breeze it was still hot and Ella shifted the collar of the shirt on the back of her neck. A small group of guinea fowl wandered in a straight line across the darkening lawn.

'They're monogamous,' Ella said, sipping mineral water.

'Who are?'

'Guinea fowl. I read it somewhere.'

'Ah.'

A waiter appeared.

'Two hamburgers with fries for me, please,' Ella said. 'One hamburger, and then the second hamburger when I have finished the first. Then each hamburger is hot, yes?'

'We have no buns for the hamburger, madam,' the waiter said, smiling broadly as she tapped the order into a small red tablet.

'I'm sorry?'

'There are no buns today. There is bread. We can toast the bread. It will be almost like a hamburger, but a sandwich.' The waiter folded her arms across her breasts and tried to frown an apology for the lack of buns.

'Okay,' Ella said. 'Whatever. But you have fries?'

'Of course, madam. Absolutely. But there is no tomato.'

Ella rubbed her forehead. 'No tomato?'

'No tomato slices for the toasted hamburger sandwich. There are no tomatoes. Not anywhere. Next week perhaps.'

'I see.'

'But . . .' The waiter paused and smiled again, a huge sunshine smile, as if she was about to impart a special secret. 'We have our own tomato relish. We made it when there were many tomatoes. Chilli. Garlic. Very delicious.'

'Excellent,' Ella said.

'Pineapple?'

'Pineapple?'

'Instead of the tomatoes. Pineapple slices. But from a tin.'

Robbie tried not to smile, and then remembered the beggar's hands holding the tin and saw, in acute close-up, the knuckles of the man's hands and his wrist bones, the wrists thin and hairless. He shook his head to clear the memory.

'No pineapple,' Ella said. 'Just the burgers in toasted bread with relish and fries. That will be okay.'

The waiter paused again, as if about to suggest something else. But she just tapped the tablet and turned to Robbie.

'The steak,' he said. 'Medium. And whatever you can put together for a salad. Whatever you've got.'

'Really, sir? Whatever we have?' The waiter's eyes gleamed with delight.

'Yep. Anything. And do you have this?' Robbie pointed to a label from a red wine bottle pasted into a thick folder full of labels from wine and whisky and vodka bottles and faded photographs of beers and milkshakes.

The waiter bent over and stared at it. There was a sweet sour smell from her breasts. 'I would not think so.'

'Then this one?'

'No, not that one either.'

She adjusted her bra strap under her top and smiled while Robbie shrugged at Ella.

'Okay,' he said. 'What red wine do you actually have?'

'Ah, actually, actually. Such a word that is.' She tapped her tablet again, then showed Robbie a picture she had called up. 'Anyway, we have the house wine from the Americas. Very rich. Smooth. There is no wine export from Europe and Australia to here at the moment. It is a rule. So there is this.'

Robbie thought he should ask what rule and why, but he suspected the conversation would become endless.

'We'll have a bottle of that,' he said.

'Technically speaking, it may not be for sale.'

'What? Then why tell me about it?'

The waiter threw out her arms in an exaggerated shrug and smiled even more broadly. 'If you can afford it, you can buy. If you cannot afford it, it is not for sale. Obviously.'

'How much?'

She tapped the tablet again and put it in front of Robbie. Four hundred dollars a bottle. He thought of his grandmother talking about buying very, very fine wine for fifty dollars and weren't those the days, and the wine cellar at the House of Many Promises. He sometimes didn't know any more what he was actually buying when he bought a bottle of wine. The hotel could have pasted new and obscure labels over bottles of vinegar, for all it might matter. He wondered again when choices and certainty had begun to slip away. Four hundred dollars was ridiculous, but everything was ridiculous.

He smiled and shrugged. 'We'll have two,' he said. 'Two bottles.'

'Then have three for the price of two?' The waiter's voice had become loud and harsh. 'Why not? Four for the price of three? A one-night-only offer. Treat yourself and the lady, sir.'

Robbie thought of the child outside the hotel with the beggar, and the sagging nappy, and the guard's boot against the child's thin ribs. At the same time, he remembered a boy in a dream. A boy on a beach, building a castle from stones and sticks and bones, waves rolling in. Now there was a bottle riding the crest of a wave, tumbling into the shore. Had there been a bottle in his dream? He didn't remember. The waiter's smile was suddenly too sharp, like a handful of diamonds tossed into the light. His eyes hurt and he rubbed them, and felt Ella reach across the table and lightly touch his wrist.

'Two bottles,' he said through gritted teeth. 'Four hundred dollars each. That's too much anyway. Now. Please.'

He looked up at the waiter, and there was only a small, neat smile as she nodded and took the wine list and walked away.

'Are you alright?' Ella asked.

'Yes, of course. Sorry.'

'Don't say sorry.'

'It's just that . . . aren't conversations becoming odd? Or people? Or something?'

Ella smiled. 'Odder than what?'

The waiter returned and put two bottles of wine on the table. There was nothing odd at all about her, Robbie saw. She was small and tired and there was a stain on her black skirt and damp sweat on her white shirt, which was fraying slightly at the collar.

He poured two glasses of wine. 'Cheers,' he said.

They both took a sip and Ella wrinkled her nose. Robbie shrugged. The wine was warm and syrupy, but he emptied his glass anyway and poured another.

They looked at the gardens while they waited for the food. In the hot and dusty evening shadows it was a grey jumble of acacias, bougainvillea, bamboo, palms, banyan and loquat trees. A flamingo stood motionless in a small pond. Robbie watched the guinea fowl return across the lawn and heard the hiss of a hose and the splutter of water on heavy leaves. The silence of the gardens was wrong, he realised. There were only muffled bangings from the kitchen and the shuffle of the waiter and the slightest bump as Ella set her glass of wine on the table. There should have been rustles in the shadows and the flap of bats' wings and cicada song, the whisper of movement even above the backdrop of the city's sounds. He leaned forward to watch the garden and the guinea fowl more closely and then he stood up.

'Something's not right,' he said to Ella.

'What do you mean?'

'I just want to have a look.'

Robbie walked over to the low wide steps that led to the garden, his footsteps loud on the tiles. Thick red ropes blocked entry to the steps. He unhooked the top rope and stepped over the lower rung. He heard the waiter call after him but he kept walking across the lawn to the line of guinea fowl.

He bent down and touched the lawn. It was plastic. Then he picked up a bird, holding it in both hands. The bird's legs kept moving, scratching through air, and its neck and beak jerked forward and back, forward and back. Robbie threw the bird on the ground. There was a thud, a sudden whirring that eased into a sigh, a last scramble of the legs and then silence. He heard Ella call out from the verandah, but he walked on to where the towering garden beds began, narrow dirt paths cutting through various groupings of plants. He reached up to pick a flower from a frangipani tree, the white and yellow bright, but the flower didn't give under his hand. Robbie laughed.

He walked along the edge of the bed towards the pond, touching each plant, leaning in to smell a leaf, bending to put his hand against the base of a palm tree. Every plant had a neat sign staked to it proclaiming its popular and botanical names. He flicked a tiny bird from the purple flower of a bougainvillea and watched it fall to the ground. He pulled a cobweb from a fern and bent it in half, and put a black widow spider in his pocket. At the start of one of the paths he knelt down to scrape up a handful of dirt and he laughed again.

'It's all fake,' he called out to Ella. 'All of it.'

'No!' Ella was leaning over the railing of the verandah, and he saw the waiter was standing at the top of the steps, hands crossly on hips.

'Everything. The lawn, the dirt, the birds.'

Robbie walked to the pond, which was simply a vast sheet of ice-blue glass supporting perfect and perfectly lifeless water lilies and white egrets and the lone flamingo.

Following the sound of a sprinkler, he turned down one path and then another, past two motionless ostriches. A man in baggy trousers with grass stains on the knees and a white shirt smeared with dirt and wearing thick gardening gloves was watering a dozen plastic mango trees. He saw Robbie approach and smiled broadly, then turned his attention back to watering, carefully directing water to the base of one tree and then another, then turning the hose onto the leaves.

'Why?' Robbie asked.

'Why what?'

'Why are you watering plastic plants?'

For a minute or two there was only the sound of water spraying and dripping from leaf to leaf.

'I'm not,' the man said.

'You are.'

'That's not true.'

'Of course it's true, man. None of this is real. It's all plastic.' Robbie reached up and pulled a mango towards him. The branch the mango was attached to stretched and stretched, forcing Robbie to take a step back and then another. He let the branch go and it ricocheted upwards, the plastic mango spinning like a little football lost on the wind. 'See. Plastic.'

The gardener began gathering the hose up in large loops. He moved down the path to the next bed, rows of high grasses, each plastic frond perfect, and carefully began to water the base of each plant.

Robbie followed. There was a smell, distinct and clean, of wet grass.

'Just tell me,' he said.

The man kept watering.

'Fucking crazy,' Robbie said and turned to go.

Behind him he heard a low keening and then a sob. 'I love this garden,' the man wailed. 'I love it. I love it.'

Robbie looked back and saw the man was squatting on the path, head in his hands, water from the hose pooling around his boots.

'This is the most beautiful garden there is,' the man sobbed. 'It's the most beautiful garden in the world.'

'Okay,' Robbie said. 'Okay. Whatever. I'm sorry.'

He started walking back to the hotel. He passed a huge screen of bougainvillea and jasmine. A small man, also in gardening clothes, was holding a large clear bottle and gently spraying each flower one by one. Next to him was a large trolley with rows and rows of small bottles.

Robbie smelled the warmth of jasmine and, for a moment briefer
than a breath, saw every simple summer day and night he had ever
known, white butterflies and yellow roses and bare brown feet on the
cool floorboards of the House of Many Promises, and the crash of a
wave on a beach and a warm blue breeze and the sheen of suntan lotion
on a woman's shoulder and smoke from a barbecue. Every image was
sharp and real and pulled hard at him so that, for only an instant, he
felt he had fallen through time to somewhere else, to places he must
have been but had forgotten, or didn't dare to remember because the
beauty of them was irretrievable. Yet here they were, dazzling, endless
summer days, one after another after another.

He closed his eyes and when he opened them he saw only a small
man in baggy dirty clothes spraying plastic flowers with scents that
were suddenly cloying and cheap and hung heavily on the still dust
of the night.

'Pathetic,' Robbie said to the man. He felt tired and angry, as if he
had been cheated of something.

The man lowered his spray bottle and looked at it carefully, as if he
was thinking. Then he looked at Robbie. 'If you choose to think so, sir.'

His voice startled Robbie. It was deep and pure, as if he had spent
his lifetime reading poetry and practising words.

'Plastic garden. Plastic perfume. Watering plastic plants. For God's
sake.'

'I wouldn't say it was necessarily for God's sake,' the man said. He
smiled and put the spray bottle on the trolley.

'You know what I mean. This used to be a real garden. I was here
just a few years ago. It was a real garden.'

The man picked up another spray bottle and studied the label. He
handed it to Robbie. 'Smell,' he said.

Robbie took the bottle. *Apple blossom*, the label read. He held it out
to his side, above his head, and sprayed the night gloom. Again, in the

time it took to draw in a breath, there was a tumble of images, each one bright and warm. Ripe red apples swaying in a chill wind on a green tree, apple slices and sugar and cloves in an old red enamel saucepan on a stovetop, an apple in a pale blue plastic lunchbox, the swoop and shriek of cockatoos in an apple orchard, an apple pie, hot and crisp, on a vast wooden table and, from the pie, or the table, a low keening, a call to home. Again, Robbie closed his eyes, and again, when he opened them, there was nothing. Everything gone. There was only where he was and the smell of old apple beginning to turn and the strange gardener standing against the wall of plastic flowers, watching him closely.

Robbie handed the bottle back. 'This all seems crazy.'

'If that's what you wish to think, sir,' the man said again.

'It's not a matter of what I wish to think. It's the reality. The garden is plastic. The watering is ridiculous. The scents are . . .' Robbie paused. There was, it seemed, something faintly magical, something hallucinatory perhaps, in the scents this man was paid to spray onto plastic flowers and fruits and leaves, but still, they weren't the real scents of real plants. 'Well, the scents are fake too. Even your clothes.' He gestured at the man's overalls, grubby with dirt and grass, his gardening boots with mud on the toes. 'What's not crazy? Nothing's real.'

The man contemplated Robbie calmly. 'A real garden is no longer possible,' he said at last. He spoke gently and slowly, as if Robbie were a child. 'That is because there was no longer enough water for a real garden, a real and beautiful garden. We can water this because every drop is recycled, because under the pond is a vast water storage, and the water just drains off and through the plastic and back into storage. We can water the plastic forever, sir, which is rather nice if you stop to think about it. A real garden would take all the water in a week and then die anyway. But the point, sir, is that people who come to eat their lunch and dinner on our verandah see trees and flowers and birds and smell water and hear it on leaves and this makes them very happy. And even people who can be bothered to come down into the garden and find out that everything is plastic, they can still see something that is perfect, despite what it is. You, sir, may find that foolish, but for most people these days it is more than enough. In fact, it is preferable. Plastic is forever. In a real garden there is the sadness of autumn leaves, or a tree that is dying, or weeds that strangle flowers, or a snake or a spider that might bite. A real garden can be a melancholy thing.'

'You're not a gardener, are you?' Robbie asked.

'Of course not.'

'Then what are you?'

The man smiled again. He had beautiful eyes, Robbie thought, a mix of dark and light.

'I am a poet.'

'I see.'

'I doubt that you do. With all due respect.'

Robbie shrugged.

'I drop words and thoughts into bottles, and when the emotions and memories they evoke are just right, as perfect as they can be, I give them to the plastic flowers and trees. I have been offered work all over the world but I like it here.'

Robbie tried to remember the images and memories that had washed through him but they were gone.

'I'm not sure I've heard of such a thing,' he said.

'Let me try something for you.' The man began taking vials and small jugs and tubes of powders and adding a pinch of this and a drop of that to a small tin. He looked at Robbie and smiled. 'You see, perhaps there is one thing, one single thing, that defines each of us. A second of something that, whether we know it or not, we are compelled to live by. The salt sting of the ocean. The powder-sweet cheek of a child. The first taste of a lover's armpit. The mown grass and the rose petals of home. Or for you, this.'

Robbie leaned in to smell the tin the man held out. Animal sweat and tears. Horse sweat and wet muscles heaving, chewed grass and hay and froth and foam on the breath. Blood, metal, and fear and anger, peppery and craven, and tears, salt.

'No,' Robbie said. 'No. No. No.'

'Oh yes.'

'No,' Robbie roared. 'You have no right. No right at all. Stop.' He thought he might be about to cry.

'I don't, of course. But you also have no right to not believe. Balance, my friend, balance. And see, it is stopped.'

Robbie shook his head and wiped his eyes. I think I might be going a little mad, he thought and he shook his head again. Everything had settled and he could smell only a subtropical garden on a warm and breezy evening.

'I am not the only one who does this,' the man continued. 'I have a friend who works on rooftop gardens on skyscrapers in China. His poems are about the stars and the moon that people can no longer see. He puts his words into plastic ivy leaves and palms and pots of cumquat trees, and people gather on the rooftops and for a brief moment it is as if the sky clears for each person and they can touch the stars. Some bring chairs and stools to stand on, he says, as if even one or two steps higher brings them closer to what they believe they are seeing.'

'Next time I'm in China I'll go and see.'

'You should. I would like to go myself, but I have a fear of heights.' The man unlatched a brake at the base of his trolley. 'Your dinner will be served shortly. And I have work to do.'

'I'm sorry I upset your friend.'

'This garden is very real to him, I'm afraid. It is hurtful to him if
that reality is denied. And I think he has breathed in too many of my
poems. That can also be dangerous.' The man locked eyes with Robbie
again and smiled. Then he set off down the path, pushing his trolley
in front of him. 'Enjoy your dinner, sir. And the view of the garden.'

'Dangerous how?' Robbie called after him.

The man turned back. 'A flower is sometimes not just a flower, is
it? You work it out. Goodnight, sir.'

Robbie headed back towards the lights of the verandah. By a large
acacia, just before the lawn began, there was a click and a humming
and from large vents at the base of the tree gusts of air blew up, so the
branches and leaves seemed to dance in the garden lights. A chorus
of frog song began. The guinea fowl seemed to have taken themselves
to wherever they went to be shut off for the night, and someone had
removed the bird Robbie had thrown to the ground.

Walking up the steps he thought he must have been a long time
and that Ella would be annoyed, but she smiled and it seemed that
almost no time at all had passed. Six minutes, according to the phone
on his wrist. But that was hardly possible. He kissed her on the cheek
before he sat down.

'So?' she asked.

'All plastic. Everything.'

'The frogs I am hearing?'

'Little plastic frogs with batteries inside.'

'How sad.'

Robbie sipped his wine and looked at the garden, its edges soft in
the garden lights. There was a faint scent of nightfall, of dewdrops,
of heavy curtains descending, of a shuttered window and closeness
and the promise of food.

Despite the steady heat, Ella shivered slightly. 'Is it getting cooler
or is it my imagination?'

'It's your imagination,' Robbie said. 'And a poet.'

'A what?'

'There's a poet in the garden. I was talking to him.'

'Was he plastic too?'

'No, he's a real poet. I think. He tries to make the garden mean something.'

Ella looked at him quizzically. 'Well, then,' she said, and leaned forward to take his hand, 'it does look beautiful, doesn't it? Even if it's all pretend, it doesn't mean it's not beautiful.'

Robbie had to agree. From the verandah, the garden looked beautiful. Perfectly and precisely beautiful.

Their food arrived and Robbie poured more wine. While they ate, Ella told him she didn't believe the new refugee station that sprawled across the borders of what had once been South Sudan and the Central African Republic could possibly work.

'Eight hundred thousand people already,' she said. 'Yes, mainly from the Northern African League States, but we're flying in people from everywhere, from Switzerland, from Germany, some of the overflow from the Cuba station. The whole point was that there was supposed to be water. In fact, all the early planning revolved around floods and too much water. I sat through endless, endless meetings talking about water. That was a first. But there is no water. It hasn't rained for three years. The new tanks are empty. The dam is just mud. There is nothing from the taps because there is nothing in the dam. And of course, this is now no one's problem. It is a nightmare. It is hideous.'

The second hamburger arrived. Ella took a large bite. 'You know, this is really very good,' she said. 'Well. Considering.'

An overhead fan came on and a different waiter lit a table candle that sat in a frosted glass jar. It scattered small shards of flickering light. Robbie ate his steak, and wondered what it was, and picked at a salad concoction of peas and pineapple and onion and thawed spinach leaves, and listened to Ella talk. He knew most of the background to the new global refugee stations and had covered some of the preliminary negotiations between the continents and countries. But he enjoyed the sound of Ella's voice and the way the candlelight caught her lips and cheekbones. He sipped the wine, which became more drinkable with every mouthful.

Somewhere beyond the hotel's walls a series of shots rang out, rifle shots and then the staccato of machine-gun fire. He raised an eyebrow but neither he nor Ella flinched. After a few minutes there were sirens, louder and closer. He noticed the businessman he had seen earlier in the lobby had come in and taken a table. A young girl, golden curly hair tied in a green ribbon, sat with him.

Ella had finished eating and was studying the wine in her glass. She was quiet for a few minutes. 'Anyway, the point is that next to the world's newest tent city we are starting to build graves. Big graves. Two hundred thousand dead or dying by Christmas. So much for all the agreements and the promises. It is not going to work. Not anywhere.' She looked across the table at Robbie. 'You should write about it.'

He shook his head. 'No.'

'It is going to prove the global population management program will fail.'

'It's already failing. Governments know it. It was always a case of too little too late.'

'But so many people are dying, Robbie. They can't get the water and medicines in fast enough, or they can't find any, but already a hundred thousand body bags are on their way. And people are just sitting in rows, row after row after row, waiting to die. It is almost as if it was a giant trap from the very beginning.'

'Perhaps it was.'

'Then write about it.'

'Oh, darling.'

'Darling what?'

He shook his head again. 'It's so hard. Really. It's not an excuse. I have so many fines piling up against me for things I've written – about the oil in Africa and the wars, and the refugee camp across northern Australia and the ERA program. I've always been grateful that I have money, but if I didn't I'd be in shit right now. I pay them off or I go to jail. I can't keep doing this. And I know it's part of the whole closing-down thing, but it's working. Anyway, no one cares any more, sweetheart. Except you.'

'Oh no. And her.' Ella nodded towards the entrance to the restaurant and Robbie turned to look.

'You're kidding,' Robbie said.

'She was on the plane. I had no idea she was staying here.'

'She doesn't look like she's changed.'

'Twenty kilos heavier. At least.'

'Hard to tell.'

'She's heading this way. Be nice, Robbie.'

'She's got the whole fucking restaurant to choose—'

But Ella was saying, 'Well, Ashley May,' loudly and brightly, her fabulous smile flashing. She got to her feet to give the woman lumbering towards the table a perfunctory hug. Robbie watched Ashley's face flush and smiled.

'Ella. Oh my, gorgeous as ever,' the woman said. Her accent was Louisiana old and deep, and it bounced off the tables and walls and set the candle flickering urgently.

'And of course you know Robbie?'

Robbie stayed in his seat but lifted his wine glass to Ashley in a token gesture.

'Oh, I most certainly do.'

'Been a while,' he said.

'Never long enough, Roberto.'

'Time to let bygones be bygones perhaps?'

Ashley ignored him and turned back to Ella. She put her hand on Ella's arm and Robbie was sure she was stroking Ella's wrist with her fat thumb. He refilled his glass and settled back to look at the garden.

'You look so well, Ashley May,' Ella was saying. 'You must be exhausted of course, and—'

'Exhausted like even you wouldn't believe, girl. I think I invented the word. Can you believe the mess up there? Can you believe it?'

'So you are here for a break?'

'One week,' Ashley said. Robbie's heart sank. 'Then I'm back there for a month. But that's it for me. Over and out. I've resigned.'

'You've resigned?' Ella sounded surprised.

Robbie was certainly surprised. Women like Ashley May never resigned. Doing something you fundamentally hated was a wonderful reason to wallow in righteous self-pity, and without that self-pity he couldn't see there would be much left of Ashley May.

'I've met someone. You surely must have heard. A nurse. From New York. Oh, we have so much in common. She's even a Scorpio, can you believe it? I'm head over heels, I truly am. So we're both homeward bound, and I'll be baking Christmas brownies in a Brooklyn walk-up. Oh, forgive me, am I allowed to say Christmas? Am I allowed to *think* Christmas?' She laughed loudly.

Robbie rolled his eyes at the acacia tree.

'I'd heard about this,' Ella said. 'And I'm so happy for you. Truly. Have you known each other long?'

'Four weeks,' Ashley May exclaimed. 'But you just know, don't you? We have so much in common. The nursing. Refugees. Death. It's as if everything aligned so that our paths would finally cross. She even loves knitting as much as I do, can you believe it? She's the one, I just know it.'

Robbie coughed.

'How long are you here for? Perhaps we could—'

'Oh, just a couple of days,' Ella said charmingly. 'And you know how it always is for me. Meetings, meetings, I'm afraid.' Ella was smiling at Robbie and moving back to her chair.

Ashley lingered for a moment, knowing she had somehow been dismissed. She smiled uncertainly. 'Well, it's a quick supper for me. I'm here to rest, after all. That's what I need after that hellhole.'

She muttered a goodbye and squeezed herself around the tables to take a seat near the wall. She pulled her bag onto the table and noisily fumbled for her phone, and then her glasses, and then her room key, and then she noisily called for a waiter. Robbie could feel her puffing and huffing.

Ella took several long, slow swallows of wine. After a moment she asked, 'What did you do to her again?'

'I interviewed her years ago for that article I did on women aid workers.'

'That's right.'

'She'll never forgive me.'

'No. Not that it matters.'

'The line about pigs at the trough of human misery was possibly over the top. But I just couldn't bear their self-righteousness.'

'A woman like Ashley would always take a line like that literally,' Ella said.

Ashley was ordering now, loudly and slowly. 'I'll have the caesar but hold the anchovies, egg and cheese and just a drop of mayo. Croutons on the side, not in the salad. And a double vodka, straight up. And a glass of ice. Oh, and a serve of fries. No, two serves. And some ketchup.'

The waiter looked at her. 'So, for the salad you just want lettuce.'

'With a little mayo. And croutons on the side.'

'Yes, madam. But we have no lettuce today.'

'No lettuce?'

'None. Not one leaf.'

'How the hell do you do a caesar without lettuce?'

'Exactly, madam.'

'Or without anchovies and egg and cheese,' Robbie said quietly. Ella smiled.

'I'd say your menu is misleading. Very misleading.'

'Well, madam—'

'You have caesar salad on your menu and that's what I want.'

'We have everything for a caesar salad except lettuce. Well, almost.'

'Almost?'

'The anchovies are sardines. There are no anchovies.'

'But I said hold the anchovies anyway. Like, hello! Are you even hearing me? Perhaps I should speak to the manager. I don't think it's too much to check into a hotel and order something from a menu and expect to eat it. Is that unreasonable?'

The big man sitting with the young girl put down his phone and banged the table with his fist. The girl was singing softly and drawing.

The man stood up. 'Actually, it is. It is extremely unreasonable.'

'Mister, I'm just trying to order my supper here. Is that okay with you?'

The man picked up the bag from his table and walked over to Ashley. 'No. You are being unreasonable and that is not okay with me. There is no lettuce for your salad.' He put his hand in the bag and took out something small and bright, brighter than the flickering of the candle. 'There isn't much food in this country, Ashley May dyke. You probably haven't noticed. But there are still plenty of these. Plenty. So. I am going to give you this diamond. And in return you are going to shut the fuck up. Deal?'

Robbie saw greed and confusion flash across Ashley's face, her small eyes squinting at the stone the man held out to her.

'But—'

'I said you are going to shut the fuck up. Now.' He dropped the diamond in Ashley's water glass. 'Eat that.' He turned to the waiter. 'Bring her fries and ketchup and vodka.'

He headed back to his table, nodding politely to Robbie and Ella. When he sat down, the girl held up the piece of paper she had been drawing on and Robbie watched the man study it intently, nodding. He said something soft and soothing and ran his fingers through the girl's fine hair.

Ashley looked across to Ella, and Ella shrugged politely. She turned back to Robbie, avoiding the woman's bewilderment, and poured the last of their wine.

'Time to go?' she asked.

Robbie lifted a finger. He watched Ashley look at the diamond in the glass. Finally she picked the glass up and, holding the diamond down with a spoon, poured the water into another glass. Then she let the diamond drop on the table. She wiped it dry with a napkin and put it in her pocket. She reached for her phone. Oh, I wouldn't if I were you, thought Robbie.

'Sugar?' Ashley called down the phone. 'It's me, honey. Me again. I'm just about to have supper and I'm thinking of—'

Robbie didn't hear or see the man move but he was back at Ashley's table. He took her phone and dropped it hard on the tiles.

'I didn't make myself clear. If I hear your voice again I will kill you. Do you understand?'

The waiter arrived with a bottle of vodka and a glass of ice. She was smiling broadly and set things down slowly and loudly. She poured a shot of vodka. Ashley reached up and took the bottle. The waiter smiled and shrugged.

'I asked if you understood?' the man said.

Ashley swallowed and nodded.

'Excellent. Now eat the diamond.'

'What?'

'I told you to eat the diamond.'

'But—'

'They didn't have what you wanted for dinner so I gave you a diamond instead. I thought that was an extraordinarily generous gesture on my part. And now you are too rude to eat it. You are obviously not hungry after all.'

'But it's a diamond. People don't eat diamonds.'

Robbie thought Ashley was near tears now. Sweaty and flushed and about to cry.

'Really?' the man asked. 'Really? People don't eat diamonds?' He leaned forward and put a finger to Ashley's lips. 'You are not a very bright woman, are you? Now, please, not one more word. Not one.' He returned to his table.

'Robbie, I want to go,' Ella said.

'Yes, of course.'

They both stood up. Ella swayed slightly. He went to take her arm but she shook her head. 'I'm fine. Just tired.'

Robbie stopped at the man's table. 'Interesting evening,' he said softly.

'Do you think so?' the man said.

'I had ice-cream,' the little girl said. 'Lots of ice-cream. Ice-cream with diamonds in it.'

Robbie smiled. 'And you've been busy drawing, haven't you?'

The girl nodded. 'Lots and lots. Look.' She spread out the pieces of paper in front of her. She wore a diamond bracelet on her wrist. 'I'm the best at drawing.'

Robbie bent over to look, and felt Ella steady herself behind him. He gasped. The drawings were perfect, almost like photographs in their crispness and clearness, although he had watched her using the thick stumps of crayons. How had she done this?

But there was more. Every drawing was of his dreams and memories. There was the boy on the beach building a sandcastle, a bottle on a wave, and, behind the boy, bones, dunes of bones. An apple pie on a wooden table, but with a woman sitting at the table, a large, very large, woman with blue eyes he didn't recognise, hands clasped. His grandmother's cat, for God's sake – what was its name? – watching him as, sitting on a chair made from bones, next to a small table with a vase of yellow roses, he read a book. And another drawing of him with another book – was it the same or different? – propped against a wall, a bag by his side, and a stranger's hand stretched out to touch the cover with skeleton fingers, and above him and the hand of bones a neat line of knitting needles hanging, ready to fall. There was a drawing of a horse, a horse falling . . .

Robbie's gut clenched. 'No,' he said roughly. 'No. No. No.'

The man and the girl smiled at him, fixed, cold, diamond-white smiles.

'What is it, darling?' Ella asked. She stood beside him, arm across his shoulders, and bent forward to look at the drawings. 'Whatever is the matter?'

'The drawings,' he said. 'I don't . . .'

'But they are lovely.' She smiled at the girl. 'Such pretty drawings. What a talent you have. Your papa must be so proud.'

The man laughed and the girl took his hand.

'He's not my papa,' she said, staring at Ella.

Robbie felt Ella straighten and look quizzically at the girl and then the man.

'Well then,' she said.

She took Robbie's arm and led him out of the restaurant, through the lobby and down the long corridor to their room. She stumbled once and laughed quietly, and she leaned against Robbie while he found the door key, so he felt the weight and warmth of her.

Inside the room, she sat heavily on the sofa in the small sitting area in front of the bed, leaning forward, her elbows on her knees. Robbie switched on the overhead fans and got a bottle of water and two glasses and sat next to her. He was sweating and thought for a moment he might be sick.

'We may have had too much to drink,' she said after a few minutes. 'Or I have.'

Robbie passed her a glass of water. She drank it slowly and then ran her fingers through her hair.

'What did you see in the drawings, Robbie?'

He tried to tell her.

'But there was nothing like that. A little girl's silly drawings. A cat. A beach. A birthday cake. They weren't even particularly good.'

He took her hand. 'Then I don't know. I saw what I saw. Or what I thought I saw. I don't know. The whole evening was strange.'

She smiled tiredly. 'Do you think we could just get into bed and sleep? I am so, so tired. I'm sorry.'

'I'm not feeling that great myself.' He kissed her cheek gently. 'Go to bed. I'm going to sit on the balcony for a while.'

'But then you will hold me?'

'Then I'll hold you.'

While she was in the bathroom, Robbie went through the minibar and found, behind a dozen cans of cola and three cartons of condensed milk, a small bottle of whisky and another of brandy. He arranged the mosquito netting around the bed and put the bottle of water and a glass on the small table on the right side of the bed, the side Ella always slept on, and took the brandy and another bottle of water onto the balcony, closing the screen door behind him. He took off his shirt and shoes. According to his phone he had forty-seven messages waiting for him. He dropped it on the small wicker coffee table.

He took a sip of brandy and closed his eyes. The night seemed thick and surprisingly quiet. Only the occasional siren and gunshot now, the occasional voice. Then he heard the scrape and rattle of a heavy trolley being pushed along the path beyond the balcony. It stopped and there was the tinkling of hundreds of little glass bottles.

'Hello again, sir.'

Robbie could see the white of the poet's teeth and the flash of his eyes.

'Hello again, poet man.'

'I have a goodnight gift for you.'

'I've had enough of everything for one night,' Robbie said. He wanted the man to leave. He wanted to be alone.

'Oh, don't say that. Never say that. Never, never. Here, something special, something just for you.'

He held out a tiny vial. Robbie leaned over the rail and took it.

'What is it?' he asked.

'It is the scent of memory. Or perhaps life. Or both,' the man said. 'Harmless.'

Robbie shrugged and sniffed. In the instant of sniffing, he smelled the scent of every woman he had ever known and wanted to know, their scent and taste, sweat and wetness, the smell of their breath and hair and the soap they used and their blood. He smelled and saw and heard voices and hands and lips and breasts, and he looked for Ella but she wasn't there, and the hands became talons and the lips covered vampire fangs and the breasts were smothering him.

'No,' he whispered. 'No. Not this.'

He threw the vial at the dark shadow of the man. The man laughed, a high-pitched ugly laugh that echoed in the night. He kept laughing as he walked away, pushing the trolley.

Robbie sat, shaking. He sat for a long time, until he remembered Ella.

thirteen

The following two days were, Robbie felt, relatively ordinary. Ella went to some meetings. Robbie interviewed a professor of economics and a professor of something called people movement management at the local university and filed a dull story on housing development and employment on Africa's east coast. He felt unsettled, as if something ominous, something dark and unknown, was hiding just out of his line of sight, but once Ella had coaxed a smile from him, and then another and another, he began to relax.

In the late afternoons and evenings they stayed in their room, ordering more beers and ever-more interesting concoctions from the hotel's kitchen.

'So, where are you taking me for our honeymoon?' Ella said, as they sat on the sofa eating dinner on the second evening.

'Hadn't thought about it,' Robbie said, although he had the entire month planned.

'If I am getting married, I want a honeymoon,' Ella said. 'Otherwise, what is the point? Oh dear. I think there is a marshmallow in the

fried rice. Look. Two marshmallows. One each. How sweet of them.
No, three. We will have to share.'

'Actually, I had a thought. No, I think I'll save my marshmallow
for dessert. But thank you. This chicken really isn't bad, you know.
Once you get used to it. Anyway, I was wondering about Greece. For
a couple of weeks.'

Ella laughed. 'Of course. Greece. And how do you plan to get us
in there? There is a two-year waiting list for tourist visas.'

'Well, sweetheart, I have a friend who has a friend who has a friend.
How else does anything ever happen any more?'

'Seriously? You have never mentioned this.'

'I'm mentioning it now. Here, you have the rest of the spinach. It's
good for you. I've taken the banana out.'

'We can go to Greece? Really?'

'We are going to Greece. It's all sorted. We're staying in a villa on
a nearly empty island that has a pathway down a hill to the beach.
There's a swimming pool and a vegetable garden, and a neighbour
will bring us bread and meat and cheese and wine every second day.
It's booked for two weeks in the spring. Here, I have some pictures
for you.'

He handed her his phone. Ella scrolled through the photographs
like a child, her eyes wider and wider, her cheeks flushing.

'Oh, Robbie! Robbie!' And she jumped off the sofa and clapped her
hands and danced around the room, out onto the balcony and back
to where he sat. 'Oh, Roberto thank you, thank you, thank you. How
beautiful. How special. How crazy.' She pushed his dinner plate aside
and sat on his lap, laughing, and clapped her hands again.

He loved this part of her; her ability to melt into a childlike joy and
wonder when something lovely and unexpected happened. It was the
reason he would spend hours and hours, days sometimes, searching for
a gift for her, something rare or beautiful or funny that would make

her laugh and cry and clap her hands and look at him in a way that made him feel how a man must have felt once upon a time when he slayed dragons and demons and returned triumphant to the woman he loved with bags of gold and pearls and silk and perfumes.

'Thank you,' she said again. 'Two weeks on a Greek island with you. Perfection.'

'There's no internet. I don't know if that will be a problem for you. The owner of the villa – well, the island actually – has spent a lot of money to make sure there's no contact with the world outside the island.'

'He must be a nice man,' Ella said. 'No, seriously, I am owed, I believe, around three months' leave. I will be allowed to be out of contact for a few weeks.'

'And then we're going to Australia.'

'Yes, of course we are.'

'Granna is looking forward to it.'

'And so am I, Robbie. Truly. What a wonderful time we are going to have. So. We get married, very quietly, at Christmas and then in the spring we are going away for a whole month, to Greece and Australia. We have a plan, as you like to say.'

'We do.'

'But . . .'

'But what?'

'But right now, at this moment in time, I don't want to eat the spinach. It still tastes of banana.'

'Okay.'

'And I don't want a fried rice marshmallow for dessert.'

'Okay.'

'Um.' She wriggled her toes and smiled. 'Would there be any chocolate? Any special chocolate maybe?'

And Robbie laughed and picked her up and put her on the bed, and then went to his bag and got out the bars of chocolate he had bought for her at the airport in Berlin and tossed them to her.

'My favourites,' she said. 'Of course they would be.' And then, after she had eaten one, 'You are just about the most perfect man, Roberto Adams.'

•

It was only at the airport two days later that Robbie watched the tiredness inch back across Ella's face, like a shadow falling. She was flying to Geneva to report on progress, or lack of it, on the refugee stations across the United Central African Federation. He was going with her and then back to London, where, he thought, he should try to make a little bit of serious money before the wedding. He'd already made a withdrawal against the trust fund, which wasn't something he really liked to do.

Now, watching Ella, he leaned over and took her hand. 'What is it, sweetheart? What's the matter?'

'Apart from saying goodbye again?' She smiled, but it was hollow and sad. She waved to a small group that had come into the business-class lounge. 'Doctors,' she said. Then after a few minutes she looked across at him, biting her lip. 'The station where I was last week . . . I mean, they are all awful. All of them. Everywhere. But . . .' She stopped and looked down at his hand holding hers, and then looked up again. 'There is a shooting range. It's huge. Well, there are two. An indoor range and an outdoor one. Both are massive. Each one, I think, maybe could fit a hundred people along the shooting line, easily. There are different target shooting ranges. You know, small-bore rifles, shotguns. There is even a section for semi-automatics. I wasn't allowed to see that. They have poured so much money into these. It is like they are for proper military or police training, except bigger. They are on the far

western side of the stations and there are separate roads and a separate
landing strip for airplanes. They have planted trees and gardens, and
there are cabins, like old-fashioned hunting cabins, and a hotel and
even a restaurant.' Ella threw back her head and laughed. 'There is a
restaurant, Robbie! For God's sake. A restaurant! It is a six-star resort
on the edge of hell.' She lowered her voice again. 'There are cages and
holding pens for the things that are going to be taken there to be killed.
What do you think those things are, Robbie? What?'

He looked at her and there was fury and fear and an unutterable
sadness in her eyes. 'No,' he said slowly.

'Yes.' Ella leaned further forward. He could feel her nails digging
into the skin on his hand. She was almost whispering now. 'It is a
refugee killing ground. Oh, they will not call it that, of course. It will
have a name like the Last Safari Resort or something. And people will
come because there have always been people who find a place like this,
or who are invited to a place like this, people who want to kill people
and who especially want to kill refugees. Don't ask me how the refugees
will be selected, the ones to be shot. Maybe the weakest, the ones that
will die anyway. But that won't be enough. There will be games as
well. Hunting games. For this people will pay huge money. They will
shoot, they will kill, they will laugh, and they will order a steak and
a thousand-dollar bottle of red wine for dinner. I asked, what will be
hunted here, or is it perhaps for the military, for training? The guard
who was showing me and others with me – there was nothing secret
about this, Robbie, nothing, it was all open and they are proud of it
– the guard laughed and said, oh, the animals, and gestured towards
the fence that we could just see, the fence around the end of the camp.
So. So.' She added something in German that he didn't catch.

'It's preposterous,' Robbie said. 'It's illegal, surely.'

'But no. No, it's not. There are no internationally binding treaties
or agreements or rules left. Not really. Think about it. Only regional,

and nothing at all I can find that has relevance for the United Central African Federation. I mean, the Federation is not even countries. It is just a . . . well, a space. It is legal, otherwise they would not do it, or they would hide it better.'

Robbie took his hand away from Ella's and stood up to fetch her a bottle of water from the bar. He gasped. On the other side of the bar, at a small coffee table, sat two men: a man in red cargo pants with long greasy blond hair, and a dark-haired man in an impeccable business suit with polished boots and wearing reflective sunglasses. They were drinking champagne and the blond man raised a glass to Robbie. He smiled the smile of an angel. The girl was nowhere to be seen.

Robbie began to shake. It's just a coincidence, he thought. Of course it is. Some of us are always travelling, always on the road. But I won't tell Ella. It's all too much.

As he returned to Ella, their flight was called.

'I should not have told you about the shooting range,' she said. 'Really, I shouldn't have.'

He knew she was reminding him that she was forbidden from discussing her work and what she saw and knew with any journalist, and especially if the journalist was her lover. It was a sign of how tired she was that she felt she had to remind him.

They were both silent throughout the flight. He made her eat some of the stale sandwich that was served and drink a cup of herbal tea, and occasionally he took her hand and kissed it. He was grateful the flight was surprisingly smooth.

When they reached Geneva, she walked with him to the departure gate for his flight to London. There was an hour's wait and she stood next to him, leaning her weight against his body, her head on his shoulder, letting him hold her upright. Robbie could see through the windows that a light snow was beginning to fall outside.

Once she took a step back to look up at him. 'Don't think about it,' she said. 'Please don't. It has all become far too much to bear, this world we are in.'

When it was time to board, he cupped her chin in his hand and spoke to her very slowly and clearly. 'And don't you think of it either, because, yes, it is too much, far too much. And I want to ask one more thing and it is a big thing: please, please, Ella, think about walking away. How long can you do this for? There are other things you can do that are good for this world, good for people. This is becoming too cruel, too big and impossible. We have money. I have more money than I know what to do with. We can find another way to live. Just think about it. That is all I'm asking.'

She smiled and shrugged, and then kissed him quickly on the lips and strode away.

•

When Robbie finally got home, he dumped his bag and then walked through icy rain down the road to a nearby pub he liked. It was warm and cheerful inside. He sat at the far end of the bar, and ordered the pâté and bread and pickles. The pâté was simply compressed meat scraps from a tin. He drank a pint and four scotch on the rocks and thought, hoped, he had two sleeping pills left in a drawer in his bathroom. He wanted the voices in his head to stop. He wanted the heavy, shapeless fear to shift. He wanted not to dream tonight, to ignore the strangeness he felt was edging closer.

Everything here soaked through and cold, he wrote in a message to Ella. *Miss you already. I am so sorry for what the world has become.*

She immediately came back with: *Don't say sorry. Hard to believe, but it is actually not your fault. Love and more.*

He smiled.

fourteen

It was one in the morning and Clare was sitting on a bench in the old town gardens. The bench was simple, made from wood that had been painted a deep green and had faded in parts. There was a small bronze plaque nailed to the middle slat: *Beloved Edith, 1986–2026. Now the night song is always yours. Margaret.* Clare hadn't noticed the plaque when she first found the bench. But after sitting for a while she had felt an odd warmth creep through her lower back, as if she was sitting next to the fading embers of a fire. She had stood up then and looked around her, and looked again at the bench and had seen the small metal square. Taking out her phone and switching on the torch, she had read the words, touching each one. The metal was unusually warm under her fingertips.

Now she came here whenever her feet brought her. She always touched the plaque before she sat down and it seemed to her the words breathed gently, swelling and shimmering and then subsiding with a silent sigh.

She saw the location of the bench had been chosen with as much care as the words. It looked across the dry river bed, facing north-west to catch the sunsets, and although the birch and oak trees that had once lined the river were long gone, what was left of the gums rustled and groaned together. Night song.

Tonight she felt the familiar light warmth beneath her. She would sit here, she thought, until the dawn began to break. Perhaps she would sleep a little, soothed by the lullaby of the whispering wind, Edith and Margaret watchful from the shadows. And tomorrow she would drive Phil up the highway as far as she dared, and then he would get out of the car and become one of the walking men.

She felt a sadness she hadn't expected. When she left the house tonight she had touched his shoulder and was surprised by the feel of bone and skin. He sat, meek and thin and grey, by the old fraying backpack she had found in the shed and had packed for him. A warm jacket. Socks and underpants. Two T-shirts and a pair of jeans. A bottle of scotch that had cost her a small fortune. Soap and toothpaste. A few tins of food and some biscuits. A knife. And a small empty perfume bottle, the heavy glass polished so clean it scattered white and golden sunbeams through the dust motes.

She had put the bottle in the bottom of the bag, under the clothes, and she wondered when he might find it, where he would be, and what he might think and remember. Perhaps he would remember nothing. Or perhaps he would unscrew the small silver stopper and smell the faintest, the almost-not-there scent, of who she had once been, and who they together had been and the simple things they had hoped for, a day they had been happy, the scent of a memory of a faded dream. Who knew, after all, what walking might do to a person.

She had showed him the bag and the blanket she had put on top, wrapped around the bottle of scotch. She didn't want him to start to panic. 'It's not much,' she'd said. 'But it'll help. And then you'll find stuff if you have to. I know you will.'

Phil had listened carefully when Clare first put the idea of walking to him.

'It's the best thing,' she'd said. 'And it's the only thing I can think of. There are so many walking. Like, there are so many people without a place to go, or a place they want to go, and so they're walking and it seems okay. I don't think it's so dangerous. I really don't. I don't think anyone cares enough to do anything about it. And there are places. Hidden places, where people are trying to help each other. I've seen one. You can be alright. Walk to Lilac Town, where I went for work. I told you about it. Look for something there. The cat. Just look. Something will come and find you, okay. Okay?'

Phil had taken a sip of sherry. He was trying to cut back, she knew. Trying to get himself ready for whatever was going to happen next. His eyes were beyond tired.

He'd tried to smile. 'How many years since I walked anywhere?'

'Could do you the world of good.'

He'd used the tip of a finger to pick up a breadcrumb from the kitchen table. He'd looked at it and then flicked it onto the floor. Clare got up slowly and got the washcloth from the kitchen sink. She wiped the table, put the cloth back in the sink and stood looking at him.

'But . . .' he began. 'I just . . .' He'd looked at her anxiously. 'Aw, shit.'

'It's all sorts of people that are walking. All sorts. Young. Old. I've seen a few that even looked pretty crook. They can't all be dying out there. I reckon they're finding places, places to stay, places where there's still food growing and where everything hasn't been cleaned out and taken.'

Phil scratched his knee. He pulled the flagon of sherry closer to his glass and looked at it. 'What if they're killing people out there? We wouldn't know. Like with the drones? Or the tanks?'

'You know what?' Clare's tone hardened. 'You stay here, you'll probably die anyway. From the booze, from sleeping rough, from someone who thinks you're a dickhead. I don't have it in me any more to keep looking after you. And I don't want to. All I know is, you start walking, something'll happen. Something good, I think.'

'Yeah,' he said. 'Okay.' He'd lifted the flagon and refilled his glass. 'Shit.'

On another evening Clare had quizzed him about the direction he should head in. Any maps of the exclusion zones seemed to have been wiped off her phone and she wondered when that had been done. She'd made hamburger patties and gravy and mashed potatoes and fried onions for dinner, a meal he used to love, and he had managed to clear his plate and even drink a glass of water before reaching for the sherry.

'North, obviously,' he said.

'For how far?'

He'd closed his eyes to concentrate. 'Dunno. I reckon Lilac Town was a couple of hours' drive from here, wasn't it? So maybe, what, a hundred and forty kays? Roads were really bad even then, when we was still driving around.'

Clare had torn a page out of her notebook. 'North for sixty or so kays, then you've got to start heading west. Don't stay on the highway. Kind of follow it, but keep maybe a couple of hundred metres off to the side. You'll spot more houses, anyway. Remember if you went north from here you reached that huge roundabout? There were the signs to the river and to all those towns up there and then to the east? From there start tracking west. There'll be the mountains on your left. Remember? Keep them there but go north-west. When the mountains are behind you, it's maybe another thirty or forty kilometres direct west to Lilac Town.'

Clare slowly wrote down the distances and then drew a road and some mountains and an arrow and then the word *cat* with a box around it. She pushed the paper to him, but as he was about to reach for it she took

it back and added the words *stuffed toys* at the bottom of the page and
drew another box around the words, and then added a question mark.
Again she pushed the piece of paper to him and watched him look at it.

'Toys?' he said.

'I don't know. Just . . . if you see any in places – like in an empty
house or in a garden or on a road or something – it's a good thing.
I think. Anyway.'

She got up and went over to the sink to finish the dishes while he
sipped from a full glass of sherry and carefully folded the paper into
a small square that he put in his trouser pocket.

Phil cleared his throat. 'You always was a good cook, Clare,' he said.

She briefly stopped scrubbing the plate and looked down at her
hands in the cold grimy water, the reddish skin. Then she heard him
switch on the TV and the slow pump-pump heartbeat soundtrack to
Race For Home came on. Clare turned around to watch. The cameras
were focused on a raft hemmed in by rubbish that stretched out in all
directions on a motionless sea. Two women were on their knees at the
front of the raft pushing aside plastic bottles and bags and cartons, but
nothing they did shifted the raft forward. The sail hung drab like a
dead thing. There was a close-up of the women's faces. Sweat and tears.
The voiceover: *The Yellow Team loses a day's provisions unless they travel
five miles by sunset. This will—* Then a piercing scream and one of the
women pulled her arm from the water. Her hand and lower arm had
been torn off, taken by something under the stinking sea, and there
was blood and a flash of bone and purple muscle. A family sheltering
from the sun under the small thatched deck also began to scream.

Phil leaned forward. Clare stepped in front of the TV, blocking
his view of the screen, and turned it off.

'I'm going for a walk soon,' she said. 'You can turn it back on
then.' She went back to the sink and shook out and folded damp tea
towels. 'Disgusting show.'

Phil bit his lip.

'You do know it's total shit, right?'

'Nothing much else, any more,' he said.

'Even a news channel is better.'

'Jesus.'

Clare thought of all this as she sat on her bench. Edith's bench. So, tomorrow afternoon Phil would walk. And then she would go and knock on her neighbour's door and ask if she could sleep in one of his sheds for a while. And use his bathroom in return for cooking and cleaning. She'd thought it through and knew he would say okay, for a few weeks at least. He liked her cooking. Once she had thought he'd liked her tits, but she wouldn't put money on that now. Rough as guts Cutter. Except he wasn't.

She wondered what she should say to Phil tomorrow. For so long they had said nothing much at all to each other. But shouldn't there be something? Perhaps not. Small lives, she thought. Poor lives. We did the best we could, she might say. It's just that for some people that's never enough. I don't hate you Phil. Not any more. I don't want you thinking that.

She felt herself drifting off to sleep and thought that she should be thankful to be sleeping. But then there was the sound of an engine behind her and she was sitting in light. The engine was cut but the light remained. She heard a door open and close, then brisk footsteps. The steps stopped in front of her.

Clare opened her eyes and raised her head. Granna Adams was standing there. The cashmere and pearls were gone. She was wearing a sturdy shapeless tracksuit and running shoes. She looked, Clare thought, like a little dark warrior from one of the computer games Phil used to play.

'Perhaps you could help me with something,' Granna said. 'If you wouldn't mind.'

She turned and walked back to the vehicle. After a moment Clare followed. Granna was untying ropes from a tarpaulin that covered the back of an old white ute. She rummaged through a pile of containers and pots and bags, and dragged a large heavy plastic bag and a sack filled with something soft and light over the side of the tray.

'Fruits and vegetables,' said Granna. 'And bread.'

Clare stared.

'For the animals. Just toss them along the path by the river bed. There are some bags of bones as well, but you'll need to make a second trip for them.' Granna was taking another bag from the ute. It looked a lot heavier. 'Seeds,' she said. 'I'll do these. I just throw them around the gardens. But I'm running very late tonight. They'll be wondering if something has happened to me.' Her voice was tired.

Clare took the bags. The one with fruits and vegetables was heavy and she almost had to drag it to the track that followed the river bed. Where the lights from the car stopped in a soft grey line she dumped several handfuls of bread. She took a few more steps and shook out half the bag of vegetables. She smelled carrots and cabbage and apples. Moving a few more steps she repeated the process, and then again. There must have been two-dozen loaves of bread. More.

As she turned back to the ute, Clare heard rustlings and steps and sighs behind her and glimpsed heavy shapes and shadows shuffling in the river bed. A brief light gust of wind carried the smell of damp animal fur and sweat. She shook her head.

Granna was waiting at the vehicle. 'Now the bones. Just throw them around the car. They'll sort it out. They always do.'

The women worked in silence. Clare could smell the blood and meat from the bones, metallic and sharp. Real bones, not falling-from-the-sky bleached bones.

When they had finished, Granna took the bags from Clare and threw them in the back of the ute, using an assortment of containers and tools to weight them down. Clare saw what looked like large soup tureens and plastic boxes.

'We need to get out of here,' Granna said. 'They're patrolling tonight. I can give you a lift somewhere.'

Clare shook her head. 'I'd rather stay here. And I like walking. Anyway, they're used to seeing me. It doesn't matter.'

There were grunts and growls and whispers from the trees and river bed, and a sharp and impatient shriek from a horse. Granna peeled off the dark rubber gloves she had been wearing, opened the passenger door, threw in the gloves, then stepped back.

'Why do you bother doing this?' Clare asked. She had to raise her voice now over the raw animal noises. She remembered the kangaroos and the disembowelled dog and shivered.

'It's not much, I know,' Granna said. 'Well, it's hardly anything. But I can't not do it. It's the same old question, isn't it? Do you bother helping one or two people because you can? Or do nothing at all because you can't help everyone? Most people just choose to think they can't make a difference. I don't see that it's any different with animals. I never have, really. Now, are you sure you don't want a ride somewhere?'

Clare looked at the passenger seat. What she thought was a small black cushion rose up and stretched and stared at her, unblinking.

'But that's Joon,' she said. Then to Granna, who was opening the driver's door, 'I know this cat. This is Joon. Isn't it?'

The cat's tail flicked, left to right.

'Not quite. This is Fravershi,' Granna said over the cabin of the ute. 'Brother of Joon. And if you have met Joon, you know more than you can begin to understand.' Clare looked more closely at the cat. Joon had one white paw, she remembered, and white gold eyes. This cat was all black and the eyes were a bright and startling green.

Granna paused. 'I see you out walking most nights. I assume you have a home?'

'Sort of. Yeah. For two more weeks.'

'Then what?'

'There are places I can sleep. Where I can stay. A neighbour. There's my car.' She thought of Phil sitting alone, waiting for the morning of the day he would walk. 'It doesn't matter. Something will work itself out. It usually has.'

Fravershi tilted his head as if listening intently, then blinked.

Granna tapped the roof of the cabin. The noises from the animals were fading. 'There will be a reason why our paths crossed tonight,' she said. 'You know, I could do with some help these days. If you'd be interested.'

She paused again, thinking. Clare waited. The wind was picking up.

'There are some things I need to get sorted. Some catching up to do. So, a week today. You know where I live. Everyone does. Come at five o'clock and we will talk. If you want.'

She went to climb into the cabin and stopped. 'Oh, and let me give you something. Please.' She rummaged through the containers and boxes and bags strewn across the tray. 'Ah!' she said triumphantly. 'I knew there was a piece left.' She handed Clare a small foil-wrapped packet. 'Enjoy. See you next week. I hope.'

Fravershi yawned as Clare closed the passenger door.

Granna leaned over the passenger seat and wound down the window. 'I'm so glad you've found Edith. And Margaret too, of course. It's actually Edith's recipe. The cake.' And with that, she reversed expertly back from the bench, turned, gunned the engine and left the gardens.

Clare went back to the bench. She unwrapped the foil and wasn't surprised in the least to find a small square of dense fruit cake that she knew would be delicious. She ate it slowly and fell asleep again. A deep sleep now.

In her dream there was a woman waving to her from the other end of the gardens. Quite a beautiful woman. Lean and tall and tanned. Each time Clare moved towards her, the woman laughed and stepped behind a tree or a shrub, disappearing briefly and re-emerging in a different place. So many more trees, it seemed, and flowerbeds too, with pink and purple flowers that danced in a golden sunshine. Her laughter was like music, and Clare knew in her dream that she would never reach this woman, that the waving and laughing and hiding would go on forever and forever and Clare would never be able to get any closer.

So, in the end, she had to wake up. And then it was time to walk home.

fifteen

O h, Clare, that's Edith of course. The beautiful Edith. And she's not waving at you. She's waving at Margaret. This is where they so often used to meet, especially in the beginning. Perhaps Margaret is carrying a picnic basket, with tomato sandwiches inside, tomato on rye bread with salt and pepper. And a half-bottle of champagne. Perhaps. Or she is carrying her computer, and she and Edith will sit together on a bench and look at the plans of the house Margaret is beginning to build and where they expect to live one day. They are discussing where the fireplace will go, and the stained-glass window that Edith wants. And some days she carries nothing and they simply wander through the gardens together, counting the ducks or worrying about the summer dry and some of the trees that are starting to die.

Edith left her husband to be with Margaret. You might think, then, that he would be the one to kill her. Some people, not many but certainly some, would say they could understand that. 'Not saying it's right, mind you,' is what they would say. 'But, you know, tough for any bloke.' But it wasn't him, not at all. He left and got himself a job at a hardware store in the next town and found a new woman and lived, I believe, happily ever after, whatever that may mean. No, no. It was an eighteen-year-old boy with greasy hair and pimples who loved God and loathed all gays and lesbians for their unnatural and sinning ways and who drew up a list called Death to All Queers of everyone he came across or heard about in town who was or could be gay. It was quite a long list, Clare.

It was his sister who told him about Edith because they knew each other through the netball club, and he began following her. Some people say the problem was he fell a little in love with her despite himself and that tipped him over the edge. He killed her over there, just there, where she is laughing and waving. Margaret was coming towards her and she was laughing and he plunged a kitchen knife into her back. Again and again. I know you cannot see the blood, but I can. Splatters and streaks and pools of it, and Edith collapsing and Margaret screaming.

Oh, the sad and evil nonsense they found on his computer, Clare. The hate. Not even his own pastor attended the trial, although people from some of those strange churches in the city came and held prayer vigils at the courthouse. For both lost souls, they were quick to say.

Just another sad little country-town story, Clare. A few years before your time here. We don't like to talk about these things too much. Except everyone certainly had their own opinion. For what it's worth, they'd say.

Margaret? Oh, she left. She went to America. Then Canada. She met someone and never came back. Why would you? All that was left at home for her was a ghost.

And him? He's still behind bars. Up north somewhere. His sister tells her friends he's HIV-positive. His Lord does indeed move in mysterious ways. I have often thought this.

So, Clare. Let us walk home together. About five thousand steps from here, I think. Phil is waiting. He is waiting for you, and he is sad.

And I am sad. The world is drowning under the weight of tears and blood and bones from all of time.

sixteen

Clare drove past the billboards and kept going for half an hour, carefully navigating the potholes in the road. She pulled in by a sign that read *No Travel Permit = Illegal. You will be caught!* The fields on either side were dry and brown. A red tractor in the far distance raised grey dust. Three kangaroos in the middle of the road watched the car, but bounded away when Clare opened the door.

She walked slowly around the front of the car and opened the passenger door. 'Come on, Phil.'

He put his head in his hands.

'Phil.'

'I thought I could do this. I really did. But I can't.'

She said nothing.

'Let me stay with you,' he said. 'Please.'

'Get out of the car.'

More silence, except for the wind whistling across the empty fields. Clare saw a car was coming up the highway, slowly. It drove past them, the occupants all turning to stare. The car pulled in a few hundred metres further up the highway and drove back. Clare initially froze, but then saw the two back-seat passengers were wearing burqas. Not the police, then.

The driver, a young blonde woman, rolled down the window. 'Walking?'

Clare nodded. 'Not me. Him.'

'Right then,' the woman said. 'As good a place as any.'

She left the engine running, got out and helped the women out from the back seat. Clare assumed they were women. A lot of people were wearing disguises these days. But then, if you were someone who wore a burqa, walking could be a good thing to do, Clare thought. The women looked young and very scared.

'Come on, Phil,' Clare said again. 'Looks like you might have some company.'

Phil finally got out of the car. He had showered and shaved that morning, and ironed his shirt. Clare could see he was shaky but he looked reasonable in his beaten-down Phil way. He nodded at the women, then looked at Clare.

She spoke slowly. 'Now listen, Phil. I'm going to get in the car and drive away. I don't have a permit for today and I can't be out here too much longer. Patrols are every four hours or so. I've got to move on. I can't afford the fine. You know that. So I'm saying goodbye.'

He didn't move.

She pulled his pack from the back seat and put it on the ground in front of him. 'I'm going, Phil.'

She saw that he was crying. Just tears running down his cheeks. No sobbing. Just tears and an astonished look in his grey eyes as it seemed to dawn on him that a price had come for all the empty bottles and empty years, a price he had never bothered to think about.

Clare reached out her right hand and touched him on his left cheek. Lightly and quickly. 'Phil . . . I'm sorry.' She cleared her throat.

'There's a note. From me. In the backpack. Okay? Read it tonight. I'm going now. I'm going.'

She looked at the two women in their burqas, which were already gathering a coating of dust. They looked as lost as Phil did, and so, so small against the endless blue sky and the endless brown and gold of the fields.

'He's harmless,' Clare said. 'Maybe look out for each other. He knows where he's going.'

Clare and Phil didn't look at each other again. She got in her car quickly and drove away.

When she passed the billboards at the entry to town, she pulled over and cried.

•

Ratbag cottage was lighter and cleaner without Phil in it. Clare stood in the kitchen and wished yet again that she could stay. Stay here alone and be safe and quiet and tend the garden and cook and sit in peace at the kitchen table and write in her notebooks. Was that really too much to ask? Really? She sighed. She heard a contemptuous sniff. 'If wishes were horses . . .' said her mother's voice.

For Phil's last lunch she had cooked a lamb casserole with potatoes and carrots and peas and some of the last herbs from her garden bed, and she was pleased that he had made himself eat it. She took a plastic container out of the fridge which held two large servings of the stew and set off on foot down Treedown Lane. She cut across a narrow gully, ignoring several dogs that were sniffing around a fallen tree and a flock of screaming cockatoos attacking some old fence posts. She saw someone had recently dumped a pile of furniture further down the gully. There was a sofa, an old-fashioned bathtub, a mirror and what looked like a huge rolled-up carpet. She stopped herself from going to have a closer look. Can hardly bring anything home now, she thought.

She scrambled up the other side of the gully and walked the boundary of Cutter's property. He'd built a corrugated-iron fence around his property, so high it almost completely hid the house and sheds on the land.

'Fireproofed it, mate,' he'd told the council inspectors who came out to have a look after a nameless and faceless complaint was made. 'Illegal? It's illegal not to fireproof the place,' he'd said with a broad and stunning smile.

And because years ago he had single-handedly saved two children and a dog from a burning house in a bushfire on the northern edge of town that had sprung up from nowhere, they'd left him alone.

It wasn't that Clare and Cutter had become friends as such, but they had sat together sometimes at the fire planning and management meetings, and Clare understood they each liked the silence and the inwardness of the other. She had come home one day to find Cutter sitting on her front steps, opening and closing a small army knife.

'Not much, is it?' he had said, nodding to the scrabbly garden and indicating the shabby walls behind him.

'Better than nothing.'

He looked at her for a minute or two and then smiled. 'Of course it is.'

After that, Clare spent two days at the start of every spring cleaning his house in return for cash, and when he came back from the hills with trailerloads of rocks and stones for his landscaping work he'd sometimes ask her to help him sort the pieces by size or colour. Clare loved that. She loved watching him with the rocks. He would look at each one as if it was a work of art, she thought, turning it over and around with a crowbar, patting it like it was a living thing. Sometimes when she was there he'd start cutting into a piece to begin to shape it for whatever it would eventually become. A table perhaps, or a chair, or a wide low water bowl for birds. He'd chip into it slowly and patiently, touching the rock after he made each cut, as if he was soothing it.

The first time she went inside his house, she gasped to see the long wall at the back of his living and kitchen area covered in an extraordinary photograph of what seemed to be two tall and slender rocks. Cutter watched her looking at it.

'That's beautiful,' she said and she meant it. The rocks had colours and shades of light and dark and indents and patterns like veins. They were each a whole landscape within themselves. Clare would have been happy to just sit for hours and stare at the photograph, writing down all the things she saw in it, the things it made her think.

'What do you see?' Cutter had asked.

'Well, two rocks. Beautiful rocks.'

He shook his head. 'That's what you're meant to think you see. Keep looking.'

And Clare had. But eventually she shrugged. 'It's two rocks. That's all I can see.'

Cutter smiled his beautiful smile. 'One is a rock. One is a man's shoulder and back.'

'Which one?'

'Not saying.'

'Not having me on?'

'I don't have people on.'

Clare kept staring. 'Well, they're both beautiful.'

'That's the point,' Cutter said.

Clare loved Cutter's house. The size of it, the emptiness and simplicity. She saw there that money could mean less as much as it could mean more, and she imagined herself living in it: where she would sit, where she would drink her morning coffee in the summer and the winter. He seemed to not have much of anything, but everything he had was beautiful, from the bathroom taps to the dozen heavy wine glasses that sat on a wooden shelf in the kitchen. She realised she liked him because of his lack of things and clutter, because she admired rather than envied how he lived. When she cleaned she looked for things that would tell her more about him, but she found nothing. He was just a very handsome man who found rocks and made things with them.

This afternoon, he was sitting on the wide decking that ran along the front of the house, staring up at the flowering gum tree that stood between the house and the shedding. In the shimmer of the early evening sunlight, the tree, with its pink-white smooth thick trunk, its curves and hollows, and its thinner graceful branches that offered some shade to the big yard, was beautiful, like a naked woman standing tall and strong against the sky, arms raised to draw in close all she loved. Another piece of art, Clare thought. Living art.

The gum's spring flowers were finished, but Cutter had hung a bird feeder on a lower branch and two red and blue rosellas were on the rim, eating seeds and spitting husks onto the ground. He didn't see Clare until she put the container of stew down next to him.

'Lamb,' she said. 'It's good.'

'Hey. Thanks.' He lifted the plastic lid and sniffed. 'Yep. Bloody good. Want a beer? Water?'

'No. No, thanks.' Clare sat down. 'Um. We're leaving the cottage,' she said. 'We have to. They've got to do all the weather stuff to it. Thing is, I've got nowhere to go right now.'

Cutter was watching the birds again. One flew down to the bird bath at the base of the tree, landing with a happy, melodic trilling. 'When?'

'Couple of weeks.'

'The two of you, looking for a place?'

'Phil's walking. Dropped him off up the highway this morning.'

To her surprise, Cutter burst out laughing. 'Never would have thought he'd have it in him. Good for him. Do him the world of good.'

'That's kind of what I said. But anyway . . .'

'I've got a tent,' he said. 'It's a good one. You can borrow it as long as you like.'

'There's not a spare space at a camping ground anywhere. I've checked. Anyway, I've only got enough money for a space for a month or so. The cheapest would be seven hundred a week just to pitch a tent.'

'You're kidding. Jeez.'

'I was wondering if I could sleep in one of your sheds. I wouldn't be any trouble. You've got the spare outdoor toilet, and if I could just have a shower a couple of times a week, that's all I'd need. I'll cook and clean and stuff, whatever.'

The words came out in a rush. Clare hated asking for anything. Asking for something that depended only on the goodness of the person being asked was a weakness, somehow.

Cutter stretched out a long leg. The cockatoos were still scrawling and screeching in the gully.

'Four weeks,' he said after a while. And then, after a few more minutes, 'Couple of rules. On a Friday, you cook enough food for ten people. Meat, vegetables, salad, whatever. You cook for you too. I'll leave a few hundred dollars out for you to buy what you need. Cook it and put it in the fridge. Friday night and Saturday night you stay in your shed or you leave early to go walking. You leave by six. And you don't come near the main house on the weekend. Not until Monday morning. And then Monday you clean. Got it? Rest of the time, I don't care.'

Clare nodded.

'Come see the shed.'

He took the container of stew inside and she saw him put it in the fridge. Then he led her behind the main shed, where he did a lot of his rock and wood work and which held a huge range of gardening tools and axes and saws and grinders and ropes and ladders and jars of nails and half-empty pots of paints, everything in its place and clean. Clare thought she would be happy to spend a month in there, looking at what he had. Next to the vast workbench was a battered old refrigerator that Cutter kept stocked with the tins of beer he sometimes sipped from dawn to well beyond dusk while he worked, although Clare had never seen him drunk. In a corner, behind a narrow wall of very old bricks, was an ancient toilet that Cutter once told her had been the old outdoor dunny belonging to the small farmhouse that had originally stood on the land when he'd bought it years earlier. 'It was a ratty old place,' he'd said. 'But I liked the gum tree.'

The smaller shed, gleaming corrugated iron, was long and narrow and ran along the fence line. Cutter opened the door, and Clare saw that it was empty apart from two large meat hooks hanging from a central beam that ran down the length of the building. There was a coil of rope in a corner. Cutter picked it up. The floor was just dirt but it had been compacted and seemed clean, and there was insulation and a power point and a small window at each end.

'Windows work,' he said. 'Just watch out for the bugs.'

Clare figured she could make herself comfortable enough. And maybe, if she cooked and cleaned really well, he might let her stay on a little longer. It was a palace compared to sleeping rough. There was access to a toilet, she could make a cup of tea, plug in the fan if a night was really hot, plug in her fridge.

'It's great,' she said. 'Thanks. A lot.'

'No worries. Just lie low.'

They walked back slowly across the yard. The sun was beginning to bite.

'Dinner time,' Cutter said. 'Bloody hottest part of the day. Soon have to start having dinner for breakfast.' He dragged the big gate open to let her through. 'So I'll see you when?'

'Two weeks yesterday.'

'You going to miss him, you think?'

Clare bit her lip. It surprised her how odd it felt to know she would be walking back to a home with no Phil in it. She shook her head. 'I don't know. A little bit maybe.'

'Well, it's what you get used to, isn't it?' He closed the gate gently behind her.

Clare was hot when she got home. She switched on the fan in the kitchen and sat in front of it at the small table. She wondered where Phil was and if he had read the note she had given him. Not that it was much. In fact, now she wished she had tried harder to find some better words. It was clumsy and sentimental, she thought.

Dear Phil, she had written. *I am sorry for this. But I think that perhaps the walking might help you. The worst will be in the beginning, but if you can try and be strong it will get easier. It might help you get healthy again. I want you to know I do remember good times that we had, not just the bad and the empty. Part of me thinks that if you get healthy and strong then I would want to see you again. We could maybe talk anyway. But that will be some time off. You were a handsome bugger. I used to say that to you, remember? Try to think of the better things about you. I know it's like neither us of have ever copped a decent break. But still. Don't give up. Clare*

She stripped the bed Phil had slept in alone these past few years and put the sheets and pillowcases in the washing machine in the tiny bathroom. The machine would shake and rattle and gurgle for several hours, and Clare often thought that a new washing machine would be the very first thing she would buy if she happened to win the lottery. What a luxury that would be. But it wouldn't happen because she could rarely afford to buy a ticket. But still. But still. Don't give up. I never have, Clare thought. And what has that got me? Fuck all.

She had a cold shower and then heated up the last spoonfuls of stew and ate it with bread and butter. The kitchen was quiet. Not even a blowfly.

•

As it grew dark, she stuffed the clothes Phil had left behind – just some shirts and trousers, a dressing-gown, a heavy winter jumper and a belt – in a couple of bags and walked through the warmth to the train station. Myamba's old train station had officially closed two years ago and the nearest commuter stop to catch a train to the city was now a forty minute drive south down the highway that required a mind-numbing array of permits and fees. The only trains that ran down the track now were carrying freight or moving people and goods from the closing-down towns. Clare had heard five-metre-high barbed wire fencing ran for kilometres either side of the train tracks leading out of the city, to try and stop the suicides. Made no difference, people said. Now in the dark night hours people gathered in the shadows of the wide and beautiful old train platform and sold or traded food and clothes, kittens and puppies, travel permits, vouchers, and odd bits of furniture. Clare had lucked out a few times, selling containers of soup or stew she had made, bags of fruit she occasionally managed to collect on her nightly walks, a petrol voucher she hadn't used. Sometimes a patrol car swept into the station parking lot and cops and guards with torches jumped out and headed to the platform. But it was half-hearted. People disappeared into the darkness of the old stone walls. Mostly they visited just to see the shadows scatter and pick through what was left behind.

On this night there were maybe fifteen or twenty people selling things: the jars of cherries and syrup and tins of loganberries and apricots from the latest Food Essentials Pack, homemade cakes and muffins, eggs, clothes, soap. And twice as many again shuffling around, looking at what was on offer.

Clare bought two slices of chocolate cake, spread out the clothes and sat and waited, her back against the old cool bluestone wall. The wall and much of the platform were covered in graffiti. Above Clare was a vicious red scrawl: *Die Faggots*; and in thick neat white letters: *If your grandparents weren't born here, get out now.*

After an hour or so an old woman, short, with dark hair in a neat bob, stopped in front of Clare. She poked at the clothing with her walking stick, turning the pieces over. Then she looked up. Her eyes were a dull gold.

'Perfect,' she said. 'I want them. How much, my dear?'

'Just one hundred and twenty for all of it.'

The woman nodded. Clare saw now that she was carrying a very large and very old-fashioned handbag with a sturdy handle and a big metal clasp. She opened it and took out a small pink plastic purse in the shape of a duck. With the handbag tucked over her arm, she counted out twelve ten-dollar coins, putting them one by one in Clare's hand. When she had finished, she smiled as if something very important had been accomplished.

Clare stuffed the clothes back into the bags and handed them to the woman. She watched her walk slowly down the platform, leaning on the stick. When she turned through the gate to the car park, a mass of weeds and rubbish, Clare followed her. She was just in time to see the woman drive away in a sleek low dark car, the kind that shouldn't be left unattended any more in a dark car park in Myamba.

Clare started on her walk home. Six thousand three hundred and thirty-one steps. A black cat followed her for part of the way.

She returned to the train station the next four nights. On two of the nights she drove down with bits and pieces of furniture to sell, two small pots of straggly herbs, Phil's bed, which she carefully dismantled and transported in a trailer borrowed from Cutter. The bed fetched more than she had hoped for, with two young mothers, bored and sullen pyjama-clad children wrapped around their legs, competing over the price.

On the third night, just after she sold the bed, a knife fight broke out when three men in grubby white T-shirts and baggy shorts, fresh out of the pub, appeared on the platform, kicking away the torches people set out on the ground for light and stamping on dozens of small pots of cuttings and seedlings a dark-skinned man had been quietly selling, along with little jars of pickled chillis and onions. Clare had bought one of the jars once and the chillis were delicious. When the man protested, they punched him and kicked his legs out from underneath him.

Clare was at the other end of the platform but she could see several people going to help, or going to help the fight along. She heard someone yell out, 'Fuck, man, don't start with the knife!' and then a scream.

There was the sound of a siren and people started gathering up their things and disappearing into the dark, onto the tracks and into the car park. Clare slipped away as well.

On the fourth night, she brought Phil's shoes and boots and socks, another belt, and a box of her own old clothes she had found in the shed from the days she had been somewhere between a size sixteen and size eighteen, as well as the pair of size fourteen red lace underpants which she simply could not remember either buying or being given, and obviously had never worn.

The woman next to her, who was selling eggs and homemade jam, nodded a greeting. 'He died,' she said. 'The bloke last night. Dee-Dee. Three kids. Oh well. Shit sure happens.' She put her earphones back in.

Clare sat, under a graffiti scrawl that read *White Australian = Great Australian*, and thought about Dee-Dee. She hadn't known his name, but when she bought the jar of chillis he had smiled warmly and said, 'Thank you, thank you so much,' in a way that made her feel she had done some wonderful and important thing for him. She thought – and then she felt a sharp tap on her knee and looked up. The old woman with the golden eyes was pointing her walking stick at the clothes.

'All of it, please. Same price as before?'

'Yes,' Clare said.

'That's not enough, my dear. Not for this lot. More clothes and nicer this time. You do need to stop being foolish. Two hundred and fifty dollars.'

And she opened the clasp on the same old-fashioned handbag and counted out from the same pink duck purse twenty-five ten-dollar coins into Clare's hands. Clare stuffed the coins into the pockets of her trousers and gathered up the clothes.

'Come along then,' the woman said.

For a moment Clare thought she was talking to her, but then she saw the black cat slip out from the shadows at the base of the wall and trot over to the woman. The cat had a white front paw and white-gold eyes. They set off together to the entrance of the car park.

When the woman had opened her handbag, Clare had noticed something slip out. She picked up her torch and looked for it. It was a feather. A red feather.

I know who you are, Clare thought. I always knew you were real.

When she got home she made herself an omelette from four eggs and sat at the table. She switched on the television and read and watched as she ate.

Bombs Kill Ninety-Four In Brussels; *Fly Europe Airliner Disappears Over Atlantic With Five Hundred And Eighty On Board, Wild Storm Blamed*; *Food Stamp Riots In New York*; *Dust Storms Shut California Again*; *Largest Sinkhole Yet For Sydney, Australia*; *World's Largest Refugee Camp In United Central African Federation Already Half-Full With*

Fourteen Million In Tent City; Experts Put Bone Sightings Down To Shifts, Tensions In Globe's Sub-Surface But Council Of Governments Deny Any Bone Fallings; Escapees From Greater Pacific Refugee Station Six Shot, Killed, Say Indonesian And Australian Presidents; Blue Team Inches Ahead In Race For Home *With Only Three Casualties To Date And Emergency Rations Intact. Vote Blue Here.*

Clare switched off the television and washed the plate and frying pan. The night was hot and sticky. There was a faint flash of fine lightning and, after she had counted to one hundred and ten, a distant rumble of thunder. Still far away. She went out onto the porch and looked at the sky. After a couple of minutes there was more thunder and lightning and she could see the storm coming in from the south-west. She sighed and went back inside and made a cup of tea and turned off every switch and light.

She lit a small candle and sat at the table with her notebook and waited, tense and tired, for the storm to move through and on. A dark shadow startled her and then Fravershi landed on the table. He was clearly surprised at how rickety and unstable it was and walked tent-atively around in circles, as a dog might, testing his weight. Then he sat and busily washed his face, right black paw, then left black paw. There was a clap of thunder, much closer, and his tail swished.

Clare was so relieved at the presence of something living and breathing that she almost laughed. Fravershi stopped washing his face and sat and regarded her gravely, his eyes a bright and light green glow. When the next sudden and sharp clap of thunder came, he put out a paw and gently batted Clare on the wrist. And then he held his paw there and looked directly at her while, for the next hour, the storm raged across the town.

The cottage shook and trembled and sagged and heaved, and light-ning flashed white, whiter than daylight, over and over. Neither Clare nor Fravershi moved.

•

Two days later, Clare walked slowly up to the gates of the House of Many Promises. Before she had even pressed the intercom, one of the gates opened for her and she walked through. She looked up at the grand old peppercorn tree, so graceful against the summer afternoon sky. She'd stood under its branches on the other side of the fence. Now here she was.

It took five minutes to walk up the driveway to the house. Granna was waiting for her.

'Good,' she said. 'This way.'

They went around to the far side of the house. Granna had backed her ute up as close as she could against a wide door that led through a big tiled laundry and into the kitchen.

Clare stopped when she stepped into the kitchen. It was as large as most houses. She saw a commercial-quality cooking range and stainless-steel benches, copper pots hanging over a bench that was on wheels, a row of sinks, knives on a rack against the wall, baskets of garlic and onions, more racks with spices, an old wooden pepper grinder as long as her arm. Everywhere there was something. And in the middle of the room, a huge dark wooden table and twelve chairs under a lazily spinning overhead fan, and on the table dozens and dozens of plastic containers filled with food, neatly labelled, and loaves of bread, and trays of cakes and muffins, and bags of fruit and vegetables. The kitchen smelt rich and sweet and abundant, of spices and hot crusty bread, and meats stewed with wine and herbs, and coffee beans.

'I need to send some emails,' Granna said. 'If you could load the truck.'

Clare was waiting in the passenger seat when Granna returned. Fravershi was stretched out asleep on the dashboard, but jumped out of the small cabin when Granna started the engine.

'Okay,' she said. 'First stop a man called Madan. Out in that new estate heading east. His partner, Dee-Dee, was killed this week. There are three children. I think they're Madan's.'

The estate was dark when they arrived. Narrow dark roads and lanes that ended in cul-de-sacs and dead ends, with small houses crowded close to the edges of the streets and cars parked by front doors, no footpaths. Slivers of light from behind blinds and shuttered windows.

'Would streetlights have been so difficult?' Granna said to herself. 'These places get more and more and more ridiculous. Ah, here perhaps . . . No, it seems not . . . Here. Yes, this is it.' She edged the small truck expertly through rows of cars on either side of the street. 'The end house there, with the outdoor light on.'

They got out of the car. Granna shone her torch over the containers and baskets Clare had packed and gave Clare a cloth bag to hold. 'So, three of the curries. A loaf of bread. A cake. A bag of fruit. Let's see . . . ah, yes, lasagne. Two. Children like lasagne. And one of those stews there.'

She marched up to the front door and Clare followed, carrying the bags. There was no front porch or alcove, no garden. Just the concrete from the road stretching to the front door.

Granna pressed the doorbell and the door immediately opened. Madan was a tall lean dark man. His eyes were red-rimmed but he managed a small smile for Granna. Clare saw a pale reflection of Dee-Dee's warm smile. Three children stood in the room behind him. Clare looked over Granna's shoulder. There was no hallway. The door just opened directly into a combined kitchen and dining area.

'I am so sorry,' Granna said.

Madan nodded. He took the bags and put them on the floor.

'So, this is how it works,' Granna said. 'You're on the list now and I'll bring food once a week for six months. Use this time to save some money and worry a little less. You're on a list for other things as well.

If there's extra food. Vouchers for a holiday or petrol or clothes. I will let you know.'

He nodded again.

'Now, I heard you looked into walking?'

Another nod.

'Don't. Please. Not now. It's too big. It's not the right thing for your children. At this time. And it may not . . . well, I am saying be patient. If you do walk you'll be on your own. You won't get the list of safe houses. You won't get the list of water collection points. I'm sorry.'

He pulled himself together. 'No, no. You are right. I had decided. And it's not what Dee would have wanted. Not now. We spoke of it. But together.' He rubbed a hand over his eyes. 'Thank you. This will help.'

'I'll see you next week.'

They drove to the next house, five minutes away, and the next and the next. Clare could see Granna had mapped out a logical route for the night, moving across the town from east to west. She counted twenty-eight food drop-offs, and at each place Granna was polite and listened and made a note if there was a problem for someone. Clare listened and learned more about walking, things she wished she could have passed on to Phil. But Lilac Town always seemed to be the starting point.

And she heard the same stories over and over. 'He couldn't take it . . .'; 'We had a business up north . . .'; 'I never, ever thought . . .'; 'I can't even make you a cup of tea. There's no furniture yet . . .'

It was well past midnight when they returned to the House of Many Promises.

'I can drop you home,' Granna said.

Clare shook her head. She got out and so did Granna. She put a container and a loaf of bread into a bag.

'Take this,' she told Clare. 'Same three nights from now.'

Clare nodded and took the bag and slowly walked home. She wondered what was more difficult: to have had close to nothing for most of your life; or to have everything – well, to have most things that normal people had, family, a partner, a job, a business – and then have it taken away from you, not through anything you had done wrong, but because you lived in the wrong place, because a country was broken, because a new system forgot, or didn't bother, to factor in how all these changes, this redesign of the map, affected people. When she and Phil lost their house in the fire, it was their own fault they couldn't rebuild. Well, Phil's fault. That was different to this. It was something she would have to keep thinking about.

When she got home, she heated up the small container of curry Granna had given her. It was delicious. And there was a hundred-dollar note in the bag.

•

Over the next few weeks, Clare worked alongside Granna two or three nights a week. She started arriving a little earlier at the House of Many Promises and helped to fill and label the containers. She took the truck down to the auto repair and certification centre and pumped up the tyres and got the engine checked over, and collected the monthly on-road and driver permits. She brought the washing in off the line before a storm swept through. She chopped herbs and dozens of onions.

'Can you cook?' Granna asked one afternoon.

'Not fancy,' Clare said. 'I can do stews. Sauces for pasta. I used to make cakes.'

'Want to do a stew next week?'

'Sure.'

At night Clare still walked, restless, unnerved by the return of summer, another Christmas to be ignored.

She had moved into Cutter's shed, sleeping on the cushions from her sofa, fridge plugged in, all her clothes and pots and pans and plates and her money box and all the other bits and pieces packed in boxes and large plastic bags and piled against one wall. The very temporariness and untidiness of them made her unhappy although she was lucky to be there. She knew this. It wasn't much worse than some of the places she was seeing on the new estates. She felt sorry for many of the people there, locked in, at the mercy of a system that seemed merciless, that lacked any logic. She felt freer here, but it was also uncomfortable. Each day and night was hotter than the day and night before it, and the shed was airless, even when she switched on the fan. She could heat up food in her microwave, and she still had her little kitchen card table and chairs but they looked odd enclosed in the iron and steel of the shed and she missed the creaks and groans and sighs of the ratbag cottage. She also missed the television. It didn't work in the shed, and she couldn't afford to watch anything on her phone.

And then there were the weekends. The first weekend Clare simply thought she would lie low. She was tired from working with Granna, and tired from cooking for Cutter, and she wanted to just be still and think about the things she had heard and seen. But as night fell on the Friday, the noise began. Half-a-dozen cars roared into Cutter's compound and she heard male voices and loud laughter and then yelling and whooping. She opened the shed door and walked slowly to the edge of the much larger shed in front, where she had a view of the yard and the wide steps and decking. There were maybe fifteen men, all big and heavy, all bearded, all naked, all drinking. She went back to her shed, turned off the light and bolted the door. 'I don't want to know,' she said. 'I don't want to know.' For the rest of the night she blocked out the noises and tried not think about what they meant.

She must have fallen asleep at some point, because when she woke it was much cooler and she could see through the small window it was that calm, not-quite-cold hour before dawn, only the faintest light in the sky, the moon fading away. She got up and went out to look at the yard. It was quiet and most of the cars were gone. She tiptoed to the toilet in the largest shed, and then went back to her makeshift bed and slept for another two hours.

The next night was wilder, the music louder, the hollering and whooping seemed to go on for longer. She sat in the dark on one of her chairs. The noise seemed to claw at her. Finally she lay down and went to sleep.

The next afternoon she slipped away and drove her car down to the gardens. She parked near the toilet block and slept on the back seat. When she woke before dawn, she got out of the car and walked to Edith's bench, where she sat, head in hands. How is this helping me, she thought. A week nearly gone and no closer to having a place to go when my month at Cutter's runs out. What was I thinking? Useless woman. Useless.

She cleaned Cutter's house on the Monday and was surprised to find nothing untoward. It was as if he had cleaned it already. Dishes were done and put away. The bed linen was already in the washing machine. She thought perhaps she had imagined the weekend to be worse than it was.

She was distant from Granna during the following days, simply because of the constant worry. Where to next? Where to next? She felt Granna watching her and she flushed and tried to work harder, faster. Keep moving. Move. Move and breathe. Move and breathe. She went back to the caravan park and paid a thousand dollars to get on the waiting list for a place to pitch a tent.

And it all began again on Friday evening. Different cars, different men, same noise, same music, same shouting. And it was too hot to be in a shed. Too hot to eat. She wanted her cottage back. She could at least have a cold shower there whenever she wanted it. She opened the door and sat outside in the dark, back against the shed wall, trying not to hear anything. She felt a familiar soft tap on her hand. She looked down and there was Fravershi. He rubbed against her, turning this way and that, watching her with his green, green eyes. Then there was a loud crash and a thump, and he darted away. Another weekend went slowly by.

She arrived early at Granna's the following Tuesday. The air conditioner would be on in the kitchen and she could stand in it. Luxury.

Granna let her in, and took in the grubby pants, the sweaty shirt, Clare's tiredness. 'Where are you living again?' she asked.

'A friend's shed.'

'It must be hot.'

Clare shrugged. She pulled a chair out from the table and sat down heavily. Granna watched her, and Fravershi sat on the table, looking first at Granna, then Clare, then back to Granna.

'Yes, yes, Fravershi. I know. I know.' Granna took a deep breath. 'Come with me, Clare.'

She walked out of the kitchen, across the vast back deck and to the garage, large enough for five or six cars and firewood and a lawnmower. At the side of the garage, towards the rear, was a narrow staircase. Granna went up it and pushed open the door at the top. Clare followed.

Inside she saw the vaulted roof space at the top of the garage had been converted into a simple apartment. In some parts the roof was low, but it was a big open space, with skylights and windows, a proper bed, a fridge and oven and some kitchen benches, two floating shelves on a wall, and a shower and toilet behind a screen. There was an overhead fan and a heating–cooling unit.

'Well? Would you like to stay here?'

Clare stared at her.

'It's empty. Has been for years. Look, it's up to you. This can be a strange house. It's so old and so overrun with memories and with

. . . well, things. But it is also quiet and rather beautiful. If you are prepared to help me, help out in the house and garden as well as the other work, and keep to yourself, then you can have this. For free.'

'For how long?'

'Oh, I don't know, dear. Until I die, I suppose, provided you behave. Then it will be up to Robbie.'

Clare was speechless.

'Well, have a think about it. My doctor's been on at me forever to get some help. I didn't like anyone I interviewed. Noisy, nosy little things. Have a look around and let me know tonight. I don't like waiting around for decisions. Do something or don't do it.'

Clare heard her walk down the stairs. She looked around. It was a simple space, sparse almost. But it was clean and bright. She tapped the walls. They were insulated. She turned the kitchen tap on and off. There was hot and cold water. She shook her head. The shower was spacious. She turned on the hot water tap and in a few seconds steam was rising from the shower floor. She walked to the bed and sat on it. It was a proper bed, with a mattress that looked clean. She could bring her small table and chairs, her television, her pots and pans. She would bring the bone-knife the walking man had sent her and put it on one of the shelves. But she wouldn't bring everything. She liked the emptiness of the space, the clean bare corners and walls. She would make it a home, not a storage unit. No clutter. No rubbish. This place was better than that.

She started to cry, the tears following the folds and curves of her face, her plump cheeks, the tired lines around her eyes. She cried and cried, her big shoulders shaking. This would be the nicest place she had lived since her house had burnt down on that summer day long ago. This place was beautiful.

Clare didn't know it yet, but the happiest years of her life began then. At that moment, sitting on the neat clean bed. A quiet and steady happiness, like a child's silent wonder at the world. It was so wholly unexpected, so surprising, that she barely dared to even think it or name it, because if it was indeed real, it could be taken away. Out of nowhere, she had been given so much that she could lose. And also at that moment she knew there wasn't anything she wouldn't do for Granna Adams. Nothing. She couldn't stop crying.

seventeen

There is Antonia – Granna, they call her – my seven-times great-granddaughter, sitting in her chair in the huge kitchen I built once upon a time. She slowly twists and stretches her hands because there are aches inside the bones. They are an old woman's hands, becoming translucent as the skin thins, and they hold time, they turn time over, they measure it, they pause it with a tremulous finger slightly raised the better to hear the relentless heartbeat of the past, to rewind it to the memory of a kiss, or a decision lightly made that changed a lifetime, or the smile of a child. The hand reels time in and casts it back to the endless silence. It caresses time, because time is all that is left.

I will sit here with her for a while, my cold and bony hand on her warm and living one. She smiles and tilts her head. She has been waiting for me. We listen together to the vast vats of water under the house whispering endlessly. Like life. Like memories. Like ghosts.

And, oh, the march of memories on these long, long nights. Her two sisters, long gone. Her own daughter, Robbie's mother, long gone. Her Daniel, beloved man. The love he brought her. She closes her eyes and remembers every flower he gave her, every poem he read to her, the jewellery and jackets and handbags he bought for her, the echo of his voice saying, 'But I want to. It matches your eyes, your hair, the shape of your shoulders, that green dress you wear.' She remembers the puppy he surprised her with. She remembers the smell of him and the way he watched her cross a room and the jokes he told and the softness of his favourite corduroy jacket. And she remembers, with a lucid and luminous grief, the bewilderment of the long years of him coming undone, the forgetting and the fading away, the handsomest doctor in town becoming a shell of a man sitting on the floor with a colouring book and a teddy bear in the huge front room of the house he had loved.

So much to remember. Granna raises her finger again to the night, letting the past weave its stories, drawing together the invisible threads of history and memory and golden time passing into a tapestry she feels every day against her skin, a promise whispered by the past. Many promises.

eighteen

Ella and Robbie were married one week before Christmas in a small registry office in a beautiful old building only twenty minutes' walk from Ella's apartment. Ella's quiet, dour parents were present, along with a neighbour from the ground-floor apartment in Ella's building, a man Robbie liked and occasionally played chess with on a real old-fashioned chessboard with heavy hand-carved pieces. The proceedings were in French and the neighbour, Thomas, translated for Robbie, smiling and nodding.

The winter's day was unusually warm and afterwards they all walked together to the restaurant Ella had chosen, enjoying the brittle sunshine. It was, Robbie thought, simple and pleasant, and Ella looked beautiful and happy and relaxed and managed to not once snap at her parents, despite having to repeat for probably the fifth or sixth time the arrangements for the honeymoon in the following spring and why Robbie would still spend some of his time in London and why Ella had to return to International Refugee Station Five for two months. The food at the restaurant was good and the wine was excellent and the background music sounded, Robbie thought, suitably sentimental.

A waiter took photographs, which Robbie sent to Granna. *Thinking of you today*, he wrote. *I know you are with me in spirit, as always.*

He also sent the photographs to Jonathon and to a few friends in London: *It's done. Life is sweet.*

Ella's parents shook his hand warmly when they left, her father even patting him clumsily and heartily on the shoulder. After a final drink with Thomas, Ella and Robbie went for a long walk through the Old Town, hands clasped. Robbie was surprised how many shops were boarded up and how many people were queuing outside what was open – a butcher's shop, a patisserie, a small supermarket.

They found a bench near the lake and sat, silent, Ella's head on Robbie's shoulder, until dusk arrived and it was suddenly cold. And then they walked home.

'Thank you,' Ella said to him as they turned into her street.

Then four months later, a flight to Athens, arriving on a hot, still spring night, the airport half-empty, the city quiet and ordered in a way it had never, ever been before the borders were locked down as much as possible and the fences built.

A private car to the port, a private boat to the island. 'I don't care what anything costs,' Robbie had said to the nameless go-between. 'I just want things to be perfect.' And everything was. Looking back, the beauty of those thirteen days and nights could bring him to tears. He wondered, sometimes, if it had been too much, if the cost of such privilege and grace was higher than he could have possibly imagined.

The villa sat low on a steep olive-green hill. From a wide white terrace and a huge swimming pool, there were views of a blue, blue sea. Opening the doors into the vast living room and seeing the terrace and the pool and the sea beyond, Ella gasped. Even Robbie was taken aback. The photographs had not conveyed the opulence, the purity of the white and the blue and the air and extraordinary sunlight and the stillness and silence.

They both walked out to the terrace and sat, speechless, staring at the sea, while the driver of the car that had brought them up from the jetty carried their bags in and seemed to check something in the pantry. It was only when he coughed loudly that Robbie realised he was waiting for a tip and to be dismissed.

He handed Robbie a card. 'If you need anything. Otherwise I return the thirteenth day of May. Also,' he gestured to Robbie to follow him back to the car, 'this man will be helping you.'

Standing next to the car was a man Robbie guessed to be, what, ninety-five, a hundred? His skin was lined and leathery and tanned and his front teeth were missing.

He held out his hand. 'I am Alec. I have placed in the kitchen for you bread, vegetables and herbs, yoghurt, a fish, some goat meat, butter and cheese, coffee and sugar. Are you happy, sir, with these things?'

His eyes, Robbie saw, were black, bottomless. His English perfect.

'Yes, of course,' Robbie said.

'So every second day, if I return with similar things, will you be happy?'

'Yes, absolutely.'

'There is a restaurant in the village, but not really a shop anywhere. The food comes from all sorts of places.'

'Chocolate?' Robbie asked.

'Ah, chocolate. Chocolate is a difficult thing.'

'That's okay.'

'No, no, my task is to find anything, anything at all, that is desired or needed. Certainly in the scheme of things over many years, chocolate would be the least of it.'

'When is the restaurant open?' Robbie asked.

'When it wishes to be. Not often. I will see you in two days, sir.'

He climbed onto an old purple scooter that had been parked behind a huge gnarled olive tree that stood near the villa creating a casual

circular driveway. The scooter had an assortment of wicker baskets
hanging off it. Alec turned the key and the scooter belched black
smoke and headed out the gates and down the hill. The car followed.

When Robbie returned to the terrace, Ella was sitting where he
had left her. He saw she had been crying and he raised an eyebrow.

She shook her head. 'I think this is the most beautiful place I have
been. Oh, Robbie, it's stunning. It's outrageous. Whatever have we
done to deserve this?'

She stood up and walked down the wide marble steps to the pool.
He watched her take off her clothes and sit on the edge. She laughed
and then slipped in and laughed again.

Robbie went inside and found a bathroom. He brought a towel out
to the pool for Ella and went back inside to explore. There were four
bedrooms upstairs, each with its own bathroom and dressing room.
Every bedroom had a king-size bed, sheer curtains that shifted lightly
in the late afternoon breeze now coming in off the sea, and an air
conditioner. Robbie unpacked their bags, and put the small gift he
had bought for Ella on her side of the bed.

Downstairs, he checked the kitchen. The fridge was full of the
food Alec had described, and on one of the benches were bowls of the
reddest, roundest tomatoes, lemons with stems and leaves still attached,
onions and garlic. Robbie couldn't remember when he had last seen
such fresh, vibrant food. From Granna's garden, he supposed. So it
would be grilled fish and salad for dinner.

He found drawer after drawer of kitchen utensils, a pantry stocked
with olive oil and vinegar and dried herbs and salt and napkins and
candles and a couple of very old cookbooks, and another walk-in
pantry with perhaps fifty-dozen bottles of wine. He laughed, much
as Ella had, like a child surprised and delighted by an abundance of
treasures. He went and joined Ella in the pool.

Much later he set the table for their dinner; two places at a long rough-hewn wooden table that could seat twenty. He lit candles and turned on the music he had brought and opened a bottle of white wine for Ella and red wine for himself and started to cook while Ella sat curled on one of the white sofas and watched the sunset, holding the handcrafted evil-eye amulet Robbie had given her, a blue sapphire for the eye.

They ate in silence and at the end of the meal Ella cried again, cried while she laughed. 'Everything. Is. Perfect,' she whispered.

Then one of their favourite songs started playing and he turned up the volume and led her onto the terrace and they danced slowly in the dark, with the wind and the smell of the sea and the pines.

•

And that was the tenor of those few perfect days. They woke. They swam in the pool. They made breakfast together – coffee and toast and cheese and honey. If the weather was good, the wind mild, they walked down a steep rocky track to a small beach where they swam and waded and sat on rocks in the sun. Each day Ella found something, a shell or a small pebble, and carried it back to the villa with her. And each day Robbie made tomato sandwiches for a late lunch when they returned from the beach hot, sweaty, sea-salt-smeared.

He was enjoying cooking for Ella and realised there was a ritual to it that delighted him, an implied security and caring and sense of home, even if the home was borrowed and, in a matter of days, would be given up. He stood in his shorts at the white stone kitchen bench, sunlight and white everywhere, toasting thick slices of crusty bread, rubbing them with garlic, piling tomato slices and their juices on top, shaking a few drops of the green olive oil over them and adding salt and pepper. I am making a tomato sandwich for the woman I love and this is happiness, he thought. This moment, which I am lucky enough to be able to repeat tomorrow and the day after that, is perfect.

They ate the sandwiches sitting under an umbrella by the pool, a beer each on the small table, laughing as the tomato juices dripped everywhere, down their hands and on their legs, onto the tiles, and when they had finished eating they would gently kiss away the tomato juice stains and breadcrumbs.

In the afternoons they would read or sleep or make love, or all three. Robbie had put some poetry collections on his tablet and occasionally he read a few lines to Ella. He had thought he perhaps wouldn't want the days to be interrupted by a story or stories, by people, even fictional people, who were outside the circle of what he might be feeling and thinking and seeing. It had been years since he had seriously read poetry and he was loving it, giving himself two poems a day to read, and read again, and think about, or let go.

And at night, after a final swim, Robbie would cook a late dinner while Ella watched the sunset, or, on several evenings, dark and wild storms rolling in across a suddenly turbulent sea. On his second visit Alec had brought a basket full of chocolate bars and chocolates of all shapes and sizes stuffed with nuts and caramel and raspberry paste. After she had done the dinner dishes, Ella would choose the night's chocolate supply, setting them out on the table along with a bottle of sweet local brandy they had discovered.

In one of the bedrooms Robbie had found several old-fashioned board games, games he remembered from the House of Many Promises, and he taught Ella Snakes and Ladders and Monopoly and Scrabble and Boggle and Forbidden Island, and Ella, who had never played anything that wasn't on a computer screen, loved them all, especially when she started winning, and said she and Robbie had to find some sets for her apartment.

'We'll bring some back from Australia,' he said. 'Granna has rooms full of games. She'll give us some.' He had just made the word *quite* on the battered old Scrabble board. 'Forty-eight for me.'

Ella was slowly tapping a finger on each of her letters. 'It would be fun, yes?' She took a piece of chocolate from the bar she had broken into pieces. 'Hmm. Forty-eight. Does that mean you are winning?' She looked at the board and then at him and smiled. 'I think I might do this.'

Robbie watched in disbelief as she added *con* in front of the *q* and then *u, e, s* and *t.*

'Conquest!' she said gleefully, and added up the score under her breath, frowning and starting over several times. 'Two hundred and twelve, please.'

Robbie tapped the number into his phone and sighed.

'I think perhaps you are letting me win.' She took another piece of chocolate.

'I wouldn't do that,' he said.

'English is not even my first language and I keep winning.'

'Your English is better than anyone's I know. Anyway, it's not mine either. I speak Australian.'

'Aussie.'

'Yep.'

'Aussie. Brekkie. Chrissy. Stubbie. Arvo. Servo. Lingo. Bikkie. Cozzie. Dinky-di. Grog. Booze. She'll be right.'

Robbie burst out laughing. 'You remember!' It had been years since he had amused her on a long flight to somewhere with Australian slang terms.

'Bloody oath,' she said. 'No, no. Bloody oath, mate!' She picked up new letters, topped up their brandy glasses and held out her hand for his phone. She looked at the numbers. 'Anyway, I have won.'

'But the game's not finished,' Robbie said. 'The board's only half-full.'

'That doesn't matter. I am in an unassailable position. One hundred and forty-eight in front. Fair dinkum.'

'But I've got a word to make.'

'And I have just picked up the *x*.'

'Oh.'

'And the *z*.'

'Bloody hell.'

'Stone the crows.'

'Okay then, you win. Start over?'

'No. Bed would be better, I think. Much better.'

As the days went by they spoke to each other less and less, and let the weight and moods and silences and shifts of the sea and the sky and the rugged grey-green hills settle on them. They slept and ate and swam and watched the view and the plants, a boat that might appear far out to sea, an airplane moving slowly far overhead, a butterfly, the bees hovering over the lavender shrubs.

'So there are still bees here,' Ella murmured. 'Of course there are.'

Robbie collected water from their showers in a bucket and watered the small vegetable bed each evening, leaning down to smell the dirt and plants. Would he ever live somewhere again where he could grow some vegetables, where he could find and cook real food, where there was time to watch a storm roll in and recede, watch a season end and a season begin? Where could they go? More and more they avoided each other's work and largely ignored what they each did when they were apart. It wasn't indifference. It was just too hard to make sense of, and the world was hard enough as it was.

Every few days he cut herbs and lavender and put them in a glass by Ella's side of the bed, so she woke up to their perfume. He washed out her swimming costume and clothes and hung them out on bushes to dry, and they smelled of sun and rosemary and lavender and fennel.

'I am doing nothing,' she said at the end of the first week.

'I'm glad.' And he was. He realised he loved taking care of her, of surprising her not with gifts and outings and adventures but simply by being thoughtful, by doing simple small things that people probably did for each other all the time but were rare for them, out of reach because of their work and their schedules and their travel.

She would catch him watching her and would reach out to touch him lightly, on his arm or his face, as if to say, *I am here, I see you too.* Once she did ask him what he was thinking, and he told her.

'A home. Somewhere. I don't care where really, but somewhere you can hear the wind and the rain, and where there is fresh food to buy and a dining table to sit and eat at each night. A space that is white and light with big doors and curtains that shift in the breeze. Places for us both to work and think and play. And a small garden. A small garden for the cat and the dog. More and more it seems to me that this might be enough.'

'A dog?' she said.

'I want to have a dog. I've said that before.'

'I know. I know.'

'Just think about it,' Robbie said. 'Please. There is Australia. My property at Granna's. It could be a base at least. What's so special about here is not just how beautiful it is, but the time. We have real time. Today and tomorrow and the day after that.'

'I know,' Ella said again. She reached out and touched his knee. 'And I am not ready. Yes, this holiday is a gift. It is something that is once in a lifetime. But all of this . . .' She made a wide gesture that included the house and the gardens and the sea and the sky. 'It does not, and cannot, stop me thinking and remembering and wanting to work. Is this all that really rich people do? Sit somewhere beautiful, buying time?' She shook her head. 'It is not enough, Robbie.'

'I have never said we don't work, just that—'

'My work is my work. Let it be.'

Robbie sighed.

•

In the second week he asked if she wanted to walk into the village.

'I really don't want to leave here,' she said. 'Is that wrong?'

'No, of course not. But I might go. See if there's anything to see.'

Robbie set off through the gates and down and around the hill. After an hour or so of walking he stopped. There was only one narrow, winding road, towards the bigger bay where the jetty was. From memory, the village was roughly halfway between the villa and the bay and he could, in fact, see in the distance some low tiled roofs. Yet even as he continued to walk, they seemed no closer. Perhaps the heat and the glare from the road played tricks with distance and space, Robbie thought. He was foolish not to have brought some water. He looked back up the hill towards the villa, but it was on the other side of the hill now.

He decided to keep going, and an hour later came to the village, or to what called itself a village but was only eight or ten houses grouped around a small square, with shade provided by several tall and broad cypress trees. Chickens pecked in the dust, and he could see behind each small home vegetable fields spreading out, some sheds. He saw a donkey and a few well-fed goats.

He had a feeling he was being watched and then noticed a very old, very small woman sitting on a red chair at the side of one of the trees. Some other chairs were scattered about. The woman's tiny brown hands clasped the top of a short walking stick. But as he looked at her, he saw that she was blind, a milky gummy grey-white where her eyes should have been, and her thin lips had collapsed inwards over toothless gums. At her feet were several cats, grey, ginger, white, and mewling kittens, and what seemed to be a pile of thin bones, chicken bones perhaps. As Robbie watched she raised the walking stick and lashed out in a low line in front of her, chuckling when she felt the stick connect with one of the cats. He couldn't tell if she knew he was there and he quietly backed away towards the buildings at the far end of the square.

He peered through the windows of a neat white building with blue-trimmed windows, clearly a taverna. He could make out half-a-dozen wooden tables, each with a vase of red plastic flowers, and a door through to what was probably the kitchen. The windows and the front door were locked.

The next three buildings all seemed to be private homes, small and neat, curtains covering all the windows. Robbie went down a narrow side path to the back of the buildings. The small fields were immaculate. He saw rows of spinach, grape vines and tomato plants. More chickens. By the back door of one of the houses was a tap. He knelt down and splashed himself with cold water and drank from his cupped hands. The water tasted faintly bitter, like cold metal. He looked through gaps in the curtains at some of the back windows and saw small simple kitchens and dining tables, but nothing that indicated the houses were lived in. No coffee cups left to drain at the sink, no plates sitting on a table, no piece of clothing draped over a chair.

Robbie reached the last house in the row. He thought he saw a faint light from the window, a flickering from a television or a computer screen. He was about to look in when there was a sharp voice behind him.

'Stop. No.'

The old woman was pointing her stick at him. He saw she was dressed in a cheap summer dressing-gown, grimy white with black-spotted dogs playing on the fabric, and wearing pink slippers. Her hair reminded him of cobwebs.

'Sorry,' he said. 'I was just looking for someone. Anyone. I was wondering when the restaurant opened and I was going to try and buy a bottle of water.'

'The restaurant never opens,' the woman said. 'Why on earth would it?'

She stared at him with her empty white eyes. Her voice was surprisingly strong and the accent was unusual, the pronunciation of each word crisp and precise but with an odd drawl on some of the vowels. One of the cats had followed her and she hit it with her stick. It yowled and hissed and backed away.

'The restaurant hasn't opened since the islands closed down,' she said. 'Well, the ones that could. We had some wonderful parties that last summer. But I am telling you, move away from that window. Now.'

Robbie looked at the flickering and flashing through what he now saw was darkened reinforced glass. There's more than one computer screen in there, he thought. And then he noticed this last house was different to the others. The back door was made of some sort of thick metal and was heavily padlocked with a security intercom, and instead of the quaint blue or red trim around the windows, there were steel rims and heavy shutters that could be pulled across. I just want one look, Robbie thought.

'One look and you will leave the island by sundown,' the woman said. 'It is that simple.'

'Okay,' Robbie said and stepped back. 'Okay.'

She seemed to regard him carefully from her dead eyes. 'This world is very difficult. I think to survive, each person and place do what they must do. And each person and place are entitled to their privacy and their secrets. So leave us, please.' She pointed with her stick to the nearest vegetable beds. 'Is there anything you want?'

Robbie shook his head.

'Come then.' She turned and headed towards the closest side path.

Robbie took a final look at the house and gasped. A young girl with fine golden curly hair was staring at him through the window. She smiled and waved. Her teeth sparkled like diamonds. She held up a drawing. It was of Timmy, lying on red-brown dirt, muscle and blood and bone exposed, eyes wild and terrified, and there was Robbie, kneeling next to him, hands cradling Timmy's straining, sweating head. And then another picture. Robbie again, but this time he was lying on the ground and it was his eyes that were wide and wild, his mouth that seemed to be screaming in agony, his back arched against some horrible internal pain. He thought he heard the girl laughing.

He turned and stumbled and followed the old woman down the path. She walked swiftly, but when she reached the edge of the square her shoulders sank and she began to shuffle. She made her way very slowly back to the red chair.

'I told you not to look,' she said. 'And, no, you didn't look through the window, which was just as well. It was really her fault. Not yours. I understand. So I will give you a small gift. Would you like that?'

'I don't know. What is it?'

He was trembling slightly and felt flushed and hot. The drawings were terrifying in their detail, their preciseness. What they portrayed was so clear, like photographs, but stretched somehow to a depth, an extreme, that a photograph, however brilliant, couldn't quite capture. What on earth was that girl doing here? Who was with her? Who else was on the island?

'It is true, isn't it, that since you and your very beautiful wife arrived on the island you have slept, as they say, like a baby every night? No dreams? No nightmares?'

Robbie nodded. It was true. He was sleeping the way he remembered sleeping as a boy, deeply, fully in the moment of simply sleeping and knowing he was deeply asleep. For more than a week now, there had been none of the dark and disconnected shapes and shadows that haunted him, sleeping and awake, more and more, and that slipped away beyond his grasp when he tried to confront them, to understand them.

'Then despite what you have just seen, what she tried to do, you will continue to sleep in peace while you are here. I cannot help you when you leave, but while you are here, everything will stay safe. The island is your home for a few more days, and it will stay safe, as a home should be.'

'Thank you,' he said. 'I'm not sure I understand. But thank you.'

'I have to say, I am very, very glad I am the age I am. Your grand-mother says the same thing. I don't think we have much faith it will all hold together for much longer. Of course, it will only be what we deserve.'

Robbie flushed. Granna? Had he misheard? He must have misheard. This was all becoming absurd, again, the way so many things became absurd.

The woman was slowly sagging lower in her chair. A cat rubbed itself against her ankle and she kicked it away. He watched a globule of spittle grow in the corner of her mouth and begin to drip slowly down her chin.

'Alec . . .' she whispered.

The front door of the last house on the left side of the square, the strange house, opened and slammed shut. Alec walked briskly across to the old woman. He handed her a pill and a glass of water, and wiped away the spit with a tissue.

'Mama,' he said.

Robbie started. Surely not. 'She's your mother?'

'Oh yes.'

Robbie looked at her. Well, perhaps she had given birth to Alec when she was sixteen or so, or even twenty. These days more and more people lived to be a hundred and ten, a hundred and fifteen.

The woman swallowed the pill and straightened in her chair.

'I'm taking Roberto home, Mama,' Alec said. 'I'll be back in ten minutes.'

He went back to the house, opened the front door and wheeled out the old purple scooter that must have been parked in the hallway. From where he stood now, Robbie could sense nothing odd or different about the house. In fact, the little square seemed suddenly shabby and dull and poor. Right now I could be anywhere, he thought, a little dusty back-of-nowhere, in-the-sticks dump anywhere in the world.

Alec started up the scooter. It belched and burped black smoke, ebbed and gurgled. 'Climb on,' he said.

'I can walk.'

'Trust me. You couldn't possibly.'

Just a few minutes later, Robbie climbed off the scooter at the gates of the villa. He stood in the sun, watching, while the memories of the last three hours slipped away. A girl. Drawings. An old woman. No, no, nothing. Nothing to dream of. Nothing to fear. A dusty little village. Another one. Gone. Somewhere else he couldn't remember. Cats. A settling. Peace.

'Ella, darling?'

She was lying on a daybed under an umbrella by the pool. 'I missed you,' she said. 'Was it interesting?'

'Not in the slightest. Tiny little old village. Nothing to see. It was hot walking on the road.' He saw she was reading one of the cookbooks from the pantry. 'Planning on cooking?'

'Well, it is my turn, surely.'

'No, sweetheart, I am loving cooking for you. It does a man good to cook. Truly. And I've got everything figured out. The oven. The grill.'

She sat up. 'No. I want to spoil you. I have looked at what is in the fridge and pantry. I am going to make,' she glanced at the page, 'feta and potato croquettes to start, with a red pepper aioli, and then . . .' she skimmed through the pages, 'fish baked with onions and tomatoes. There. Delicious. You just have to choose the wine.'

He looked at her bright eyes, her smile, her golden skin, her softness with the little bit of weight she had put on. 'It sounds like a feast,' he said. 'I will be in charge of wine and music and dishwashing. And for now, I will make tomato sandwiches for lunch.'

It wasn't that Ella was a bad cook, he thought, as he made the sandwiches. Once she mastered a recipe she was brilliant. But as far as he knew, she had only mastered five recipes in her lifetime. In their early years she had earnestly explained the story behind each dish: why she liked it, the mistakes she'd made with early versions, the pitfalls in the recipe, what secret ingredient she had added that had enhanced the recipe far beyond what any professional chef had managed to do. It astonished him that a woman who could oversee the establishment of kitchen facilities to feed a million refugees in a desert could be reduced to tears by cooking steak and vegetables.

On one of his first visits to her apartment, he'd arrived to find Ella swearing passionately in French and German at, apparently, everything in her tiny kitchen. 'But look, Roberto. Look, look. The meal is supposed to look like this.' She showed him a series of photographs on her phone of a small beef roast with crisp vegetables and red wine sauce. 'And then look at fucking this.' On the bench was a plate holding a piece of beef that sat in a bloody puddle and was burnt black on top, and onions and potatoes in a similar state. In a small saucepan on the two-burner cooker was a thin sauce overwhelmingly pungent with garlic.

Ella saw him looking at the sauce. 'The recipe was three shallots, but I couldn't find any so I used garlic, but garlic is smaller than shallots, I do know this, so I used six cloves. I know you like garlic.

But it does smell a bit too much, doesn't it? And the beef – I just don't know. Okay, okay, so I am stupid!'

'Ella!' he said. But he didn't know her well enough to say much more.

He'd moved into the kitchen and looked at her wall oven. It had taken him a long time to get used to the size of kitchens in homes in Europe. Granna's kitchen and its adjoining pantries would have been the size of Ella's entire apartment. He'd looked at the dials and knobs and arrows for a few minutes. Then he looked at the beef dish. 'I think that perhaps you set the oven to the grill setting, not the roast setting. Perhaps. I could be wrong.'

'So you are agreeing that I am stupid? That I would do such a thing? It is my oven, after all.'

'Yes, but if you don't use it often, if you're not used to using it, it can be very confusing. But that is why the meat has burnt on top.'

She sniffed. 'I am not a very good cook. I am telling you this now.'

'Well, no, it's just—'

'Please don't be reasonable. Especially when I am being unreasonable. It will always annoy me.'

Robbie bit back a smile and looked at her kitchen curtains, which were orange. After a couple of minutes he'd said slowly, gently, 'Let's start tonight again. I'll come knock at your door and we'll go out for dinner. And tomorrow night we'll cook this beef dish together because it does look very delicious.'

'Reasonableness.'

'I think you need to throw out the sauce and the beef. We'll start again tomorrow.'

'Okay. I will clean up the kitchen. You go for a walk and then come back and we will start anew.'

Ten minutes later he knocked on her door again. When she opened it she was wearing a sheer lace gown that hung open. She took his hand and pulled him gently inside.

Robbie remembered all this while he made the tomato sandwiches, toasting the bread carefully, rubbing the cut garlic over the toast. One small thing at a time. He made an extra sandwich, just in case dinner was not quite edible, and put out a small bowl of olives as well.

'Perhaps I should make dessert also?' she asked while they ate.

'I think two courses is enough. And there is still chocolate. Lots of chocolate.'

Ella spent most of the afternoon in the kitchen, music playing softly, and Robbie swam in the pool and read and fell asleep on the daybed.

It turned out that dinner was indeed delicious, and Ella clapped her hands in delight when Robbie helped himself to a second serving of everything. Then it took him nearly three hours to clean up. It seemed Ella had managed to use every pot and pan and utensil and cutting board and measuring cup the kitchen held.

On the second-last night, they watched a storm roll in. It was as if a black cape had been tossed over the island. The sky was black and cold. Thunder and lightning raged directly overhead, and torrential rain soaked the terrace and some of the rooms where windows had been left open. Power was lost as soon as the storm started and Robbie scrambled to find a torch and candles and matches. They sat together on one of the sofas, a rug over them, and Ella trembled slightly with each lightning flash and roar of thunder.

'I hate these storms,' she said. 'It doesn't matter where you are any more, out of nowhere there is a storm.'

'I know.'

'Make it stop.'

'I wish I could.'

They fell asleep before the storm was over. When they woke, dawn was breaking across a sky of the clearest, palest blue.

•

There was nothing to say on the morning they left the island.

'We can come back,' Robbie began, but Ella cut him off with a look.

'This was enough for a lifetime. I have already said.'

From the island to Athens, from Athens to Rome, from Rome to Melbourne, Australia, where Robbie had decided he would stay on for an extra few weeks after Ella left. He wanted to write about the closing-down towns, about the upheavals and the unravellings, but to do that in any meaningful way he had to see for himself what was happening, talk to people, talk again to Jonathon. Similar things had happened and were happening in other parts of the world. Canada State, for example. Parts of the Americas. Greece. But they weren't his country. He thought of the landscapes he had known as a boy, as a young man, the rocks and hills and the white and grey gum trees, the cold and echoing footy ovals, the smell of smoke on a searing northerly wind blowing in on a summer's night that was like a furnace, the endless roads, the train rides to the city because it was Christmas or a birthday or there was a show to see. He wanted to know where all of this had gone, if indeed it had gone. Everyone was tired now, worried, and the smallest things often seemed worse, more difficult, than they really were. Sometimes. Perhaps it wasn't quite as bad as Jonathon had described it, as some of the stories and pictures he had seen.

Robbie and Ella took enough Valium before they boarded the flight in Rome to manage to sleep through most of the turbulence. When they arrived in Melbourne it was mid-morning. The airport seemed odd to Robbie. Strangely empty. He looked at the arrivals board. Only two flights coming in from Europe all day. Fourteen from China. Three from Indonesia. That was all. In the customs hall there were as many armed guards as travellers.

'Why are you here?' the customs officer asked as he checked their fingerprints.

'Family,' Robbie said.

'Good luck, mate,' the officer said.

Robbie left Ella with their bags and a strong coffee while he went to sort out the hire car. It was autumn and the air was cold. There didn't seem to be any heating in the airport terminal and he saw now that things looked tired and dirty. Some of the shops were boarded up or had closed signs hanging on their doors. There were empty bottles and paper cups and food wrappings on the ground and the smell of something stale. He walked past a group of people asleep on an assortment of blankets and pillows.

Only one hire car desk was open and only one type of car was available. He collected the keys and returned to Ella, who, he was relieved to see, seemed cheerful enough. He sent a message to Granna: *Two hours away, tops x.*

Robbie hated the car. Electric, of course, but an older model with very little real power and too small.

'A car for short people,' Ella said. 'Oh well.'

It took only a few minutes to get clear of the airport, something that used to take what felt like forever, and Robbie headed north. Everything on the drive to Myamba and the House of Many Promises surprised him: the potholes on the road; the new housing estates that spread out either side of the highway, tiny bare boxes of houses and apartment buildings, grey and drab; the long convoy of military vehicles, trucks mainly, which he overtook cautiously and saw were branded in big red and yellow lettering, *Brightest Star Agribusiness, Greater China*; the lack of traffic heading north and the jammed lanes of the highway heading south; the checkpoints; the helicopters overhead; and, strangest of all, to his left, people walking, people with backpacks and suitcases on wheels or pushing a trolley. No one walked along the verge of a highway. Anywhere. Did they? Unless their car had broken down. It wasn't a huge number of people but it was noticeable, and they all had about them a certain look, a glazed, furtive, weary determination.

Despite all this, so much was familiar. The few low hills that hadn't been built on were turning green again with the help of autumn dew and frost. The sky was big and low. The mountain range that divided the southern plains from the harder, rougher, browner northern country loomed large. Robbie could see scorched patches through the mountains. Last summer's fires, he guessed.

He saw the turn-off to the town in the foothills of the mountains was blocked with heavy chains and razor wire. *GOLDHILL TOWNSHIP CLOSED. This is NOT an Inclusion Zone. KEEP OUT.* Robbie remembered driving to a winter solstice festival in Goldhill when he was about eighteen, along with his girlfriend at the time, his very first girlfriend. She played the banjo and harmonica and was a vegan, and was planning on studying massage therapy and crystal healing when she finished school at the end of that year. There had been some good music and huge cauldrons of hot soups and homemade breads and baked potatoes. It had been a pretty town. He couldn't remember the girl's name.

Just before they reached Myamba, Robbie asked Ella if she wanted to stop for another coffee or some food.

She shook her head. 'I am sure your grandmother has that well taken care of. Let's just get there.'

So he took the turn-off and drove along the familiar roads towards his grandmother's house, the car barely coping with the climb up the final hill. As they approached, the iron gates swung open and he edged up the driveway to where he could see his grandmother waiting at the foot of the steps. A big, broad woman stood well behind her. That would be – what was her name? – the new helper woman.

He squeezed himself out of the car and, laughing, gently picked up Granna and held her close, smelling the rose-petal softness of her,

her hair, her cardigan. When he put her down, both of them wiping away a tear, Ella stepped forward, smiling warmly.

'Antonia,' she said.

'Ella. Beautiful Ella. Welcome. Welcome again.'

Robbie looked at the rambling imposing house, the driveway stretching around to the buildings behind, the beautiful gardens.

'You lost a tree,' he said, pointing.

'The oak,' Granna said. 'There was a swing on it, remember? Two summers ago. Poor thing. It was just too dry. Now,' she continued, 'I want you to meet Clare. Clare, you come here. Clare is helping me with, well, everything really. We'll talk about that later. Clare, this is my Robbie. And Ella.'

Robbie shook Clare's hand. She was a little taller than him, and her hand was big and warm and soft. He had a memory of a big strong woman waving at him. Someone like Clare. Was it Clare? What was he thinking of?

'Nice to meet you,' he said.

She nodded, and nodded as well to Ella. Shy, Robbie thought.

'Clare will help you to the cottage while I sort out lunch,' Granna said. Then to Robbie, 'Have you told her?'

'Who?'

'Don't be silly. Ella, of course.'

'No.'

'Oh dear. Well, perhaps you should. Right now, probably.'

'Tell me what?' Ella said.

Robbie scratched his head and cleared his throat. 'You know the old studio at the back of the gardens that used to be the stables? I told you that I'd bought it off Granna? Well, I've kind of had it done up. For us. I've always loved that building. I just thought . . . Anyway. It's a lot nicer than it was. It's just a place for us to have. If we need it. Or want it.'

'I see,' Ella said, in a tone that suggested she didn't. 'Well, then. Let's have a look.'

She started up the driveway at the side of the house, followed by Clare, and Robbie brought up the car. Behind the house was a huge covered deck and then a series of gently terraced garden beds. A wide gravel path meandered between and around them, leading eventually to the rear border of the property, where the old stables and tack rooms stood. Part of them had been converted to a studio decades earlier by Granna's mother, who had wanted a quiet place to paint and read. A toilet and shower had been installed downstairs, alongside what Granna's mother had called her private parlour. Upstairs, reached by a ladder, was a bedroom. A few years earlier Robbie had knocked out part of a wall and added a rough kitchen space, somewhere to make a coffee and toast and keep some beer cold. It was where he stayed, alone or with Ella, when he came back to the House of Many Promises, and it was quiet and private and quaint. Ella had told him several times that she liked it. 'It is peaceful,' she'd said. 'Simple.'

Now she stopped on the path and gasped. She turned around and looked at Robbie, shook her head, and turned back

The building did look, Robbie thought, impressive. It had been completely remodelled. The old stonework gleamed, and wide French doors running the length of the ground floor were pulled open to reveal one big room, with a kitchen in one corner, bathroom in another, a small wooden table set for six, big old sofas, a television, a long desk area with two chairs against a wall, an oversized wood stove for heating.

A new spiral iron staircase now led upstairs. He watched Ella climb it slowly and then followed her. A big bedroom, another bathroom. An upstairs verandah running the length of the building had been added and it held chairs and a small table. In the second room there was a piano and a bookcase and two armchairs. Robbie looked at the bookcase. There were his books from when he was a boy, adventure

stories mostly and books about animals. A shelf of board games. Ella
played a few notes on the piano and they were clear and true.

They climbed down the staircase and went outside.

Ella looked at the building. She shook her head slowly and folded
her arms. 'Robbie.'

'All I've done is renovate something that belonged to me anyway,'
he said. 'I owned this building for years.'

Robbie didn't understand why he felt and sounded defensive. There
was a part of him, he knew, a very small part of him, that had half-
hoped she would say, 'Oh, of course, Robbie, let's live here, for a little
while,' even as he knew this was ridiculous and would never work. Not
yet, anyway. There were a lot of things about Switzerland she enjoyed,
and a lot of things about Australia she found jarring or difficult. And
he knew he would become bored here. He always had. It was why
he'd left in the first place.

But as he'd approved the plans for the renovations and looked at the
photographs Granna sent through regularly, the new doors, the new
windows, the new floors, he understood that at the very least he liked
the *thought* of a home, a real home, not just a base to which he returned
now and then to unpack, rest a little, repack. And a home, a more or
less permanent home, didn't have to mean Australia necessarily. There
was Switzerland, and they could also probably qualify financially for
one of the new secured cities and communities springing up in some
countries. But then, what would those places mean to either of them?

The other option was to muddle along, as they had been doing.
He could tell himself home was wherever Ella was, and wherever he
amused himself or worked while she was travelling. It could be kept
that simple. Except that wasn't working very well any more. I'm tired,
Ella, he wanted to say. Let's just stop.

'It's nothing more than I've already said,' he explained now. 'One
day, somewhere, I want to live in a place that is ours. Your things, my

things. Time. It doesn't have to be this place, but we have it anyway. I will never not ever come back to here. And you told me you liked it.'

'Robbie, I do like it. Or I don't not like it. I just wish you had told me. You've made it beautiful. Of course you have. I am just surprised.'

'It's for us,' he said.

She kept her arms folded. 'No. It is for you. No, don't interrupt. "Us" is a conversation about doing something like this. "Us" is me paying for some of it.'

'You don't like it, then.'

'You are not listening. I do. I know we can spend happy times here. We always have. But this is not somewhere I have ever thought about living. Not seriously. Please don't sulk, Robbie. You have done a lovely thing. Let's let it be for now.'

Robbie shrugged. 'We should go in for lunch,' he said. 'We'll unpack later.' He saw Clare had left their bags by the dining table.

As they walked to the main house, Ella laughed. 'I am not so worried,' she said.

'What do you mean?'

'At least you have not got a dog yet.'

•

By unspoken agreement, they avoided any further discussion of the Stables and the renovations that had been done. The autumn weather was cooler than expected and Ella went into town and bought herself some heavier jackets, some socks and boots and another pair of jeans.

'I will leave most of these here,' she said when she returned with the new clothes. 'If that would be okay.'

'Of course it would be okay,' Robbie said. And that was all.

They spent most of their time with Granna, sitting at the huge kitchen table or in the front lounge room, where Robbie lit a fire every afternoon. He also lit a fire in the wood stove at the Stables before going over to the main house for dinner and when they returned to the Stables they would open a bottle of wine and sit on floor cushions in front of it, Ella stretching like a cat in the warmth.

Robbie thought his grandmother looked absurdly fit and well for her age and wondered what regime of age-defying pills and serums she was on. He loved eating her meals again, the food as nourishing and rich and warming as he remembered.

In the mornings and afternoons Granna and Clare cooked and stacked up the food parcels and containers in the refrigerators, and Clare disappeared early every evening to her room or to make deliveries.

'How did you find her?' Robbie asked over dinner the second night.

Fravershi sat in an empty chair between Robbie and Ella. Occasionally he leaned forward to nudge Robbie's wrist or elbow with his head.

'Our paths crossed,' Granna said. 'And thank God. It was getting to be too much.'

'So she's sleeping over the garage?'

'Aunt Mildred's rooms,' Granna said.

Aunt Mildred had died before Robbie was born, although he had seen photographs. Eight generations of the same family had lived at the House of Many Promises, each adding rooms, or updates, or a new shed or a studio.

'Do you trust her?' he asked.

'Aunt Mildred? No, I never did. She was a handful. Oh, you mean Clare? Well, what's not to trust?'

'She's very quiet,' Ella said.

'Times have been difficult for a lot of people. Clare is one of them. When you don't have much, there's sometimes not much to say.'

'How many food parcels are you doing every day?' Robbie asked.

'I don't always keep track. It's not every day. Maybe forty every few days. More some days. Less on others.'

•

One morning when his grandmother was in town, Robbie wandered through the ground floor of the house. When she married, Granna had created a retreat for herself and Daniel, knocking out walls to make an oversized bedroom, and a reading room, dressing room and bathroom. He opened the door to the space now. It was as beautiful as he remembered it. Elegant. Simple. Polished floorboards, cream curtains. And still, the small table behind the bedroom door with a vase of roses, yellow and white. Hanging from two hooks on the back of the door were a brown corduroy jacket, worn at the elbows, and a man's heavy blue dressing-gown. They had belonged to Daniel. He had been dead for more than forty years.

From the door he could see through a wide arch into the reading room. The bookshelves were gone, and instead there was a long bench and a bank of computers. Robbie frowned and went in for a closer look. Two very large, very serious computers. Two printers. He didn't dare touch anything. The computers were switched on.

Leaning down to look at the screens, he saw a small dark-haired elderly woman with a blue budgerigar on her shoulder. She was standing at a kitchen bench, passing something out the window. A cat that looked very much like Fravershi sat on a kitchen table in the foreground, tail swishing. An old movie perhaps, Robbie thought. On the other screen, another old woman, in profile this time. Grey hair like cobwebs, sunken chin, spit in the corner of her mouth. Robbie shivered. She looked vaguely familiar. Strange, he thought.

But it wasn't really any of his business whether his grandmother had one computer or twenty. What a person does in private is his or her own business and no one else's, she had always said.

He wandered back to the Stables, where Ella had been making some business calls.

'All okay?' he asked.

'Oh yes.'

On most days Robbie and Ella went for a walk together. Down to the town, where they would have a coffee and wander. Or to the botanical gardens, where Robbie marvelled at the number of trees that had come down over the years. Some days they helped Granna in the garden, pulling weeds, raking leaves, planting winter vegetable seedlings.

Ella had never had a garden and she especially loved this. 'More, please,' she would say. 'I can do more.' And she would plant each tiny thing meticulously, measuring the distance between each plant, measuring out the fertiliser and the water.

The days rolled on and Robbie was pleased they continued to enjoy and share something of the easiness and peace that had been theirs on the island. Ella seemed determined to stay happy, although she began a countdown. Eight nights. Then seven. Then six. She made more business calls, began checking her emails.

He also made calls, most of which weren't returned. But no, he would not be given a permit to travel into an exclusion zone. No, he could not visit Goldhill. No, there was no one to interview about the progress of the closing-down program. The government gave regular and detailed updates and these made it clear that progress was excellent.

At night Granna shared stories plucked from the overgrown family tree, stories that amused Ella. Robbie's great-great-great-aunt Myrtle who ran away to join a circus and then found God and went to China as a missionary. Chen Ling, who built the original six rooms of the House of Many Promises and the furniture for it and the hundreds of metres of water channels and shafts that continued to carry and store water under the land and house.

'It was extraordinary,' Granna said. 'He engineered it along the lines of the qanats in Persia and no one ever knew how he knew about these things. But to this day, we have more water here than we could ever possibly need or want. He could never have imagined just how valuable this would be.'

She talked of her own parents, William and Maria; her sisters, Marie, who left Myamba to teach at a school further north, and Elena, who went to Greece for a holiday and decided never to return; her daughter, Susan, who died in a car crash when Robbie was just a toddler. 'Let's see, there'd be Chinese, Irish, Italian, Scottish, English and a bit of Greek in you, Roberto Adams.'

She talked of the ghosts she saw, in the house and the gardens. Chen Ling, of course, his son Christopher, and Christopher's two sons who both died in the stinking freezing trenches of Flanders in World War One. Granna's own Daniel. On and on the stories went. Generation after generation.

'There seem to be many ghosts,' Ella said playfully one evening.

'Well, yes, dear. They don't all stay, of course. They come and go. Has Robbie shown you the Chinese temple Ling built? It's very small. But there is always food for them there. I think they quite like it here. I know you're laughing at me, young lady, but that small wooden chair next to the bookcases in the front room? Chen Ling sits there reading most afternoons.'

'And what is he reading, Antonia?'

'Oh, it could be anything. I've kept several rows of his books for him. He preferred reading Chinese and Persian. Not English, really. People back then must have thought he was very peculiar.'

Sometimes Clare would be in the kitchen with them, but she rarely spoke. Just nodded. For a big woman she moved quietly, Robbie thought. Quietly and quickly, like a shadow.

One afternoon, as Robbie carried wood and kindling into the big front room to lay a fire, she was standing by the sideboard, holding something.

Robbie nodded. 'Hello,' he said.

Clare looked at him. 'What is this?' she asked, holding out the object.

He put down the wood box. 'Ah. That's an opium pipe. It's very old. It would have come from China once upon a time.'

'And this?'

'A brush, to write Chinese characters. Chinese letters. Calligraphy.'

Clare put it back on the sideboard. Her fingers were thick, Robbie saw, but she touched the antiques and the wood they rested on gently. Her eyes were a very clear grey-blue.

'So many things,' she said. 'Beautiful things.'

'Yes. I guess this is different for you, from where you were before? From what my grandmother has said. Well, it would be different for most people, I know.'

She looked at him. 'You could say that,' she said slowly. 'Very different, I would think. For just about everyone.'

'Yes, of course. You were married?'

'Still am, technically.'

Robbie waited for her to say more. He wondered if she was a little slow. Or just very shy. 'And?'

She shifted on her feet. She was wearing a dark green shirt and it stretched tight across her large breasts. Robbie thought he could see some cleavage. He cleared his throat.

'He walked,' she said finally. 'There's a lot of walkers.'

'I know. But where are they going exactly? How much do you know about it?'

Clare picked up a small porcelain bowl and turned it around gently in her hands. 'Not much. I don't think anyone knows much about anything that's happening. The walkers. The bones. The closed-down towns. That's how they want it.'

'I want to do a story about it,' Robbie said.

'Your grandmother showed me some of your stories. She keeps them all, you know. Prints them out. Puts them in a folder.'

'I didn't know that.'

'She showed me. I tried to read some but they were difficult. I didn't really understand them. Things, the world, they're complicated.'

'Well, I'm not sure I understand half of what I write any more,' Robbie said with a smile. 'Yes, the world is complicated. Very complicated and mostly very sad and strange.'

Clare shrugged and put the bowl on the sideboard.

He bent to start laying the fire, then straightened. 'Maybe you could help me? Show me where your husband walked, where the walkers are. I don't know . . . maybe I could talk to people? Ella leaves soon, but then, if you'd be interested?'

Clare looked at her feet and then back at Robbie. 'Sure. I don't know much, but sure.'

She headed towards the door and turned back. 'Your grandmother is a really, really good woman. Kind.'

'Yes. I know.'

She stared at him. 'Good, then,' she said.

Robbie watched her leave the room.

•

Three nights. Two nights.

On the last night, they ate dinner alone, sitting at the dining table in the Stables. For the first time in a month Ella only picked at her food, finally pushing her plate away. 'I am sorry, Robbie. It is delicious, but I'm not hungry.'

While he tidied up she went upstairs and after a few minutes he heard music from the piano. Slow and soft, haunting. He knew she was saying goodbye and he sat on the sofa, tears in his eyes. The music went on and on, the same notes over and over, but at a different tempo, then in a different key, the repetition making it sound like a lullaby, a lament.

When it finally ended, he climbed the stairs and took her hand. They lay on the bed fully clothed, wrapped around each other.

'I will always love you,' he whispered.

'I know,' she said. 'Same. Always.'

Golden time passing. Promises. The words too small, far too small to say what was needed and wanted and meant.

And then the sun came up and the magpies began their singing, and Robbie drove her to the airport.

nineteen

Robbie was happy to spend the next week or two helping his grandmother. He painted the sunroom for her because she said it needed it. He chopped more firewood. He went with her on a couple of evenings when she delivered food and listened to the stories.

'I had a business,' one woman said to him as she put on the kettle and put away the food Granna had brought. 'A good business. Oh, we weren't rich but we didn't want for anything. The girls had all they needed. But when they close down towns, they close down lives with it. And do they think of that? You just start your business over is what they said. Well, my business was bloody poultry farming. Chickens. Quail for a few years. Eggs. All free-range. I said to them, how do I start a poultry farm when I'm living in a shoebox townhouse inside an inclusion zone. You tell me how, I said. Well, no answers to that, of course. What they gave me barely covered the cost of moving here. The savings are gone. The girls miss the farm, their dogs, their friends. I never was one to live week to week, I always saved, put money aside. Now here I am, taking handouts.'

Just four doors up, an even smaller townhouse, dark and cold. A middle-aged man sat at the cheap kitchen bench, just big enough for two, staring at the box Robbie had put down.

'I heard it was a good funeral,' Granna said, and touched the man's shoulder lightly.

'He would have liked it,' he said. Then he put his head in his hands and wept. For twenty minutes Robbie and Granna stood there, listening to the sobs, until the man finally looked up. 'I'm sorry,' he said, as Granna handed him some tissues. 'You tell me it's no coincidence. The day we moved here, he gets told he's got three months to live. Tops. They killed him with this move. Would have been kinder to shoot him.'

On two nights he went walking with Clare and was surprised by the pace she kept, the back streets she knew, the distance she covered. She took him to the old train station and showed him the men and women and children selling food and clothes and junk by torchlight. She took him to the billboards on the edge of town and they stood in the cold and watched as people walked past, sixteen one night, twenty-five the next. Young, old, women, men.

'There's more than there was,' she told him.

She took him to Maisie's Café and let him buy her lunch and told him just to sit back and listen. 'It's where the old-timers come now,' she said. 'It's good here. The food's good. And you can just listen.'

And Robbie did and he realised he was hearing the voices from his childhood and youth, the accents thick and from the land, men and women talking about the farms they had left behind, the few chickens they now kept, when would the winter rain come and what if it didn't, again, the cost of petrol, the cost of gas, and coffee and beer, the school fair this coming weekend, the oval still too hard for football.

As Robbie listened he watched Clare slowly eat a meat pie with chips and peas and gravy, putting her knife and fork down carefully on the plate while she chewed each mouthful. He liked being with her, he thought. Her silence. The simplicity of her. The way she watched and watched and watched her small world. He noticed the cuffs of her shirt sleeves were frayed.

As they walked back to the House of Many Promises Robbie understood there were more stories than could possibly be told. There always had been, of course. But for too long now, people had been left out or forgotten. Things happened. Dreadful and cruel things. Things that could barely be imagined. They were each noted, briefly, but they had no meaning because they were given no context. A catastrophe was only a few words flickering quickly by on a screen.

I need to write about people again, Robbie thought. When did I stop doing that?

•

On the day before he was to fly to Sydney to talk to Jonathon, Robbie delivered firewood to a woman who lived in a small wooden shack on the edge of town.

'Last winter I'll be here,' she told him while he unloaded the wood from the back of Granna's ute. Two young children, barefoot despite the cold, and grubby, tried to help him stack the pieces. 'Have to move. They'll bulldoze this place. Shame really. Pretty quiet out this way. We've been happy here.'

She prattled on, twisting a strand of mousy hair around her finger, and when he was finished she offered him a cup of tea, but Robbie said he wanted to get back into town before it was completely dark.

He drove slowly on the back roads, careful of the kangaroos. When he turned right onto the main road, he didn't see the black car roar around the corner, swerve, right itself and swerve again, crashing into a truck travelling in the other direction, and then both turning, spinning and colliding with Robbie. There was a screeching thunder noise as the truck rolled, and the scream of metal on metal and glass smashing, loud enough to bring people tumbling out their front doors, torches in hands.

Robbie heard his own scream as the car spun, turned, and the front collapsed down. Then things seemed to be quiet and he understood that he was alive. Trapped somehow. His legs. Couldn't move. His shoulder.

People were opening the door. There were voices. Shouts. He vomited. There was a crushing pressure and a feeling that he was falling. Falling slowly. Falling towards a golden door. Falling. Falling.

•

Afterwards, Robbie tried to remember the sequence of things – where he was and when, the faces of the surgeons, the worst days and nights, the worst of the pain, when Granna came and went, what Ella had said, and when he began to believe he might learn to live again. He always gave up. He decided there was no point remembering. The memories came and went as they chose.

But one memory persisted, always. The falling, the slow falling, and the golden door. He wanted to open the door and he was coming closer and closer to it, or the door was coming to him. A simple door, wood perhaps, and a soft light behind. So easy to just gently push it open, go through and leave everything behind, the mess of it all, leave it far, far behind and sleep forever. But then the door would fade, fall away and disappear. Robbie's eyes opened. Not yet, he remembered thinking, or trying to think. No. I am not going there. Not yet.

Then there was light. And loud voices. Too loud. A siren far away. He smelt his own piss and shit, his own blood and bones. Always blood and bones. He was lying on cold ground. So cold.

'He's back,' a voice said.

'He's back. He's with us,' said another.

A man knelt beside him. Short black hair, black eyes. He wore a blue uniform.

'There was an accident,' the man said, very slowly and clearly. 'Do you remember? Quite a bad accident. You've done some damage to your legs. And you had a heart attack. But you're coming through, mate, you're coming through.' He raised his voice. 'Another round of morphine. And I want the oxygen here now. Now.'

He turned back to Robbie. Someone else, a woman, came to kneel at Robbie's other side. He saw a needle. She put something on his arm and reeled off numbers. Someone else was saying, 'Good, good, good.' Someone else was on a phone: 'Cardiac arrest. Stable. Left leg broken ankle, right leg multiple fractures, possible dislocation to hip. ETA two hours.'

The man in the blue uniform with the black eyes put a hand firmly on Robbie's shoulder. 'We're taking you to Melbourne. Nod if you understand.'

Robbie nodded.

'It's too windy to chopper you in. There's another ambulance on its way for you. How you feeling?'

Robbie rolled his eyes.

The man smiled. 'Glad to have you with us, mate. We know who you are. Someone's gone to tell your grandmother.'

'Water?' Robbie asked.

'Sorry, mate, not yet.'

Robbie thought he would die unless he had a mouthful of water. That was all he wanted. All there was. He closed his eyes. Water. Blood. Bones. A door. Then there were more people and Robbie was lifted onto a stretcher and slid into an ambulance and strapped in. Someone told him his phone and wallet were on the stretcher with him. There were too many people, Robbie thought. There was too much noise.

Another man in a blue uniform climbed into the ambulance and sat next to Robbie, slipping an oxygen mask onto him and attaching wires and cables to his wrists and chest. A steady beeping and blinking of lights began, steady like a heartbeat, like a living thing. Robbie closed his eyes. He saw the door, the door with the gently glowing golden light behind it. It is too late now, he thought. Too late. I let it go.

Through all the days and nights that followed, the weeks and months of agony, and then only hurt and, finally, healing, Robbie thought of the door. He would think of it for the rest of his life.

•

The paramedics took Robbie from the ambulance into emergency admissions. They found a place for his trolley down a corridor behind the admissions desk next to the toilets. People were crying. People were screaming. People sat or lay in silent shock. People were talking loudly on phones. 'He cut his fingers off, one by one,' Robbie heard. 'High as a kite. Said God made him do it.' Someone was singing loudly. Orderlies and nurses and doctors walked past and around the patients waiting for help, for treatment, and barked out instructions, but nothing happened or seemed to happen. There was the smell of accidents and death: blood and piss and vomit.

On a trolley on the other side of the corridor, an old, old man lay curled under a soiled sheet, bony shaking fingers picking at his lips, which were scabbed and bleeding. His eyes were huge and bright and vacant, and Robbie saw that he was crying, a river of tears down his bony face.

Robbie looked at the ceiling and closed his eyes. He opened them a long time later when he heard a voice saying his name.

'Roberto Adams?' A young orderly, dark circles under his eyes, was looking at his health insurance card. 'This is you?'

Robbie nodded.

'Date of birth?'

Robbie gave it, his voice a croak, and asked for water.

'Not my job. Not allowed. This is current? Paid up?' He held the card in front of Robbie's face.

Robbie nodded again.

'Man, aren't you the lucky one. You don't know how damn lucky. I've got to make some calls and I'll be back.'

Robbie was hurting now. His legs. His chest. Pain shooting and darting from one place to another. He gritted his teeth. He would die if he didn't have a glass of water.

The old man opposite was whimpering. 'I want to go home,' he called out. 'I want to go home.'

Robbie looked at him again. He wanted to tell him about the door. Just let go, he wanted to say.

'I want to go home, mister. Been here a whole week now. No one even helping me to the toilet.'

The orderly returned with two others. 'Lucky day, like I said. Taking you upstairs. A doctor's going to look at you.' He put the card back in Robbie's wallet. 'Take him up. Cardio. And orthopedics need to know.'

They negotiated Robbie's trolley through a maze of corridors, squeezing past people in queues and sitting on the floor. 'Four days,' a woman was shouting. 'Four fucking days.' There were a series of elevators, more corridors, then a merciful silence and dimmed lights.

•

Two people came towards him from the shadows, one tall and big, the other small and elegant, her eyes shining with an ancient grief.

'Robbie. Oh, Robbie, darling,' said his grandmother.

He began to cry then, quiet tears, exhausted and in such pain, confused and uncertain of what was to come.

'Clare drove me down. I'll be staying for the next little while. There's a hotel across the road. I'll be here while we get you fixed up.'

Doctors came, serious men and women with tired eyes. He was wheeled into a room and there were tests and scans and machines and screens and more oxygen and he was, finally, given water and more drugs. Two young nurses cut away his trousers and underpants, took the ring Ella had given him off his finger, and sponged him clean where they could. Someone else shaved his chest and groin and left leg and forearms.

There was a surgeon in an immaculate grey suit, white shirt and red tie, who looked him over for half a minute, looked at the bank of monitors for even less, and gave him a dazzling smile. 'Tomorrow, three o'clock,' he said.

Much later, two more surgeons, one in a medical gown smeared with blood, the other in a tracksuit, came and spent a slightly longer time looking at Robbie's legs and hip, touching him lightly, looking at X-rays. 'We'll talk to you in a few days,' one said and they left.

Two other doctors and a nurse set his left leg in plaster, and the cool dampness of it was almost pleasurable.

He was finally left alone to sleep and as he drifted away he thought that this whole thing was preposterous, ridiculous. A few hours ago he had been a man tossing logs onto a woodpile, a man driving a car, a man going back to his family home to eat a roast lamb dinner and enjoy a bottle of excellent red wine. How was he now here? How absurd. There had been a mistake, an outrageous mistake, and he would have to get it sorted in the morning.

•

The following day, Robbie had double-bypass heart surgery, and three days later his right leg was amputated at the knee and his right hip was replaced. To survive it all, to come out the other side, he decided to ignore everything that was happening. He ate when he was told to eat;

he swallowed the pills and medicines. He listened to what the doctors and surgeons said, he nodded, he told them he understood. He watched the nurses take blood samples over and over and over again and take his temperature and give him sponge baths. He smiled at them and nodded. He refused, for now, to look at his own battered body, the brown and black and purple bruises that seemed to be everywhere, his mangled legs and then his missing leg, the scar along his left arm where they took the veins for the bypass surgery. He blocked out the noises from the ward, the moans and groans and calls for help, the constant clatter of the nurses, the hum of the monitors, the rattle of the food trolleys, the physiotherapy class underway across the hall, white-faced, shuffling and shocked patients in baggy and slightly grimy pyjamas with their tubes and wires and portable monitors. He heard doctors talking by his bedside once or twice a day about which ward he should be in, the ward for his heart or the ward for his legs, about a slight infection and elevated blood pressure, about constipation, about rehabilitation. He heard coughs and snores from the person in the cubicle next to his, and muted conversations when there were visitors. He kept his eyes closed. He would live or he would die. Either way, this would pass. It had to.

The day of Robbie's surgery, less than twenty-four hours after the accident, his grandmother held his phone to his ear. There was Ella's voice.

'Roberto. Oh God. Sweetheart.' A half-laugh and a sob. 'I want to say God damn you, but you know I don't mean that. You know what I mean. I know you have a big operation today, a very big operation, but they do this all the time. They know what they are doing.' Another pause. A deep breath. 'I will be talking to Antonia every day. Okay? Do you understand? I am so sorry. I am so shocked. I don't understand . . .' Another sob, or a gasp. 'I just . . . Robbie, darling, I can't be there right now. There is just so much . . . You know how it is . . . I love you. I love you so much, Robbie. Goodbye for now. Just for now.'

He gave a weak thumbs-up sign to Granna to indicate that he had heard, and he carried Ella's voice and words with him through the doors of the operating theatre. I love you too. I love you. There is a golden door, Ella. A door somewhere. Let's open it together.

Every day there was a message from Ella. He was too tired, too drugged, too sore and sick to begin to hear or understand anything except her lovely voice saying over and over, 'I love you, Robbie. So much. I love you. Be strong. You are strong. You can move through this. You are doing so well.'

As the days passed, he could not believe how much worse he felt. Several times a day the cardio rehabilitation team made him breathe and cough and it felt like someone was splitting his chest open with a rusty axe.

'No, I can't,' he said. 'I can't.'

The nurse rolled his eyes. 'Couple of broken ribs from the CPR. Way it is. What I wouldn't give for the drugs you're on. You've got to breathe, man. Breathe. Deep breath.'

Robbie steadied himself. Breathe in. Breathe out.

'Now cough for me. Come on. Cough for me.'

Robbie let out a low scream. 'I fucking can't.'

'Whatever,' the nurse said.

And then there was the rehabilitation team for his legs.

'Little walk, Mr Adams,' the physiotherapist would begin.

'I don't think so.'

'Okay. Another day here for you. No skin off my nose.'

And Robbie would relent. This will pass, after all. Sit up. Agony. Legs over side of bed. Manageable. Not bad. Left leg down.

'It's healing well. It can support you. Trust it.'

Standing up, but shaky. Take the crutches. And the stump, what was left of his right leg, just hanging. Heavily bandaged.

'Take a step.'

One step.

'You're going to turn and walk to the end of the bed.'

Seven hobbled, shuffling steps in five minutes, propelled by the crutches. Robbie was pouring sweat.

'Now back.'

A muffled sob. Fuck this hurts.

'Well done. Looking good.'

As much as he possibly could, Robbie slept. He slept and slept and slept. His dreams were wild and extraordinary. He woke up reluctantly, not wanting them to end.

In one dream he sat on the floor with a dog by a blazing fire in the front room at the House of Many Promises. Cold rain pelted the windows and the wind gusted and receded and gusted again. The old windows rattled. The dog was handsome and big and clean, and its head rested heavily on Robbie's lap. Robbie's hand stroked the dog's head and he touched and gently squeezed the dog's ears, which were soft and lovely, like silk. In a low armchair pulled close to the fire, an old man talked, a black cat curled in his lap and a pot of tea and two cups on a low table next to him. Meaningless chatter about where the gold was hidden and the vegetables to be picked for market tomorrow.

But when Robbie looked up it wasn't an old man at all but a skeleton, rattling bones, talking still, jaw working and chattering, hands gesturing, new stories tumbling out and spinning around. Robbie saw the thousands and thousands of men swarming out over the low hills that surrounded, for miles and miles, the House of Many Promises, scurrying relentlessly like ants, looking for specks of gold and ferrying them back. Mud in winter. Dust in summer. 'Money,

money, money, money,' said the skeleton of Chen Ling, rocking back and forth, laughing, laughing.

Robbie smelled the gold and the mud and the smoke from small damp fires burning beside sagging tents. There he was with Ling, standing in a waterlogged laneway, drinking from a silver flask. Two women were walking slowly towards them, long skirts dragging through the mud. One woman was Bernadette, Ling's wife, small and red-haired. The other woman was dressed in a heavy old-fashioned blue taffeta dress drawn in at the waist, her hair in a bob. A small blue bird that matched her dress was fluttering above her left shoulder. She glared at Robbie and shook a finger at him. 'Fool,' she muttered. 'Fool of a man.' A narrow door opened in the rough stone wall behind her and there was Ella, in jeans and a white shirt, laughing. 'Why on earth are you out there, Roberto darling? Come inside. Come.'

And then it would be dawn and time for a blood test, or time for medicine. Or it was late afternoon and time for another blood test, time to swallow fourteen tablets, time for dinner. As soon as he could, he would go back to sleep.

Another dream. The poet man, in clean and crisp work clothes and gardening boots, came into Robbie's small cubicle, wheeling one of the hospital trolleys which was filled with the poet man's small vials. Robbie was waiting to sleep, lying on his back and he smiled when he saw the poet man and the poet man smiled back. They seemed to be friends.

The man sat on the bed, looking at Robbie, and shook his head. 'What do you want?' he asked.

'You know.'

The poet man spent a long time studying his vials. He sighed. He seemed to be thinking, brow furrowed. Then he took an empty vial, selected a full one and carefully tapped in a drop, then selected another full vial and added another drop. In the dream the process took forever, the poet man slow and steady, and Robbie content to watch. Finally the small vial was full and the poet man put a cork stopper in the top. He shook it, took out the stopper, sniffed, almost laughed, then seemed to think again. Another vial was selected, another drop added. Another shake. The poet man smelt again and smiled.

'Here,' he said.

Robbie took the vial and sniffed deeply. Ella, Ella, Ella. There she was. Dancing with him on the terrace of the villa, his lips pressed to her hair. Having a shower, the smell of soap and her shampoo. Leaning out the window of her small apartment, watching him come up the steep narrow street, waving when she sees he is looking at her. He lifts the bunch of flowers he is carrying – tulips, blue tulips that smell faintly of an early summer day and cool soil – and she laughs. And there she was again, eating curries with him in a small restaurant only a few blocks from his London apartment, talking intently, fork jabbing the air, drinking beer from the bottle, and the smell of cardamom and ginger and hot oil and grilled chicken.

'Try it another way,' the poet man said. 'Think of a colour.'

'I don't know. Blue.'

There was a vast, still blue sea. A naked Ella walked slowly into it and he could touch the salt and sun. There was Ella lying on her stomach on the pale blue sheets he had owned long ago, a younger Ella, breathing heavily, and he smelt her sweat. Ella picking a shirt from a rack, blue pinstripes, holding it against him, nodding, and he smelt laundry powder and crisp ironed cotton. On and on, over and over. Moments and memories on constant replay.

'More,' Robbie said, like a child. 'More.'

Finally the poet man snapped his fingers. 'Enough.' When Robbie opened his eyes there was no sign of the poet man, only a young dark Indian woman shaking him awake and telling him it was time for a blood test.

•

'You're sleeping a lot, I'm told,' the surgeon said during an unexpected visit one morning. 'That's one of the best things you can possibly do.'

'I'm having all these crazy dreams.'

'Oh, that's common enough. Good dreams or bad?'

'No, no, good. I *want* to go to sleep. It's better than being awake.'

'The intense dreams are something to do with the surgery and the drugs. It's well documented. But you're lucky. I've seen grown men screaming over the nightmares they've had.'

Robbie looked at him. The man was admiring his polished shoes and then, it seemed, his fingernails.

'Who knows?' he said, looking directly at Robbie. 'We pull open your chest, turn off your heart, use a machine to pump your blood around while I do what I do. Playing God. Perhaps it shifts things. Creates another little fault line somewhere, somehow.'

'Could be.' Robbie just wanted to go back to sleep. But it was nearly lunchtime. He tried to remember what he had ordered. Sandwiches? That was yesterday. Meatloaf? He remembered ticking meatloaf. Maybe that was for today. Meatloaf could be good, if there was real meat in it.

The doctor consulted his phone for a couple of minutes and scratched his chin. He looked back at Robbie. He was Middle Eastern, Robbie saw now. Clipped grey hair, dark eyes, thick eyebrows. Handsome. Strong.

'I know who you are, Mr Adams. I've even read some of your pieces. I like your articles on finance and currency in particular. Good analysis, clearly written. Tell me something: are you glad to be alive? Because, in the scheme of things, you really shouldn't be. Alive, that is.'

Robbie reached for the strap attached to the end of his bed to pull himself into an upright sitting position. The pain across his chest when he moved was extraordinary. He gasped and closed his eyes. He had forgotten what he was going to say.

'Of course I'm glad I'm still alive,' he eventually managed. 'Of course I am. And you've done a wonderful job. Your colleagues have done a wonderful job. I'm grateful.'

'Good. Gratitude is good. We like gratitude here.'

And I am glad, Robbie thought, when the surgeon had left. Of course I am. Aren't I?

twenty

Every day there was a message from Ella on his voicemail.

'You are doing well, Roberto. That is what they tell me. You are doing so well. So strong and so brave and I love you very much. So much. I am in . . . well, I am in Indonesia now, Refugee Station Three. I mean, that was always the plan and there just isn't . . . well, there are not the resources for me to . . . well, for me to not be here. But you are doing well, sweetheart. You really are.'

New message: 'I am going to come back to Australia to see you in a couple of months. Everyone says that is the best. There will be things I can do for you then. We can start to work some things out. Remember I love you. There are so many storms here. Remember that storm in Greece? We held so tight to each other all night long. I am still holding tight, Robbie, I really am.'

New message: 'I have been reading so much, Robbie. About the amputation and the heart surgery mainly. I know it is big, so big, but people get through this. I know we know this, but it is good to read and to understand there are so many people going through the same things. And, of course, there are so many things to start thinking about. I do love you.'

New message: 'I am confusing my times, Robbie. Every day. How is it that for so many years we have spent most of our time away from each other in different countries in different time zones and always managed to talk? I am so sorry. I am sorry. Anyway, I am calling to say I love you. You know that.'

New message: 'I heard something today you might want to know. Two thousand refugees were killed on the shooting range at the refugee station in Africa yesterday. Just a trial, they are saying. They have built a crematorium. For the bodies. There is some talk about adding a real hunting element so the guests can stalk the illegals through a jungle. Whatever. This upsets me so much. I hate it. You have to write about this, Robbie, please! You really do. When you are better. You are not dead yet . . . I am sorry. You know what I mean. I love you.'

New message: 'Also, why am I now the one who is saying always that I am sorry? Perhaps this makes you smile? I do miss you. Oh, and I am home by the way. For a few days. There is a conference – refugee transfer arrangements. Thomas sends his very best wishes. He says to get in touch at any time. The geranium is in bloom and looks beautiful. It is so hot here now.' There was a photograph of a rich red geranium against a blue sky.

In the hours that he was awake Robbie tried to call Ella. He didn't care what time it was wherever she was. The phone rang out again and again and again. Because his dreams mostly sustained him, he let things be. He knew he was furious and hurt but he had no energy to begin to understand how to deal with either emotion. The fury and the sorrow grew and rose like a wave and then crashed and ebbed away.

He composed a message for her. 'Ella,' he said to her voicemail, 'I am not angry. I'm too tired to be angry. Too sore. There are more important things for me right now, like getting better. And I am getting better. I will be better. Yes, of course I wish I could see you. I wish you were here. But I do know there is nothing you could be doing that would be useful. So I don't mind, really, that you are back home and back at work. I am just asking: can we talk, please? Please. I do need to understand what you are thinking and feeling. I need a conversation with you. I've been in an accident, Ella. That's all. You and I have seen and heard of far, far worse things. Our world hasn't ended. Something bad has happened, but in a few months' time it will be over. Let's talk about that time, Ella. Please. Let's talk and make plans and I will come to you when I am well again.'

He lowered himself onto the pillows, exhausted.

•

After the first fortnight, when it was clear that, bruised and bloody and broken as he was, Robbie would pull through, Granna asked him what he needed from home.

He tried to think. 'My computer,' he said after a while. 'The small one.' He tried to think some more and began to fall asleep again.

'Robbie. Wake up. Talk to me.'

He stared at the television on the wall opposite his bed. That reality refugee show was on. Who had put that on? Women were in some sort of a swimming race. Why?

'And a charger. For the computer. And there's a computer case. A brown one. Leather. There'll be a book in the side pocket. It should be under the desk. Bring that.'

'I'll sort out some clothes for you,' Granna said. 'You'll need track-suits, things like that. For a little while.'

'And can you choose a couple of books, any books, off the main shelves in the front room?'

His grandmother smiled. 'Remember when you counted those books that winter it rained every day for two months? You were so determined.'

'I remember. More than eleven thousand books,' Robbie said. 'And you told me there were more books in boxes in the attic.'

'You asked me if we had all the books in the world.' They were quiet for a few moments and then Granna stood up. 'I'll be back the day after tomorrow, latest. I'll bring some food too.'

He smiled at her. 'That would be good.' He knew how much weight he had lost. She was almost out the door when he asked, 'How often do you speak to Ella?'

Granna turned. 'She calls me. Often. She is very upset, Robbie.'

He said nothing.

'People cope in different ways when something like this happens. Or don't cope. She needs some time, that's all. Let her be.'

She turned to go again.

'Granna.'

'Yes, Robbie?'

'Thank you. I know you've been here every day. Thank you.'

'I love you.'

'I know. I love you too.'

'And I know that. Now rest for me, my boy.'

'And thank Clare too. I'm grateful. I know she's been here, and I know she's made it possible for you to be here.'

•

Occasionally Robbie turned on the television. The tennis was on in London. For a few years he had gone to the tournament, until it was stopped because of the heat and then delays in building the new indoor courts. He managed now to stay awake for some of the matches. He also watched a documentary about changes to migration patterns across the Atlantic by birds and fish, but he couldn't follow what was being said or what the point was. He tried to find the weather channel so he could track the weather in London and Switzerland, but it was too much effort.

He regularly came across *Race For Home* and he watched it once, for a few minutes. The boats seemed to be gathered at some sort of marshalling station and the cameras were panning across the players. Old men and women, children, women with babies. Indian-looking, mostly. A few north Africans. One boat, the blue boat, with a mix of blacks and white, mostly overweight westerners. Robbie turned the volume up: they were participants from a US prison's death row. Everyone seemed to be waiting for something. Then two helicopters came into view. They swooped low, between the boats, and churned up the water. They were dropping parcels, Robbie saw, in different colours to match the boats and teams. He turned the volume down.

When the helicopters left, there was a gunshot and the boats began to scramble to retrieve their parcels, rowing this way and that. It would be easier, Robbie thought, to swim to the parcels, but then he saw the sharks' fins.

A helicopter returned and dumped large plastic bins clearly filled with blood and bits of flesh and bone, and then, through the door of the helicopter, two or three men seemed to be dragging and pushing something.

Robbie leaned in. My God, he thought. A calf fell into the sea. Then another. The animals fell clumsily and the cameras caught the frozen terror in their eyes, their bawling, the twitches and jerks of their thin legs. The sharks, already frenzied by the blood, went crazy, circling and darting and leaping through the water. One hurled itself against a boat with the rear leg of a calf in its jaws. And the people on the boats clung on and screamed as the water turned a frothy red and heaved and churned.

The screen froze. *Race For Home. Season Four. Starting NOW.*

Robbie turned the TV off. The person in the next cubicle began coughing – deep, wheezing, laboured, gasping coughs. Robbie went to sleep and in his dreams the poet man came visiting.

•

The day before he moved to the rehabilitation centre, Clare arrived with a small suitcase. It had an old-fashioned plastic name tag attached to the handle and Robbie could see Granna had written his name on it in spindly letters. He had a sudden memory of wandering off to school, lunch and computer in his backpack which also had a name tag on it, the letters stronger then and bolder.

'Clothes,' Clare said. 'Your grandmother chose them. All new stuff.'

Robbie looked at her and smiled. 'Thank you.'

She stood tall and straight, like a rock. I could lean against you, he thought. Any man could. But he had also seen her smile like a child when Granna praised something she did, or when she was doing something she clearly enjoyed, like baking a cake. And he had seen her flinch, almost cower, if she thought she had made a mistake or was confused, again like a child, a child expecting punishment. He suspected she would lash out if she felt cornered.

'And how is my grandmother?'

'She's alright. She said to say sorry she couldn't come today. Busy with something. She'll come to the rehab place when you've settled in.'

'How was the drive down?'

'Long. Roads are a mess. Big queues at the checkpoints.'

'You can make yourself a cup of tea in the kitchen if you want,' Robbie said. 'That's what visitors do.'

Clare shook her head slowly, as if weighing up whether going to make a cup of tea and possibly being required to talk to another patient

or a nurse was worth it or not. 'Should head back. Got some things
to do for your grandmother.'

'You still like working for her?'

'Yes. Of course.'

There was a very small cupboard in one corner of the room, and
Clare put the suitcase in it.

'You want anything else?' she asked.

'What's the weather like out there?'

'Really cold. Going to rain again tonight, they reckon. People
around town are pretty happy. Water tanks filling up.'

She ran her hands up and down the railings at the end of his bed.
The person in the cubicle next to Robbie began coughing. Again.

'Noisy here, isn't it?'

'Do you like coming into the city?' he asked.

Clare considered this carefully. 'No.'

'Why's that?'

More thought. 'Too big now. Too many buildings. No light gets
in. Can't see around the corners.'

'A bit like life then,' Robbie said.

She smiled slowly. 'Well, yeah. There's no seeing around corners
most of the time, that's for sure.'

She was attractive when she smiled, Robbie thought. Like a big
flower opening. The small lines around her eyes and lips crinkled.
He wondered what would make her laugh, and suspected she hadn't
laughed a great deal during her life.

'Oh,' she said. 'I almost forgot. Two things.'

She picked up her backpack from the floor. He saw that it was
frayed at the corners and along the straps, and noticed now that the
shirt she was wearing had a button missing.

She was rummaging in the pack and produced a small heavy block
wrapped in foil. 'From your grandmother. Her fruit cake.'

'Of course.'

'And this came. Only yesterday. From Ella.' She handed the small parcel to him warily.

'Thank you.' He didn't open it.

'Well, then,' Clare said. 'I'll be off.'

He watched her leave and then looked down at the parcel. Couriered from Ella's address in Geneva. He opened the plastic wrapping. There was a small box inside. Her fingers touched this box, he thought. Just a few days ago. He held it in his hands for a few minutes before opening it.

Inside was the evil-eye amulet he had given her in Greece. And a note. *Darling man. One day you'll bring this back to me.* That was all.

He smelled the piece of paper. Nothing. Just paper. He ran a finger over the letters. Then he cried.

He was wiping the tears away with his forearm when he noticed a woman standing at the end of the bed, watching him.

'Yes?'

'I'm Dr Vaanavaraayer.' She smiled.

'Yes?'

'The amputation. I was one of the doctors. I'm here to do a final check so we can release you into rehab. Someone else will be by to get you measured for a prosthetic.'

Robbie watched the curtain that divided his cubicle from the next while she undid the bandages. Her fingers felt cool on his leg.

'Hurting?' she asked.

'A little.'

'It's healing well. Very well.'

A nurse wheeled in a trolley with fresh bandaging and towels and lotions.

'I'll leave you then,' Dr Vaanavaraayer said. 'And it will be off to rehab for you tomorrow morning.'

There was coughing again from the cubicle next door. Gasping coughs. Then a gurgling and choking. The doctor paused. She strode over and drew the curtain. 'Oh dear,' she said.

The nurse who was gently smearing a lotion over Robbie's knee and the stump where his leg now ended went to join the doctor. Robbie heard the ghastly wheezing and coughing again. 'Please help . . .' said a frail voice. More coughing and gasping.

One of the ward doctors came into the room. 'Oh, her,' he said. 'Nothing we can do. She's just dying.'

Robbie stared at the ceiling. Ignore this, he thought. Ignore it.

'I am thinking some oxygen,' he heard Dr Vaanavaraayer say quietly. 'And some—'

'No way,' the ward doctor said. 'She's taking forever to die as it is. I've got a quota to meet. And I need beds.'

'For God's sake,' Robbie said loudly. He glared at the doctor, who turned and winked at him.

The wheezing and choking continued but softer, ever softer. A final burst of coughing, then laboured breaths, each inhale and exhale too long and slow and rasping, and then becoming softer and more brittle. Robbie closed his eyes.

The nurse returned and resumed work on his leg. No, Robbie thought. It's not a leg any more. It's a stump. Get used to it.

'Excellent. She's gone,' the ward doctor said. Then into his earpiece, 'Trolley to 28B. For the basement.'

Robbie watched them wheel the body past his bed and out into the hallway. It was a tiny old woman, grey hair thin and shiny like cobwebs. She was wearing a grimy grey-white dressing-gown. For a moment she seemed absurdly familiar and he shivered.

It wasn't until after the nurse had left that Robbie realised he couldn't find the amulet. He knew he had been holding it when the doctor arrived but it must have slipped out of his hand somehow. He searched the bed as best he could, but his chest was too sore and he couldn't reach the corners and lower half. He pressed the emergency button. A nurse came in.

'I've lost something,' he said. 'I need help. Please. It's just a small thing. Round. Blue mainly.' He was almost sobbing.

'You need to calm down,' the nurse said. 'Just breathe. This won't be doing you any good.'

She rang for some colleagues and a wheelchair, which they lifted him into while he moaned from the pain in his chest. He was sweating and his hands were shaking. Rationally, he knew they would find the amulet. Of course they would. His whole world was no bigger than a narrow bed. And when they did, everything would be fine. But in his panic, amplified perhaps by the shock of the strange old woman with the cobweb hair, he felt only that disaster was imminent, that there could never be a happy ending. If he didn't have the amulet, he didn't have anything, and most of all he didn't have Ella.

'This it?' One of the nurses held out the amulet to him.

'Oh my goodness, that's beautiful,' another said.

'Is that a sapphire?' asked another.

'Thank you, thank you,' Robbie said. He closed both hands around the amulet and put them in his lap.

'We might as well make the bed up fresh for you now,' the first nurse said.

She fetched him a glass of water and made him drink it, and kept up an aimless chatter while she made the bed, something about the bar she'd be going to after work with her boyfriend where you got three cocktails for the price of one for thirty minutes from seven o'clock, and how her boyfriend was a builder who was working seven days a week because there was so much construction going on with the new apartments for all the people moving into the city, so a Friday night never felt like a Friday night any more, the way it used to, and it was great Robbie was moving to rehab where there would be better food, a nicer room.

As soon as they lifted him back into the bed Robbie fell asleep, hands clasped tightly around the amulet. He dreamed he was riding Timmy, and Timmy was cantering slowly across rolling green hills, ears high and alert, Robbie's hands buried in his thick mane.

twenty-one

I keep Antonia and Clare company through these days. It is the least I can do. What has happened to Robbie reminds me again that there is a great deal to be said for being dead. Just go through that door. Step across the threshold. Let it all go. Let it go now.

The grief my seven-times-great-granddaughter has known. Ridiculous. Daniel. And then a sister. Her daughter, Robbie's mother, killed on that very same road where Robbie had his accident. Not the same spot but near enough, and the town knowing it and talking about it. Grief holds Antonia together. The memories. The need to find a way through, to keep going. Grief and love. That is all there is.

'No, Ella, I don't understand,' she is saying into the phone, foot tapping impatiently. 'No. I do not have to see it from your point of view. For heaven's sake, this is about Roberto. It's not about you.'

And a few days later: 'No, actually, we haven't bothered asking yet when he can get on a plane. Let's see, Ella. Six weeks at least in rehabilitation, then home to here and more rehabilitation. We need to get through all this first . . . At the very least, just talk to him. Please . . . It will help him . . . I don't see that being angry is of any use . . .

239

Well, Ella, sometimes the things we think will never break, that aren't supposed to break, just do and yes, it's too much but it is what it is . . .'

I watch her do what she has always done: work. And then work some more. Back straight. Eyes bright. Meals and money for those who need it. Advice for the walking men and women. Plans for Robbie. One foot in front of the other.

Clare understands this. It is also what she has always done. One hundred and fifty-eight thousand four hundred steps from this big old kitchen down the winter roads to the teeming city and the building where Robbie lies sleeping, an amulet and a little note from Ella in his hands.

Sometimes, late at night, when she is sure that Clare is in her own room, Antonia calls her sister who lives in a small green cottage only some people can find in an empty closed-down Lilac Town. On some nights there is no connection but often she gets through and they can talk of the walking men and women and falling bones and shared memories of how things once were before the unravelling began.

And that is the thing. It is hard to close things down. They have always tried, in different ways and using different means. Tried to close down a voice, a movement, a town, a country. But people find ways. They always have. Ghosts find ways too. They even find ways together.

twenty-two

Clare loved living at the House of Many Promises. She loved that she felt useful. That she could have a hot shower every day. She loved the bed in the big airy room, and the bedside table that had a lamp on it. She loved switching on the split system and feeling the room cool down or warm up in minutes. She loved the table and two chairs Granna had given her from an upstairs room in the main house.

'That's not a table,' Granna had said when she saw Clare unload the folding card table and plastic chairs from her car. 'There's a table upstairs somewhere. Pine. Round. It should look quite nice. Take that.'

The kitchen was small but she could make a simple meal there – sausages and eggs, a fried sandwich – and she could eat whatever she wanted in the big kitchen. She would sit at her table at night and move her hands across the surface, a surface that was smooth and clean and that reflected the light, while she watched television. And then she would turn off the television and listen to the silence, to the windows that didn't rattle, the roof that didn't shake.

During the first few weeks, anxious that Granna would change her mind, guilty that, somehow, she had a room at the finest house

in town while others added their names to waiting lists for tents and
caravans or a camp bed in one of the churches, she asked Granna over
and over what else she could be doing to help.

'I'm a good cleaner,' she said.

'Other people come in for that,' Granna said. 'Just help keep the
kitchen clean after cooking.'

'I can rake leaves. Weed.'

'Well, if you want to. But people come in to do that too, when
they remember or when they need the money. Really, I've been paying
people to do these things for years. They'll get very upset if I stop
now. And I'm not actually paying you anything. So, please, shopping,
cooking, helping me with deliveries – that's quite enough. And that's
what I need.'

Sometimes, when Granna went out, Clare would stop what she was
doing in the kitchen and wander through the house. Twelve rooms
downstairs, and a small upstairs wing of four rooms and another bathroom. Three or four of the rooms downstairs seemed to be Granna's
private rooms: a bedroom, study, dressing room, bathroom. Clare stood
in one of the doorways and looked through. It was another beautiful
space, open and light, long sheer curtains at the windows. She was
too nervous to go in.

There were three other bedrooms and two more bathrooms. All
quite ordinary. Tasteful. Very nice, but nothing that screamed money,
Clare thought. Old-fashioned heavy wood furniture. Wooden bookcases in every room, full of books. And then there were the beautiful
front rooms: two huge lounge rooms, one with sofas and stools and
small tables and sideboards that Granna set vases of cut flowers on,
no matter the weather or the season, and mirrors that threw light,
rich cream walls and curtains, and the other more like a library, or
what Clare imagined a library to be, with shelves on every wall from
floor to ceiling and two wooden ladders on hinges, four reading chairs

upholstered in green leather, and floor lamps; and the dining room, with its wooden table and twenty chairs and more bookcases. There was a reception hall as well, with a bench for coats and one wall covered in photographs, mostly black and white and, Clare saw, very, very old. She walked through these spaces almost holding her breath in case it disturbed the beauty and the elegance, too nervous to touch anything.

After her initial visits, as she took in more details, she noticed each room had small cameras blinking from the high cornices. Granna hadn't mentioned a security system. It certainly wasn't connected at the kitchen door. Oh well, she thought, I am just looking. I could look forever.

As the weeks stretched to months, she grew bolder. She sat on one of the green reading chairs. She smelled some orange and yellow roses in a vase. She looked more closely at the books on the shelves and the photographs in the hallway. There were several of a tall lean Chinese man with a thin moustache, standing on the wide granite steps that led up to the front porch and double doors, and standing by a horse and carriage at the foot of the steps. He was frowning. In another photograph he was standing outside the entrance to a shop, apparently a fruit and vegetable shop, his hands on his hips. Another photograph was of a woman Clare was sure was the woman at the Lilac Town house, young, actually quite beautiful, but with the same hair and hairstyle, the same eyes, the same tilt of the head. But the photograph looked to be a hundred years old at least, Clare thought, so she must be wrong.

She stopped to look at a photograph of a woman who was so beautiful she gasped. It was one of the few photographs that was in colour. The woman was standing on a low cliff with the bluest sea and sky behind her, wearing a white swimming costume with a white sarong tied loosely at her waist, and dark sunglasses. The sea and sky joined seamlessly behind her, becoming one. The woman was smiling and waving at whoever was taking the photograph. The blue of the sea and sky made Clare think the photograph had been taken in Europe, somewhere like Italy or Greece, a long time ago.

There were also lots of photographs of cats. Black cats with golden eyes and green eyes. Clare began to count them. They couldn't all be Fravershi, clearly. The photographs spanned at least two hundred years. But the more closely she looked at the photographs the more she spotted a small black cat somewhere, winding around someone's foot, sitting in an empty chair, walking along the back of a sofa, in the distance in the garden.

Clare thought about the photographs when she was alone in her room at night. About who was who, about Granna's family, about her life, and all the stories the House of Many Promises could tell. Sometimes she added a few lines to her notebook, or sketched a cat or a vase of flowers, or started a list of things to do the following day, or took the walking man's bone-knife down from the shelf and held it, but mostly she just sat. One night she wrote *I am happy* and looked at the words for a long time.

She grew used to the people who came and went from the great house, from the cleaners and gardeners and builders who would make themselves a cup of tea or coffee in the kitchen and look through the huge and always full biscuit tin Granna kept on the table, to the shadows in the night who stood in the kitchen and took the small food parcels Granna offered, listened to instructions about roads and Lilac Town and where they could find water, and then slipped away.

'If you see or learn anything you think others should know, be sure you ask for a message to be sent back from Lilac Town,' Granna would say. 'And there is a communications line all the way north. Use it when you have to and when something will help others.' And then she might laugh as Fravershi jumped onto the kitchen table and looked up at the visitors expectantly. 'I do believe Fravershi plans to see you to the edge of town. Or beyond.'

Granna said very little to Clare about her role in helping the walking people. Clare felt Granna hid nothing in particular from her, but neither did she explain or elaborate. Clare tried to understand whether she was bothered by this. She suspected not. She had been given enough. There were already so many new things to think about. More things to think about, in fact, than she could have ever known.

•

Clare was surprised by what she thought of as Granna's resilience after Robbie's accident. Apart from the first two weeks, when she was waiting for Robbie to be moved out of intensive care and given the all clear, she mostly maintained her schedule in Myamba: the cooking and deliveries and trying to solve problems for people she barely knew or didn't know at all. She was grateful that Clare could drive her to and from the hospital – 'That is something I really am too old to do,' she said – and could deliver things to Robbie. The books he asked for. The little parcel that arrived from Ella.

On the day that Robbie was taken to the rehabilitation unit, Granna asked Clare to walk with her to the Stables.

Granna unlocked the door and looked around. 'We'll need to fix this up for him. That staircase will be impossible. The bedroom will need to be down here. And a better bathroom. I don't know . . . it's very small. But I do want him to have his own place.' She walked outside and pointed to the side of the building. 'I suppose they could extend out a little here. Anyway, could you pack up their things? You'll find suitcases somewhere. Just put them in the garage when you're done. Or anywhere.'

On the way back to the house, Granna made a call. 'Hello, Chad. I have a building project . . . Well, no, I can't wait three years. Six

weeks . . . Good to hear someone your age can still laugh like that . . .
Chad, all this time and I've never called in the favour and I don't like
doing it now. But it's the way it is . . . it's for my boy . . . Thank you.
He's pulling through. Doing well. But he's lost a leg, and he's going
to have to live with a bad hip. I just want his rooms reconfigured . . .
Five o'clock? Thank you.' Granna snapped off her phone and turned to
Clare. 'Well, I can't fix Robbie. Or Ella. Or the two of them together.
But let's fix what we can.'

•

Because she was not paying any rent – every time she remembered
this, Clare felt the tears begin – and because many of her meals were
from food she cooked at the House of Many Promises, Clare had more
money than she'd had in years. She rarely touched any of her Under-
Employment Assistance Allowance and she still collected her Food
Essentials Pack because cancelling it might have drawn attention to
herself but now she often just left it down at the station for someone
who needed it. She still kept her money in the old biscuit tin and
often spread it over the table and counted it.

After some consideration, Clare decided to buy herself some clothes,
and worked out this would be first time in fourteen years that she
had bought anything new. Completely new. Not previously worn by
someone else and then discarded. New! She had also noticed Robbie
watching her when they talked, with that calm and patient gaze he had,
and she was very aware that her trousers were grubby and worn and
the cuffs of her shirts were frayed, and some had a button missing or a
stain that wouldn't wash out. She didn't want him to ever mention to
his grandmother that she seemed scruffy or – what was the word her
mother had liked to use? – unkempt. Clare did not want to be unkempt.

The shop she went to in Myamba wasn't fancy. The clothes were
cheap, practical, sturdy and mostly dull, and Clare couldn't have cared

less. Best of all, they had a large section called For Bigger Women. She spent three hours trying things on and deciding. A pair of jeans, baggy, with an elastic waist. Comfortable. They looked nice, she thought. She'd have to let down the hems a little, but that was easy. She decided to get two pairs. It felt a little greedy but it meant she could always have a clean pair of nice trousers ready to wear.

Then she chose two shirts. One was white with blue flowers on it and lace on the cuffs. Pretty, she thought. The other shirt was from the men's department, an extra-large checked flannelette. It felt warm and soft.

Finally, a jumper. She wanted a winter jumper with no holes in it. In the end she chose a dark blue turtleneck, thick and floppy. She worried that it made her breasts look too big, but anything else felt too tight. When she took the jumper off she stood and looked at herself in the mirror. Her bra strap was grey and fraying. Her underpants were sagging and had worn patches. Well, they could be the next things to buy. Perhaps in the spring. If she was still at the House of Many Promises. If nothing had gone wrong.

And yes, her breasts were big. So were her stomach and her hips. And her legs were thick but they were long. Her skin was pale. Some stretch marks. Some veins. Some folds and sags. But wasn't this what most middle-aged women looked like? Was she really fat and ugly? She didn't know.

Anyway, I am what I am, she thought, as she put her old shirt back on and gathered up the clothes she would buy. I am what I am. She checked again that she had done the sums correctly and counted out the notes from the money in her pocket.

The sales assistant looked startled to receive real money, as if she didn't know what to do with it, and she counted it out twice before folding up the clothes and packing them in the bags Clare handed over. Two bags of new clothes, Clare thought, walking down the street.

Five things. Isn't that something. She walked to her car, which she'd had to park over five blocks away. Then, on a whim, she turned back and went into the hairdresser's.

'Shampoo and cut, please,' she said. 'Not too short.'

While a young man cut her hair, she worked her way back through the years again. Twenty years since I've done this, she thought. Been cutting my own hair for twenty years.

The next day she wore the new flannelette shirt, and blow-dried her hair with a dryer she had found in one of the spare bathrooms in the main house.

Granna was sitting in front of a computer at the kitchen table when Clare went in to work. She looked up and nodded, then looked up again.

'My goodness, dear. You look nice. Very nice.'

Clare smiled.

•

Two weeks after Robbie went to rehab there was a knock at her door one evening. Clare opened it to find Granna standing there, a plate of food in one hand and a glass of wine in the other.

'I thought you might like this,' she said. 'Roast lamb. I've got a friend coming for dinner and I've cooked far too much. As usual.' She followed Clare into the room and put the plate on the bench. 'This is looking nice. Good to see it being lived in again.'

Clare nodded.

'Anyway, I have something to show you.' Granna scrolled through her phone and gave it to Clare. 'Look.'

It was a photo of a man grinning. He was tanned and lean, shirt unbuttoned, standing somewhere that looked very flat, very hot, bright red, red earth and rocks against a blue sky. Next to him was a small table and a portable barbecue. She could see cans of soft drink and a

loaf of bread and a bottle of tomato sauce. Under the table there was
a tangle of stuffed toys. A giraffe. A koala. An old-fashioned teddy
bear. Something that could have been a wombat. In the distance
there seemed to be one or two other men, one particularly tall with a
beard, but the details were blurred. Clare wasn't sure what she should
be seeing so she looked more closely.

'Phil!' she exclaimed. 'And that man, the tall man, he could be the
walking man I met, the first walking man.'

'Phil's doing well,' Granna said. 'Struggled the first few weeks, but
Marie got him sorted. New man now.'

Clare could see from the photograph that Phil's eyes were clear
and he had put on a little weight. His hair was bleached almost white
but it was thicker and cleaner. His smile was cheeky and real, like
his old smile.

'Phil,' she said again.

'It's been a bit over six months, hasn't it?'

Clare nodded.

'I can get a message to him.'

Clare thought for a few minutes. 'No,' she said slowly. 'Thanks.
Not yet. But I'm glad he's doing well.' She thought for a moment and
asked, 'Where is he?'

It was Granna's turn to shake her head. 'Not saying. Not for any
real reason. It just always feels safer this way.'

When Granna had left, Clare removed the foil from the plate and
carried it to the table. She couldn't remember when she had last eaten
a meal like this. When she was young, probably, and she and Phil
sometimes went to a restaurant.

She sipped the wine and enjoyed it. It was rich and soft and she
saw that it perfectly matched, or complemented, the meat and the
light gravy flecked with herbs. She ate slowly and carefully and then

she used a finger to wipe the last of the gravy from the plate. While she ate she thought about Phil.

•

Clare drove Granna once to the rehabilitation centre to visit Robbie, but it was nearly five hours there and five hours back, and even Clare, who loved driving, especially one of Granna's nearly new cars, became more and more anxious. The highway and city roads were shocking. Detours around sinkholes, recklessly driven oversized trucks, stray dogs, traffic lights out of order.

Robbie looked surprisingly well. While he and Granna talked in an overcrowded living and dining area, Clare wandered around the facility. She glanced in rooms and through windows that looked out on small, bare gardens, she read the notices and rosters pinned to a wall near the entrance doors, she made herself a cup of tea in what seemed to be a communal kitchen. It was all quite pleasant, she thought, apart from the number of people with no arms or legs or both, and people who'd had a stroke or just sat, motionless, in wheelchairs. She sat near the kitchen for a while and watched a young girl at a nearby table work busily on a drawing, using short thick crayons. She had golden curly hair. Pretty girl, Clare thought.

When she went back to where Granna and Robbie were sitting. Robbie seemed angry – it would be about Ella, Clare thought – and Granna was leaning forward, shaking her head and patting his arm. Clare decided to wait in the car.

Finally, Granna climbed slowly in, next to Clare. She was pale and her lips were thin and tight. Clare drove away slowly.

'I think we need to eat,' Granna said after half an hour or so. 'If you take the next right, there used to be a shopping complex in there somewhere. Goodness, these buildings are ludicrous.'

It took Clare another half an hour to cut across the highway and turn down a side street. It took them to a walled-off range of high-rise towers, Jasmine Village, that seemed to cover several large blocks.

'I must have made a mistake. I'm so sorry,' Granna said. 'Let's just go home. I don't recognise anything. There used to be some wonderful restaurants around here. We'd drive down just to eat and then walk on the beach.'

Clare found her way back to the highway. Just before they left the outskirts of the city, she pulled in to get petrol. While she paid, she got a coffee each, a packet of potato crisps and a small bar of chocolate.

'I'll give you some money,' Granna said.

'No,' Clare said proudly. 'My treat.'

Granna ate the chips and the chocolate. 'That's better,' she said. She was quiet for the remainder of the long drive home but as they reached the House of Many Promises, she spoke again. 'I am trying to understand. I really am. But I don't. I want to slap her. As hard as I possibly can. There. I've said it.'

Clare helped her out of the car and into the kitchen. The night was bitterly cold and she built up the fire, then carried more wood in from the garage. She warmed up some soup, cut a piece of bread and some slices of cheese, and set the food in front of Granna, who was looking at the fire.

'Thank you,' she said. She cleared her throat. 'I'm glad you're here, you know.'

Clare ran the tip of her boot over a floorboard. She looked at Granna before she turned to leave the kitchen and she saw an old, old woman, tired, frail, bowed down, a tremble in the hand that picked at the bread, a tremble in her pale lips, eyes sad and looking far, far away. It was all wrong, Clare thought, whatever was happening with Robbie and Ella. The accident was wrong, and Ella's reaction was wrong. It was all wrong and sad. She thought she'd like to slap them both, too.

And yet she liked Robbie. He was polite and had looked her in the eye when he talked to her, not just at her breasts. He had shaken her hand when they first met. There had been something very sad and knowing in his pale blue eyes, a haunting, and now this – a leg gone and a heart broken in so many ways. Did bad things always happen to good people? Or did people always deserve what happened?

She climbed the stairs, turned on the heat, and sat in bed with her notebook. *Robbie*, she wrote. Then, *Phil*. Then a question mark.

In the morning Clare looked out the window. She gasped and then laughed. Snow had fallen overnight. She walked carefully down the stairs in her dressing-gown and slippers and scooped up a handful. It was cold and crunchy. She laughed again. She had never seen snow before. It was beautiful. She spent the morning watching it melt away.

twenty-three

R obbie would never, ever tell anyone but he loved rehabilitation. He tried to work out why. It was something to do with the complete lack of responsibility to do anything except get well and to make full use of all the resources available to help him do that. There were the simple healthy meals, a decent enough room of his own thanks to his insurance, massages, hours and hours of sleep, and a hundred stories around him to listen to, to watch. There was also the relief and the thankfulness that the pain really did begin to ease and fade. Not completely, not yet. But in his fourth week he could lie on his side to sleep. And a week or so later, he suddenly felt comfortable on the crutches, able to walk swiftly and turn. The posture still hurt his chest but it was manageable. The prosthetic leg arrived and, yes, it was difficult and strange at first, but he grasped immediately that it would work, that of course many people walked on prosthetics, travelled the world wearing them, played sport wearing them.

When he entered rehabilitation, Robbie was taking nearly twenty pills a day. By the sixth week, he was down to eight. He began to work out with weights in his own time, and asked to be taken to extra swimming sessions. He walked in the small gardens, despite the cold. Apart from the scars and aches and the side effects of some of the drugs, he was beginning to feel, strangely, very well.

And then there was Ella. He'd realised in his first few days at the centre that however much he missed her, however much he longed for her, however much he wanted to wind back time, he couldn't cope with daring to hope or believe that tomorrow might be the day she decided to speak to him, or the day after, or that she might appear at the door to his room, crying and saying sorry.

She continued to leave messages for him. He was still far too tired to stay up at night waiting for her calls – and anyway, if he answered, she would hang up – but the first thing he did each morning was to check whether there was a message. They were mostly simple. Work. Where she was. The heatwave across Europe. Hello from Thomas. Tears sometimes. She always told him she loved him. That was something, he thought.

On his ninth day at the centre he called her, now at a point where he felt it might be possible for them to talk again, to get this strange, immovable hurdle between them dismantled somehow. He timed the call for when she was at work. She never, ever answered her phone when she was at work. When her voicemail kicked in, he spoke as gently as he could.

'Hello, Ella. How are you, sweetheart? So, they've moved me to rehab. It's not so bad here. Much better than the hospital. I'm doing all these exercise classes and programs and I'm not taking nearly so many drugs. I'm still sore but I'm okay, you know. I've been thinking – we're obviously each in a tough place. I know you're in shock, I know this isn't what we planned, but trust me, I feel the same, twice over. So I'm thinking, I'm here for the next eight weeks or so and then I'm going home to Granna's for a bit. Let's talk then. Okay? I'll know exactly how I am, what the outlook is, any issues. And for now I can concentrate on getting better, on healing. I just need one thing to focus on – it's all I can deal with. And you don't have to worry about calling me, about what to say in a message. Just try and look after you, try and figure out what's going on for you. Okay? I don't know what else to do, Ella, I don't. I just want to be well. I want to be glad I'm alive. And I want us to talk on the first day of September. That's the first day of spring here – when things start over, when new life begins. Can you promise me we'll talk then? Please? I love you. Let me know, and then no more messages. They don't mean much any more. I love you.' He hung up.

When he woke in the morning there was a text message on his phone. *September 1, I promise. Thank you for having a plan. You always do. I love you too. Good luck. Heal well.*

The first of September. Fifty-six sleeps.

•

He paid extra to stay on at the centre for a final fortnight. He wanted to use the equipment for as long as possible. He knew he was eating well, and was allowed to have a glass of wine at night. He was sleeping too, often still with the help of tablets, but he was sleeping. And walking well on his prosthetic. Slowly and with an awkward limp, but walking. He had overcome his revulsion at this leg. It was what it was. Half a leg. That was all. He had learnt to clean it, strap it, rest it when he was tired or it hurt. He understood that he was beginning to compensate for his injuries and broken bits in other ways, slowly, day by day, building up strength across his chest, in his arms, across his stomach. He could look at himself in a mirror again, scars and all.

He called his grandmother regularly and heard the relief and happiness in her voice at his recovery. During one call he asked if there was still a gym in town and she told him there were three. When he hung up, she called Chad. 'A small gym. Weights mainly, I think . . . I don't know. Just fit a space in.'

He spoke to Jonathon. He played chess online with Thomas. He spoke to a friend in London and arranged for his rooms in Chelsea to be aired and cleaned monthly. He paid the rent through to the end of the year so he wouldn't have to think about it. He didn't know any more where home might be. Would be.

One night he was watching TV and his phone rang. It was Thomas.

'Is everything okay? Is Ella okay?' he asked.

'Hello, Roberto. Yes, yes. She has not been home all week, but she said she would be travelling. It is so hot here. I would leave if I could. In fact, this is why I am calling you. Would you like a visitor?'

Robbie laughed. 'Thomas! You have never left Switzerland.'

'And so why not leave it now?'

'Well, why not? Yes, it would be wonderful for me to see you.'

'I would like to meet your grandmother. We have spoken a few times now. And I think you and I could play chess again in the real world. And go for walks perhaps. I have looked at the weather forecasts, for what they are worth these days. I am thinking September or October?'

'October is usually lovely. Or it used to be. Not too hot. The roses are coming out. But whenever is great. Whenever.'

On another day, he was drinking coffee in the living area and watching the news stream on the communal television – *Death Toll Rises As Heatwave Continues Across Western Europe; Tornado Smashes New York City And Sea Wall Breached Again In New Jersey With Hundreds Missing; Record Cold Snap Across Southern Australia; Summer Cricket To Return With State-Of-The-Art Indoor Stadiums in Australia and India; Confused About Your Medical Bills? Information Session In Dining Room 2pm Tomorrow; One-Currency Talks Resume; Former First President Of The Greater Americas Loses Appeal Against Death*

Penalty – when he felt a presence behind him. He turned slowly and there was Clare.

'Hello,' she said.

He smiled. It was good to see her. She was wearing a big checked shirt, blues and reds, and it suited her.

She sat down on a chair next to his. 'You're doing well, your grandmother says. You look good. Stronger.'

'I am doing well . . . I think. There are still the days that aren't so good.'

'It'll sound silly, but you look better than before what happened. Before the accident. Calmer, somehow. Less worried.'

'Maybe nearly dying can do that for you,' Robbie said. But he agreed with her. He could see the changes himself in the mirror. 'Anyway, you've come a long way for a visit.'

Clare shifted in her seat. She was wearing new boots, he saw. Her feet looked small and neat.

'I had to come to the city to get something. Actually, it's a present for you. Well, for all of us really, but especially you. I had to think for a long time what I could get you because you kind of have everything, but then I thought of this, and when I asked your grandmother about it, she said it would be perfect.'

She spoke slowly, as if she'd thought about the words before saying them, or had practised them in her head. It was the longest speech he had heard from her.

'I see,' he said. 'But you didn't have to give me anything. You've been very kind and helpful. Really.'

Clare stood up. She bit her lip and looked at him. 'It's in the car. Come have a look.'

'You could bring it here.'

'I can't. Not really.'

Robbie stood up slowly and stiffly. Clare saw his crutches leaning on the chair opposite and handed them to him. She watched as he got himself organised, the crutches in place, back straight. He saw there was no pity on her face, not even sympathy, just a steady watching.

He followed her slowly down the wide hallways, through the double glass doors at a side entrance and into the car park. She had parked near the doors and now she unlocked the boot of the car.

'Have a look,' she said.

The back seats had been lowered and in a large wire cage sat a dog, watching him curiously. A golden retriever, Robbie saw. Beautiful coat. Golden-brown eyes.

'She's nearly a year old,' Clare said. 'Your grandmother helped me with the paperwork and the permit, but I found her. And when you go away again, I'll take care of her for you. Really good care of her.'

'What's her name?'

'She doesn't have one. The owners knew they couldn't keep her so they didn't want to give her a name. Here . . . you can pat her.'

Clare undid the wire door at the front of the cage. Robbie edged closer and leaned forward. He put out his hand. The dog sniffed it, each finger, his wrist. Then she licked him and looked up at him and smiled. Robbie put his hand on her head. He could feel the bone beneath the thin skin, the softness of her ears.

'She's beautiful,' he said. He felt the tears begin and turned away. 'She's just beautiful,' he said again, but his voice broke. Clare patted him on the shoulder. 'Okay,' he said after a few minutes. 'So. This is one of the best presents ever. Thank you. Thank you.'

Clare's face lit up. 'Well, she'll be waiting at home for you. Just give her a name. I'll start training her.'

'Timmy,' Robbie said. 'I want to call her Timmy.'

Clare nodded. 'Okay. See you back home soon.' She closed the boot and moved towards the front of the car. 'I'm glad you like her.'

Robbie reached out and took her hand. He raised it to his lips and kissed it. 'I do. Drive carefully.'

Clare blushed. She climbed into the car, switched on the engine and drove away. Robbie limped slowly back inside.

Well, that's something, he thought. I have a dog. A beautiful dog.

•

There was one more surprise for him before he went home. He woke from an afternoon sleep and there was Jonathon sitting beside the bed, sipping a takeaway coffee. In the few seconds before he was fully awake, Robbie was in a room in a long-gone house far away on a warm evening and he was just a boy, hurt and sad, and Jonathon sat patiently by his bed for hours and hours.

'Hello Robbie,' Jonathon said softly.

Robbie blinked away a tear. 'Let's go for a walk,' he said.

Jonathon waited patiently while Robbie pulled on a jumper and a coat, and found his walking stick. Together they walked slowly to a garden area and sat on a bench.

'It's a long way to come to say hello.'

'I was bored.'

'That's what you always say. But I saw you on TV a few days ago. Opening that museum complex and memorial for the Great Barrier Reef. How could you possibly be bored?'

Jonathon smiled. 'You are going home soon,' he said.

'Yes.'

'And will it be home? Do you think?'

Robbie stretched out his good leg. 'I don't know,' he finally said. 'There is a part of me that would like it to be. And that's a big thing to say, as you know. But . . . well, there is Ella, of course. She and I need to talk.'

They looked at the garden. The few plants, some ferns and clumps of native grasses, were mostly dead. Frost-scorched. The bare branches of a small tree, black against the red brick of the building and the heavy grey sky, bent and bobbed in the chill breeze. Robbie shivered.

'You can always move on,' Jonathon said. 'Nothing's forever, after all.'

Robbie straightened. 'Some things are,' he said. 'I've been doing a lot of thinking. Of course some things are forever. Whether they're meant to be or not.'

Jonathon sighed.

'How many towns now?' Robbie asked.

'Eight hundred. As of this week. Halfway.'

'Well, then. That's a forever thing.'

'Let's go inside,' Jonathon said. 'I can't believe how cold it is here.'

He stayed on for a few hours. They talked about Granna and Sarah and the new tent city that had been built on what had once been Sydney's Botanical Gardens and the weather and Robbie's exercise programme and they shared Robbie's dinner, ham with gravy and pineapple and a potato salad that tasted like tin.

It was only when he was leaving that Jonathon told Robbie he had resigned.

'Why?'

'Because it's unbearable. More than I can possibly explain.'

Jonathon bit his lip and stood up. He looked in his pockets for the key to his hire car and he walked over to where Robbie was sitting. He bent down to kiss the top of Robbie's head. Then he left.

That night Robbie dreamed a young girl with curly golden hair sat cross-legged on the end of his bed, drawing pictures on a notepad with big thick crayons, all the while softly singing an endless lullaby of old, old songs and nursery rhymes, a softly, softly whispering that lulled Robbie into an ever deeper sleep. When he woke there was a large sheet of stiff white paper on the bed. On it was a drawing of

Jonathon and Robbie, the older man leaning down as if he were about to give Robbie a kiss. The colours and details were perfect, down to the birthmark on Jonathon's cheek, the sadness in his bright blue eyes, the strands of Robbie's hair, and the crease of his collar. Drawn on the wall behind the men was a small black pony, eyes proud and bright and over the top of the pony, in flowing red letters, was the word *forever*. Robbie looked at the drawing for a long time. Then he folded it carefully and put it on his bedside table. 'Thank-you,' he said to the quiet room.

•

All the time he was in rehabilitation, Robbie watched and listened. The people at the centre reminded him of the people he'd grown up with when he lived with Granna. People who managed to smile or laugh, no matter what outrageous hand life dealt out to them, people who knew how to just keep going, no matter what. He listened and thought, he ate, he worked out. On the day he left, he knew he was on his way to being as strong as he had ever been.

Clare picked him up from the centre and drove him home. They sat in silence at first while she navigated her way through the crowded city streets, Fravershi in the middle of the back seat, watching them.

Robbie looked at the people on the roads, the dark buildings, the shops. I am here. I am alive. I am glad, he thought.

Once they hit the highway, Clare relaxed a little and they talked. Timmy knew her own name now, she told him, and 'sit' and 'stop' and 'no' and the mats she was allowed to sleep on. She and Fravershi pretended to hate each other but they didn't really. Clare had found them sleeping together on a mat by the fire in the big front room. She told him about the last of the winter vegetables his grandmother was stewing and pickling, and the first early wattle she had spotted.

Now and then she pulled over to let tanks pass or a convoy of trucks, and she was stopped at a couple of checkpoints, where her phone and fingerprints were verified. She warned him his grandmother had planned a feast for dinner, and he laughed and looked forward to opening a bottle of wine again.

When they reached the House of Many Promises, he assumed he would be sleeping in one of the rooms on the ground floor of the main house. But Granna and Clare walked him slowly up to the Stables. The steep slope was difficult but not impossible, and he knew it would become easier.

He could not believe the changes his grandmother had made. A bedroom and big bathroom on the ground floor now, a small kitchen with a wide bench for eating and working, and a comfortable living area. A wall knocked out to extend the space, and a new staircase, straight up, not spiral, with sturdy hand rails on both sides.

'Oh, Granna.'

'What, my boy?'

He shrugged. 'Everything.'

Clare came in, with Timmy. The dog was beautifully proportioned, lean and strong and smiling.

'Timmy,' Robbie said softly. Then louder, 'Timmy. Come.'

The dog trotted to him and sat on his left foot, leaning against his leg. She looked up at him and he stooped awkwardly to pat her head.

He saw there was a dog bed in the corner of his bedroom and a packet of dog biscuits on his bed. 'Come, Timmy.' He limped over, took a biscuit and walked over to the dog bed. She watched him, unblinking, then trotted to the bed and jumped in.

Robbie smiled and gave her the biscuit. 'Good girl.'

That night, long after Robbie had gone to sleep, Timmy jumped up onto his bed. When nothing happened, she edged a little closer and curled by his left foot. And, aside from the many times she slept in Clare's room when Robbie was away, that was where she slept for the next fifteen years. Sometimes Fravershi joined her.

•

On the first of September, Robbie's phone rang at seven in the evening. It was dark and still cool.

'Robbie.'

'Hello, Ella.'

Silence.

'I miss you,' Ella said.

'Then talk to me. What's happened?'

Another silence.

'What are you wearing?' she asked.

'Does it matter?'

'I want to know.'

'Jeans. Black jeans. A black T-shirt. And that blue jumper you bought me in Paris. The V-neck. Cashmere.'

'Yes, I remember that. And where are you sitting?'

'At the Stables. My cottage. Our cottage. By the fire. It's still cold here.'

'Yes, I have been following the weather. And you are well? Thomas says you are very well.'

'I'm fine. I'm mending. In another month I can get on a plane and go anywhere. I can come to you. I can go to London.'

'And what is it you want to do?'

'I don't know. I am actually happy here, in a way. It's a good place to be. What is it you want me to do? And what is it, perhaps, I would like you to do?' Timmy pushed her head against Robbie's knee. He scratched it. 'What is it, Ella? Tell me. I truly don't understand.'

'Oh, Robbie.' He could tell she was beginning to cry. He could picture her pushing her hair back, her eyes wide and damp. 'Don't you see? Nothing was ever supposed to happen to you. God. There are enough broken things all around us. You were perfect and you were supposed to stay perfect. And I can't bear it. I truly can't. I can't bear anything that is happening any more. But it's not just what has happened. It is that I especially can't bear that you will die one day, that you will leave me. I am not strong enough any more. I used to be, but not now. I thought that if we got married, perhaps, somehow, there would be something extra taking care of us, that we would be given an answer. I don't know. This sounds stupid. I don't know anything. But look . . . you nearly died. You have only one leg. Everything is breaking. Everything will break. And I can't bear it. Don't ask me to. Please don't.'

Robbie didn't know what to say, She was distressed. She had been distressed, sad and tired for a long time.

'Ella. Just come here. For a few weeks. It will do you good.'

'Work is too busy. It is not that easy.'

'Work isn't everything. Come on.'

'And if I come, what will we do? Talk, talk, talk, talk. The same old things. Over and over.'

Robbie liked that she was angry. She sounded alive. 'Well, no. We'll walk the dog for starters. Every day. Twice a day.'

'What dog?'

'A beautiful dog called Timmy.' Timmy's tail thumped the floor and she pressed her head against Robbie's left foot. 'A present from Clare.'

'Wonderful. Another thing to love and then have to leave.'

'Ella.'

'How can you say you would ever come back here when there is a dog?'

'Ella, there are people here to take care of her. Anyway, she's very lovely. You'd like her.'

'Where does she sleep?'

'In a basket near the bed. Maybe on the bed sometimes. Is that important?'

'A little. You have called a dog Timmy?'

'Why not? Another Timmy to love after all these years.'

Robbie heard her sniff.

'Ella, darling. Listen to me. Are you listening?'

He heard her sniff again.

'Okay. Something really bad happened for us. And I am so sorry. But this is life. Now I've recovered and I'm healthier than I have been for a long time. Yes, part of one leg is gone, but it's not so bad, sweetheart. I am not broken. I am nowhere near broken any more. I am strong enough for us both.'

Ella mumbled something, then started again. 'My mother has cancer.'

'Oh, Ella. What? When?'

'Just after your accident. It is treatable. For now. But she is not well. My father is not coping. It is the beginning of the end, he keeps saying. Something happens, a switch is flicked, the end begins. And perhaps that is us too.'

'Ella, I'm so sorry about your mother. I didn't know. Obviously. But this is why we have each other. Until the moment that switch is flicked, we have each other. And, no, a switch has not been flicked for us. Sorry, maybe it has . . . for me. There are some things that aren't as important as I thought after all. That's what I have learnt. What is important is you and me, and you and me together. We have time. We have love. We have a dog to walk. And even when something happens, something awful, it is not always the end. Not at all.'

'I was so upset about you. And my mother.'

'Of course you were. Are.'

'Everything has been too much.'

'I see that now. I understand.'

Silence. Robbie heard a possum scurry across the roof.

'Thomas is going to visit you.'

'Yes.'

'He is looking forward to it. He invites me to dinner and tells me fifty things about Australia.'

'That must annoy you.'

'It does.'

Silence. The fire crackled. Robbie got up and threw on another log. Ella sniffed again. He thought she might still be crying.

'Are you really not broken?' she asked.

'A little bit of my leg got broken off. That's all. Ella, I am truly well. Strong. Eating. Drinking. Walking. Everything working. Didn't Granna tell you?'

'Yes, of course. But you don't believe what people say. Not when it is so serious.'

He could imagine Ella considering everything she was being told and then dismissing it and drawing her own conclusions. He sighed.

'Sweetheart, it's beautiful here. The cottage is beautiful. Come in the late spring, before it's too hot. Come for a holiday. Come to rest and talk. And I could come back to Switzerland with you perhaps.'

And then they both cried.

twenty-four

On a hot and windy November evening, Robbie and Clare and Thomas and Granna were eating dinner on the wide porch on the eastern side of the House of Many Promises, an area sheltered from the burning late afternoon and evening summer sun, and cooled by overhead fans and the sound of water trickling over rocks into a pond. Thomas had arrived three weeks earlier and avoided any questions about when he planned to leave. He seemed charmed by Granna, which amused Robbie, and startled and intrigued by the landscape around him: the shimmering summer heat, the scents in the sun from roses and the leaves of trees and rocks and gravel, the birds that played and rested in the ponds and bowls of water Granna and Clare set around the garden.

Robbie was mostly happy. Ella remained elusive, but they talked regularly and he was confident it was simply a very difficult year for her. He could bide his time, wait her out. He had enjoyed the last couple of months. He'd helped Clare plant spring vegetables, and watered them in every second evening. He'd written a piece about his stay in hospital, adding details he'd researched about how the existing hospital system was unlikely to cope under the inclusion-zone plans and had sold it to the news stream and paid another fine. He went with Granna on some of her food deliveries, and began drafting a series on the closing-down towns. He worked out, lifting weights every day. He rested. Slept and dreamt. He waited. He played and walked with Timmy. He reread the books he had read as a boy. He cut spring flowers for Granna. He cooked barbecue suppers. He took Clare for lunch occasionally at Maisie's Café and learned a little more about Phil and her mother and her father, and that the only real holiday she'd ever had was a one-week stay with Phil at Bondi Beach in Sydney when they were both young and she had found everything about it overwhelming – the lights, the noise, the cost of the food, the fancy cars and beautiful women and the blue glitter of the sea and surf. He was touched by her composure, her lack of self-pity, the way she tried to think her way through things.

But on this hot November evening everyone was rattled, on edge. The previous night, lightning strikes had started a bushfire in the scrublands west of town and it was now officially designated out of control, fanned by a hard, dry wind coming in from the north-west. Twenty houses gone, then thirty, now nearly fifty. There was a faraway whine and wail of sirens and the thump-thump of helicopters. Clare had spent the day filling the bathtubs and every bucket and bowl she could find with water.

Robbie checked his phone. He hadn't heard from Ella for over twenty-four hours. It didn't mean anything, but yesterday was her birthday. He had sent champagne and messages and normally she would have been in touch.

Granna had made pavlova with fruit salad and cream, Robbie's favourite dessert. 'This is our national dish,' Robbie began explaining to Thomas, and then he smelled the smoke. Timmy smelled it too. She got up and he felt her trembling. The lights flickered.

Robbie dragged Timmy inside and quickly helped Granna clear the table. They moved the old wicker furniture settings from the verandahs to inside the house.

'I think we can start turning on some of the water,' Granna said. 'It's probably too soon, but still . . .'

The House of Many Promises had long ago been fireproofed, as much as it was possible to fireproof any building. The roof and gutters of the main house and all the other buildings had a spray system that drew from town water initially, tank water when the town water failed, and then, finally, the qanats beneath the main house and garden. Walls of water would fall from the roofline when activated, and shoot upwards and outwards from key points in the garden. As well, the qanats could be emptied to flood any fire that began to move up through the gardens towards the house and garage. Now Robbie went to the water tanks at the rear of the house and pulled some levers. A fine mist began spraying the roof of the house. He unrolled a long hose from a tap at the back of the house, another at the western side and one in front and turned them all on. Water began to slowly pool around the main entrance points to the house and trickle down the driveway and towards the gardens. Robbie could smell the water. And the smoke.

Clare appeared. She looked terrified, Robbie thought. 'If you could hose down the front of the house.' She nodded and walked away slowly. Robbie picked up the hose nearest to him and began spraying the garden beds, window frames, the pathway that ran down the full length of the house. He saw Fravershi bound towards the house in great leaps.

With little warning the smoke got thicker. The night was very dark but there were flames in the distance. Tall, angry flames. Robbie could smell things burning now, wood and rubber and fur, and sounds and noises collided and intensified – sounds of things falling, breaking, crashing. Waves of sound. The sirens were close now. Very close. He heard dogs howling. The wind roaring. The flames were coming up the hill. Were they? Yes.

Clare had gone inside and now he followed. Granna had opened the trapdoor to the basement in the broom cupboard behind the kitchen. He saw Clare disappear slowly down the ladder.

'There's a dead rat down there,' Granna said. 'People will complain. I should remember to check these things. Oh well, at least they'll be perfectly safe. You do think people would learn to be grateful.'

Robbie smiled, despite the heat and noise and stinging of the smoke.

'Timmy?' he asked.

'She's in the small back bedroom, with Thomas. She's safe there. Fravershi is in there too. There's water for them.'

Granna took Robbie by the hand and they went to the entry hall. Robbie opened one of the doors.

'My God,' he said. The wind was a living, demented thing now, a screaming fury, whipping through the flames and the black smoke.

'I think it looks worse than it is,' Granna said. 'It's not as close as it seems. I hope. Fire plays awful tricks.' He saw her answer her phone. 'Yes, yes. Of course. Two hundred,' she shouted into it.

A few minutes later, people started arriving, mainly on foot, some in cars.

'Fifty in the basement – children, families. The rest in here.' Granna flung open the doors to all the rooms in the House of Many Promises. 'You will be safe here.'

Robbie watched the flames and smoke curl over the town, beaten back in many areas, clearly winning in others. He saw the giant peppercorn tree at the base of the driveway catch alight, but a fire truck arrived and hosed it down. Another truck arrived and Robbie could see they were trying to keep the entrance and driveway to the house clear and safe.

'Oh dear,' Granna said. 'Time for the water walls, I think.'

Robbie returned to the back of the house and lifted the cover off the old keypad that either opened or closed the pipe system connected to the massive water tanks and entered the code he had learned as a boy. It appeared from the hoses that they were still on town water and that was a hopeful sign, he thought. He keyed in the final digit and hit 'enter' anyway and there was a huge hiss and spray and suddenly it seemed as if the House of Many Promises was standing in a giant fountain, water jetting in all directions.

Robbie returned to the front of the house soaked through. There were more people on the verandah now and animals too, panicked dogs, a wombat on the front stairs. He saw kangaroos coming up the driveway, heading further up the hill, behind the Stables. Please God, don't let the fire head up there, Robbie thought. Please.

From the verandah it looked as if Myamba was circled by fire, and embers were starting flare-ups across the town. Even as Robbie thought this, a strong sustained gust of wind brought embers and sparks hurling down on the house's front gardens. They spattered and fizzled out, then there was another wave. He began to feel very afraid. This was too savage, too fierce. He saw now that the fire was clearly at the edge of the property, that it would climb the hill. Everything below seemed to be screaming flames and wind. Even on the verandah there was ash and embers, and the water jets were no longer completely cool. They were warm, and then warmer still.

Granna was tugging on his arm. 'The qanat,' she shouted. She saw his expression. 'Now. Now!'

Robbie went to another trapdoor, in the floor of his grandmother's private study. He pushed aside the rug and there it was, exactly as he remembered it. He pulled up the door and fastened it. On the top step was a thin torch and he held it in his teeth as he climbed down the ladder. His prosthetic was hurting and his heart was pounding but he could manage.

He reached the small control room and prayed that he would remember. He stared at the bank of levers. Up for down. He was sure. And then the left row, down. He felt the water beneath his feet and beyond the walls shift and sigh.

He pulled each lever one by one, his full weight behind every effort. He wondered if he had the strength to do it, but slowly each lever shifted inch by inch. He felt as much as heard the roar of the water as it came awake, the shuddering of the house. Another lever. Another. The water was at chest level as he pulled the last one. Then he grasped the ladder tightly as the water swirled and gurgled away, trying to suck him down with it.

He climbed the ladder slowly, gasping, and closed the trapdoor and limped to the front of the house. The water was cascading down to the town. Not a trickle or a spray or a stream, but thin sheets and sheets of water, drowning the fire, the embers, the sounds, snaking into streets and gutters and gardens. People were quieter now, sensing the shift and change.

Robbie saw a fire truck inching up the driveway through the smoke and water. It pulled in at the verandah. The driver got down. Robbie saw it was Chad, his grandmother's builder. He looked tired and sweaty and grimy.

'Delivery for you, mate.'

Robbie walked down the steps carefully.

'I didn't know you were a fire-fighter.'

'Not supposed to be but who the fuck did they think would end up doing it? The ones that always have. Anyway . . .' He pulled open the rear door to a small cabin behind the front steps.

'Come on, love. You're safe now.'

Robbie watched a woman climb down from the cabin, hair wild and tangled, face smudged. His breath caught in his throat. 'Ella,' he said. 'Ella.'

She slipped and fell into the water pooling around her feet. Robbie sat down next to her and held her. He felt her sobbing.

'Oh, Robbie. Really,' she whispered, 'fire and flood. Very biblical.'

'Where on earth have you come from?'

'The supermarket. That's as far as the taxi would take me. The taxi I got at the airport. The driver said she didn't know the town, and it was too dark and frightening. I couldn't blame her. Anyway, I tried to start walk . . .' She started crying again.

Robbie looked up at Chad, who had brought Ella's bag around from the other side of the cabin.

'Thanks, mate,' he said.

'No worries. Could have been worse all round tonight, that's for sure.'

'How bad is it in town?' Robbie asked.

'We managed to hold the town centre pretty much. Few spot fires. Most of what you would have seen from up here was that new subdivision to the west. Bit of a mess out there, I reckon.'

He climbed back into the truck and, once Robbie and Ella had got to their feet and climbed up the steps to the verandah, he edged the truck slowly back down the driveway.

Ella took Robbie's hand. There was a sudden howl of the wind and then a shift in tone, a growl and a final chaotic gust, as it swung around to the south. Then there was a sudden coolness.

'The worst is over, Ella,' Robbie said. 'Truly, darling. The worst is over. Forever.'

'Oh, Robbie. When was there such a thing as forever?'

Robbie laughed. 'Come and meet Timmy,' he said.

twenty-five

It took Clare days to stop shaking after the fire. Too many memories. Too many precious things taken from her in the past. But not this time. Everyone and everything that mattered to her were safe. But still. Still.

Her own room was completely untouched. There was the smell of smoke but it began to fade quickly. Clare sat on her bed, holding the walking man's bone-knife in her trembling hands. 'Thank you,' she said to the white walls. 'Thank you. Thank you.'

Nearly two hundred homes were lost in Myamba, mostly in the two new housing estates on the western edge of town. Thirty people dead. Three hundred and twenty people to be added to Myamba's homeless register. Scores of other buildings damaged. All considered very minor, in the scheme of things. Within a day, most attention was on a fire that had started in bushland near Sydney and had already burnt out six hundred homes and killed more than one hundred people, including a busload of school children returning from an excursion to the coastline. *Inferno Closing In On Sydney* the news stream read. *Fire Started Deliberately. Death Toll Certain To Soar.* Apart from a lingering smell of smoke and scorched things, and the throb of bulldozers razing the wreckage of the burnt homes, Myamba's small tragedy was done with, forgotten.

'Could've been far worse,' said a man to his companion at the table next to Clare's in Maisie's Café.

'Hell, yes.'

'Summer's got a long way to go, though.'

'That's for sure.'

'Problem is, they reckon, all these new homes and townhouses are built from such cheap shit they're just waiting to explode if there's even a whiff of smoke.'

'Probably built that way on purpose. Kill off a few people.'

'It'd make sense.'

•

Within just a few weeks there were few signs that fire had come anywhere near the House of Many Promises. Granna rounded up a dozen men and women who wanted and needed to earn some money, and they pruned out charred tree branches and plants, raked the burnt grass and took away the scorched garden furniture. Clare helped, and made platters of sandwiches – far too many, so people would have to take some home with them – and carried out jugs of cold water. She was hugely surprised and proud when Granna told her she would be in charge of paying everyone.

Granna showed her the safe under the floor of the pantry and gave her the combination. 'Makes sense for you to have it anyway,' she said. 'Something has to happen to me one day, surely.'

Clare spent that night sitting at her small table, notebook in front of her, carefully calculating the payments. Twelve people. Eighty dollars an hour. Three days. Eight hours a day. She did the sums over and over again to make sure she had them right.

Robbie and Ella kept to themselves at the Stables, although Robbie came down to the big house at least once a day, to say hello, or to take the keys to one of the cars and head off for a drive with Ella.

Granna kept cooking and making up food parcels and doing her delivery runs. She worked on her computers and received and made odd calls. It was all normal, Clare thought. Safe and normal.

Some evenings she and Granna and Thomas ate together. Thomas was a good cook and often prepared the meal. Cold meat, a salad, pickled cucumbers. He made cordial and cakes and pastries and stewed fruits.

'This is how we would eat at home in Switzerland in summer,' he said. 'Well, of course, there is not so much food as there used to be. But in the old days.'

Despite the fire, one of the three large water tanks on the hill heading to the Stables was still half full and Clare used the water to keep the vegetable gardens and strawberry patch alive and the birdbaths and water bowls full. She asked Granna what happened now the qanat had been emptied.

'But that's the beauty of it, dear,' Granna said. 'It is extraordinary. It will fill up again. Slowly, steadily, drop by drop.' She paused. 'It is like life, I think. It *is* life.'

She didn't elaborate and Clare spent a long time wondering what she meant. Maybe it was just that there was always a little bit more to draw on, a little more than you had thought, if you were patient enough, strong enough. If you just waited.

•

The night before Ella returned to Europe, Robbie invited everyone to the Stables for dinner. He cooked sausages and onions on the barbecue, and Ella made a salad from cabbage and apples and celery. Robbie

piled the sausages and onions onto bread rolls and passed around a
bottle of tomato sauce.

'Your favourite meal when you were a boy,' Granna said.

'Yes. Sausage on processed bread. A gourmet delight.'

'It is very good,' Thomas said. 'Very good.'

'We must do this at home, Thomas,' Ella said. 'We will go into
the mountains and have a barbecue. Robbie has shown me how to
get the burnt bits exactly right.'

Clare thought Robbie looked very well. His limp was barely noticeable; the scar down his arm only a thin, pale line. He seemed at peace,
she thought. A man who was sleeping well at night.

Robbie gave Timmy a sausage and cleared his throat. 'I'll be taking
Ella to the airport in the morning,' he said. 'But I've decided something.
Well, we've decided something. I'm going to be staying here. For good.
I'll visit Ella, of course, and stay with her, but this will be home. My
home. Our home. I want to be home. And Ella will spend as much
time here as she can. It will work itself out. So.' He leaned towards
Granna. 'Are you happy?'

Clare thought she saw tears in the old woman's eyes. Then Granna
laughed her laugh that was like water playing on stone.

She reached for Robbie's hand. 'Of course I am. Of course. So very
happy.' She looked brightly around the table. 'I always knew it. I knew
this would be how it ended. I just had to be very patient.'

Clare smiled. She was relieved. And, she realised, happy as well.
Possibly too happy. If Robbie lived here, for a lot of the time anyway,
there might be more walks together on the cooler days. Meals or coffees
at Maisie's Café. There would be talks. Moments in the kitchen in the
big house when they would pass each other and brush shoulders, or
she would hand him a plate or a knife and their fingers would touch
and he would smile at her. Something might happen to make him

sad and she would pat and rub his shoulder again. That would be all. Nothing more. A simple touch. Enough to hope for. Everything.

•

A few weeks after Ella left, Granna appeared at Clare's door early one hot evening. She handed Clare a stiff brown envelope that was smudged and crumpled in places. Clare's full name was printed on it in messy red letters.

'Happy Christmas Eve,' Granna said.

'Same.'

'Busy day tomorrow.'

'Yes.'

'Come down and have a drink with us in a little while, if you want. Thomas and Robbie are seeing who can make the best champagne cocktail. It is Christmas, after all. For what that's worth.'

When she left, Clare sat at her table and opened the envelope. A piece of cardboard fell out, ragged on all its edges as if it had been torn out of a bigger piece. On one side was part of a picture of a bowl of cereal. On the other side was a short note. It was from Phil.

Dear Clare. I have heard you are well, with a nice place to live. Good. You deserve it. I am thinking you don't want me back and that is alright. But I want to say sorry. Not just for the things I done but for the things I didn't do. I didn't notice when your hair went grey and I didn't tell you it still looked nice. I didn't notice your eyes go tired. I stopped holding your hand. I stopped seeing you. So I am saying sorry. For all the not done things. They're the worst things and the saddest too, I reckon. I also want to say thank you because you were good to me. You are a kind woman. Love, Phil.

Clare read the note several times, and ran a finger around the rough edges of the cardboard. She put it on the shelf next to the bone-knife from the walking man.

twenty-six

Ilike to walk at dawn through the gardens of the House of Many Promises. There is a moment before the first magpie sings and the light reaches the low hills to the west that can be magic in its stillness. An illusory moment of unwound time, so that everything is brought back to its beginnings. And with that there is a fleeting hope, too brief to be held.

There is only the palest light this morning, struggling against a rush of the first dark autumn clouds. The clouds throw high-dancing shadows across the grand old lemon trees heavy with fruit, the quince trees and apple trees, the magnolia and lavender. This wild and grand and beautiful garden with its secret paths, the roses and foxgloves, herbs springing from cracks in rocks and chipped pots. There is the scent of sage and rosemary and the leaves readying to turn. A hint of frost. The tease again of rain.

I sit on a low wall of stone that I built once upon a time, as cold as my cold bones, and listen patiently for the story of the day to begin. There is a flash of weak sun as the clouds part. For just this moment – ah, watch it slip away – it is as it all was nearly two hundred years ago when I built this wall and these pathways and laid out the fruit tree groves. The first magpie sings.

Beneath my feet is the ceaseless whispering of the water in its vast underground vat. My gift. As good as any gold. Better.

Acknowledgements

There are many people to thank here.

Closing Down may never have seen the light of day had the first few chapters not won the inaugural Richell Prize for Emerging Writers in 2015. I will be forever grateful to Hannah Richell and the Richell family, Hachette Australia, The Guardian Australia and The Emerging Writers' Festival for establishing the award in memory of the late publisher Matt Richell.

Heartfelt thanks also to all at Hachette Australia who have shown such support and enthusiasm throughout the journey to publication. I especially thank my publisher, Robert Watkins, but also Fiona Hazard, Karen Ward, Jessica Skipper, Vanessa Radnidge, Justin Ractliffe and Louise Sherwin-Stark. And huge thank-yous to editors Chris Kunz and Nicola O'Shea for their invaluable insights and ideas and to designer Grace West for the wonderful cover design.

I am also grateful to Sophie Cunningham, who read a very early partial draft when I was fortunate to be in her Faber Academy course and provided supportive and helpful feedback. And thanks also to friends and early readers Kath O'Connor, Anne Forden and Elizabeth Rider. To the friends I cook for and share meals with, thank-you also.

I would like to acknowledge my mother, Anne Abbott, formidable teacher of English literature in her day. I was lucky to grow up surrounded by books and I am even luckier to still be enjoying our conversations about writers and reading.

Thanks to Jill Gibson, who should have been here in this world to read this. I know you were proud and I'm glad.

And finally, and always, all thanks to Mary Kidd, who has never not believed, and whose patience is apparently inexhaustible.

THE RICHELL PRIZE

The Richell Prize was established in 2014 to assist emerging unpublished writers who are looking to take the next step in their career. Offered annually, it invites writers to submit three chapters of a new work in progress. The winner will receive prize money to support their writing as well as a mentorship with a publisher at Hachette. The goal of The Richell Prize is to help new writers find their voice and have their work reach the attention of readers everywhere.

The Richell Prize was established in memory of Hachette Australia's CEO, Matt Richell, who died suddenly in 2014.

 **EMERGING WRITERS' FESTIVAL** **theguardian**

The Prize has also been made possible through the support of Simpsons Solicitors and Joy.

For more information about
how to enter The Richell Prize, please head to

hachette.com.au